Grave-Reaping Shrew

by

Everlyn C. Thompson

Grave Reaper Series

Grave-Reaping Shrew

Cover Art by *Kristian Norris*

The Wild Rose Press, Inc.
PO Box 708
Adams Basin, NY 14410-0708
Visit us at www.thewildrosepress.com

Publishing History
First Edition, 2023
Trade Paperback ISBN 978-1-5092-5008-0
Digital ISBN 978-1-5092-5009-7

Grave Reaper Series
Published in the United States of America

"Farranen?" I asked, even though I knew exactly who those pain-filled eyes belonged to.

"*Theo?*" He blinked again and some measure of alertness returned to his face.

"Shhh… It's me."

His shirt hung in tatters from one shoulder, black with dirt and sweat and blood. Cuts of varying ages crisscrossed his chest and arms, some still oozing blood. The fact that he hadn't been able to heal himself was a testament to how badly he'd been injured. I blinked back tears at the sight of his ravaged skin. The damage was spread across his entire body, like someone had tried to inflict as much pain as possible. I'd already known the queen was one sadistic bitch, but this…this was worse than anything my imagination could have come up with. I quickly removed my cloak and draped it across his cold body, the same way he'd wrapped me in his cloak when I'd been attacked by Lebolus.

"My lady…" He lifted a hand and weakly caressed my cheek.

I couldn't help it, I let out a hiccupping sob that refused to stay bottled up any longer. And my magic, already sparking anxiously under my skin, erupted with all the finesse of a dump truck plowing into a cement wall.

Dedication

For Bryan Twinkle-Toes Hammer, the strongest man
I've ever known.

Chapter One

"Put your *damn pants* on!"

I kept my exasperated gaze on the scarred hardwood floor to avoid the blatant display of male nudity.

"Pants. *Now.*" I enunciated each word clearly, as if I was speaking to a toddler.

A low growl came from the other side of the bed, and I looked up to meet Dog's defiant gaze. It took a few seconds before he quieted and lowered his amber eyes to the floor. He caught the balled-up pair of sweatpants I threw at him as I strode out of the bedroom.

I hid a small smile as I scooped coffee into my ancient percolator. This wasn't the first time we'd had the same ridiculous argument. We both knew my irritation was just a bluff to cover my awkwardness.

Because awkward didn't even begin to describe what it was like to find that Dog had shifted to his human form sometime during the night, after he'd gone to sleep at the foot of my bed looking like a normal wolf.

Which doesn't sound normal at all—but for me, that was as normal as it got.

And while I was considered slightly prudish by modern day standards, all kinds of warning bells started ringing in my head when I was faced with a naked adolescent boy. Shifter. Whatever. It was just plain *wrong*. So, pants had become mandatory in my cabin.

Dog emerged from the bedroom as I cracked eggs into a mixing bowl; his glower told me exactly how he felt about being forced into the confining fabric. I wanted to sympathise; being a bigger girl made most clothing feel uncomfortable and restrictive. I'd bought him the softest, loosest pair of sweatpants I could find—and really, there was no such thing as uncomfortable sweatpants, so he was just going to have to learn to suck it up if he wanted to roam around on two legs.

"Want to go for a run after breakfast?" I asked.

His head swiveled up, and I caught a flash of teeth. I liked to tell myself it was his version of a smile. Dog wasn't big on words. And that was fine with me. I figured, if he had anything important to say, he'd say it. Until then, I was good with the nonverbal cues he used. He spent most of his time as a wolf anyway.

****

After being forced to literally run for my life more often than a scantily clad bimbo in a psycho movie, I'd concluded that I needed to be prepared for the next time I was attacked by a hungry vampire or psychotic fae. So, despite the fact that it was the middle of December with two feet of snow on the ground, Dog and I went for a three-kilometer run every second morning. And just in case you're wondering, "freezing your ass off" isn't actually a thing. Even with all the exercise, my butt still filled out the new size twelve workout pants I'd bought.

My cabin, located at the back end of a dead-end road, aptly named Broken Road, wasn't technically part of the hamlet of Tamarac, so the gravel roads hadn't been plowed. The only people who used the road in the winter were myself and a handful of deliverymen from town that brought groceries and supplies for Mrs. Swazle next door. The twin tire ruts were hard-packed and slick with ice; my old sneakers didn't offer much in the way of traction, so I nearly fell half a dozen times. Someday soon, I'd have to invest in some high-quality footwear.

Dog didn't have the same issues with balance, probably because he was back on four legs, and he bounded through the loose snow. By the time we reached the halfway point, a power pole at the top of Gervais Hill, I was panting and sweating like it was thirty-five degrees above, instead of fifteen below. Summer was going to be hell. I bent over and put my hands on my knees while Dog sniffed the power pole before marking it.

"You could just carve your initials into it; then you wouldn't have to pee on it every time we're here."

He shot me look that said I was an idiot for not understanding the importance of peeing on all things outdoors.

It must have been a male thing. Or maybe a wolf thing. I can't say I understood either. These days, I couldn't even manage to act like a human.

Three months ago, I'd been attacked by an ankou fae and infected with his magic. My body had started the transition from human to changeling but never finished. Dying had also been a very real possibility, but thankfully that hadn't happened. Obviously.

So, I was stuck in a weird sort of limbo, the magic lingering under my skin but no longer growing. It was like having a dormant cavity that your tongue kept poking at; it was a constant awareness that I couldn't get past. Even now I could feel the low-level buzz moving through my blood, sluggish and sullen. It wanted to be acknowledged, wanted to be used.

I had to think about something else; the magic knew it had my attention.

Before I had a chance to completely catch my breath, Dog head-butted the back of my thigh to get me started toward home.

"Just give me a minute," I told him, only to receive another head-butt that nearly knocked me over. "*Stop!* I'm not ready yet—"

He nudged me again, and this time my feet shot out from under me and I fell backward into the snow.

"Ow!" The loose powder was softer than I expected, but I'd probably still get a bruise on my backside. "You are such a *nag*," I said in my most affronted voice. Seriously, he had no patience. Running wasn't easy when you're overweight; it was even harder when the ground was frozen and slippery. You'd think he could cut me some slack—at least I was out here trying.

After brushing off my wet tush (and dignity), I followed Dog back down the hill.

****

Living next to your ex is a lot like witnessing a train wreck in slow motion. You'd do literally anything to look away, but you find yourself helpless to point your eyeballs in any other direction.

I had the unfortunate luck of living two doors down from my sort-of ex, Farranen. Since I lived at the very end of the street, I was forced to pass his neat white cabin every time I went for a run.

Please, not today, I thought to myself. *Please don't let today be the day I run into him.*

And while I knew seeing him again was probably inevitable, I didn't want it to be when I was a hot sweaty mess and breathing like a cow in labor. There was absolutely nothing cute about my plus-size workout pants or the way my pale skin turned bright pink with even the smallest amount of physical exertion. The long brown hair I'd scraped into a ponytail was stuck to the back of my sticky neck, and my citrus breeze deodorant wasn't even coming close to doing its job. Not that I should care what my ex thought, but still, a girl had to have some pride.

His driveway and sidewalk were shoveled, even though I'd never seen a vehicle there. Actually, I don't think Farranen knew how to drive. Not that I really knew him all that well; we'd been neighbors for over a year, but I'd only just met him about three months ago.

I couldn't help it, I turned and stared at the tidy little cabin as I jogged past.

My complete lack of willpower was shameful. I really didn't want to be *that* girl, the one that kept constant tabs on someone she was no longer involved with. Sadly, it was turning out that I was, in fact, *that* girl.

Movement in one of the windows caught my attention. It was a face—someone was watching me. My foot slipped, and I had to jerk my eyes back to the slick road so I wouldn't break an ankle, but not before I caught the fine features of a woman with big beautiful green eyes.

There was a woman in his cabin. A *woman*. And

not just an ordinary human woman. Judging by the quick glance I'd gotten, she was fae. That kind of perfect bone structure and luminescent skin couldn't be faked by any amount of cover-up or plastic surgery. The small electric snap of my magic reaching for her confirmed that she was fae.

Dog whined and rubbed his head against my hip. I hadn't realized that I'd stopped running, but there I was, standing in the middle of the road like an idiot. I must have had a dazed look on my face because Dog head-butted my hand until I absently wound my fingers into his silky fur.

"Sorry, buddy, I was just…daydreaming." That was the best excuse I could come up with. It didn't sound believable, even to my own ears. I didn't bother to elaborate; Dog probably already knew the treacherous road my mind had turned down. He'd been witness to more than one of my meltdowns over a pint of mint chocolate chip ice cream.

It took effort, but I finally got my feet moving again. If only my heart could be so easily convinced.

****

Cold showers in the middle of the winter sucked ass. Big hairy ass.

The royalties from my six previously published novels brought in a decent paycheck four times a year, but I still wasn't going to pay for a new water heater until my current one croaked. I was frugal to a fault.

Even with a fire blazing in the fireplace all afternoon, I still had a chill, thanks to the tepid shower I'd taken after my run. Dog had disappeared through his doggy door once the cabin had reached twenty-eight degrees, and I didn't blame him. Having a built-in fur coat during the winter sounded handy, but I had a feeling that next summer was going to be hard for him. Maybe he'd let me shear him like a sheep.

I knew he wouldn't be gone for long; it was nearly suppertime and I was just starting to clean up the dishes from the cake I'd made. We didn't actually need cake, but it had been a convenient excuse for me to rationalize turning the oven on. And it's not like it would go to waste. Cake never lasted long at my place.

"Hello, Theo."

The gruff words cut through the silence and startled a shriek out of me. The soapy mixing bowl fell back into the sink with a clatter as I spun around with my hands clutched to my chest.

"*Ozzy!* What the *hell*?" I demanded in a voice that sounded like I was being strangled.

Oscar Alderidge, an agent of the Paranormal Intelligence Maintaining Peace Agency, stood on the other side of my small kitchen. He towered over my measly five foot four by at least twelve inches, and I had to fight the urge to back up. I would not give in to his pathetic male posturing in my own house.

"Don't call me that."

"What are you doing in my cabin, *Ozzy*?" I intentionally used the nickname he hated, just because I could. Poking the surly giant was one of my more perverse hobbies.

The last time I'd seen him, we'd had a fun little conversation about the night my husband had shown up after a six-year disappearance to kidnap me and turn me into a vampire so I could join his brood. For some reason, Will seemed to think that I'd want to be part of his big happy vampire family. Imagine his surprise when I wasn't on board with being inducted into his new undead way of life. In the end, it hadn't mattered what I wanted since his sire, Marissa, had cut his throat and quickly ended any possibility of me being turned.

Unfortunately, the carnage had resulted in some of his tainted blood spraying me in the face. It hadn't been enough to turn me, but ever since then, I'd been accused of "smelling like a vampire." I still didn't know if that was an insult or a compliment. I guess it varied, depending on who it was coming from.

Farranen had said something about my magic changing, but I'd been too busy trying to wrap my head around the idea of having *any* magic to really notice the subtle changes Will's blood had caused.

"Just stopped by to follow up with you about your husband." His slate-gray eyes gleamed, reminding me of a shark looking for prey. There was no chance I was going to enjoy whatever he'd come here to say to me.

"*Ex*-husband. *Dead* ex-husband," I reminded him. I left out the part about Will being a vampire, since I didn't want to sound like a bigot or racist toward the undead, even though I hadn't met a nice one yet. Did all vamps turn into assholes because of their transition? Or were they like that when they were still human?

"I need you to accompany me to the property where Will's sire was living."

"What? No!" As far as Ozzy knew, I'd never been to Marissa's abandoned mansion in the woods. After Will had knocked me out and kidnapped me, I'd woken up to find myself locked in a filthy house of horrors that I eventually escaped from.

"I don't even know where it is." It was the truth, since I doubted I could find it even if I wanted to. I'd hauled butt as fast and as far as I could once Marissa had released me.

"I do. Grab your coat; I'll drive."

I stared at him in disbelief. "What? *Why?* Sightseeing a vampire torture chamber is pretty low on my list of things to do tonight." Definitely not top ten; I'd rather scrub every square inch of flooring in my cabin with my tongue than go anywhere with Ozzy. I crossed my arms defensively, and he must have realized I was digging my metaphorical heels in.

"Christ, can't you just listen for once, woman?" He ran a hand through his bright red hair, making the mess even more unruly.

"Nope."

"All supernatural creatures are subject to the laws of the Paranormal Intellig—"

"Unless they are under a direct charge by the queen of the fae. Royal fae ruling trumps any legislation by your agency." I followed up my argument with a cocky grin. I'd heard Farranen use those exact words against Ozzy and come out victorious. Although, if anyone bothered to look too closely, they'd find out the queen's original directive only included sixty nights, so technically her orders had long since expired.

It made me a little sad that I was starting to sound like a fae myself, bending the words just enough to slip through the hidden loopholes without ever breaking them.

Ozzy growled something under his breath about stubborn women before wiping the frustrated grimace off his face. "Fine; must I seek permission from your guardian then? Or should I inquire with the fae queen in person?"

Damn. The man had called my bluff. I hadn't told him in so many words, but Ozzy must have clued into the fact that Farranen's absence in my life was permanent. And he likely knew I wouldn't want the queen's attention on me for any reason. I was under the assumption that she'd forgotten about me, and I planned to keep it that way.

Stupid supernatural politics. Ozzy sure knew how to play the game.

"Fine."

I stomped off to find my coat.

Chapter Two

True to his word, Ozzy did indeed know the way to Marissa's abandoned mansion and insisted on driving.

"What's wrong with your car?" I groused from the passenger seat of my old truck.

He shrugged. "Nothing."

"Then why did we have to take my truck?"

"It handles back roads better than the boring piece-of-shit car the agency issued to me."

I glared at his stoic profile. He actually looked like he enjoyed being behind the wheel of the forty-year-old antique.

I held onto my indignant anger, letting it percolate so there was no room in my head for anything else. If I didn't, I'd be forced to acknowledge the small edge of fear worming its way into my thoughts. Letting myself get bullied into a late-night joy ride wasn't the smartest thing I'd ever done. And the fact that Ozzy was a vampire wasn't even the scariest part.

Nobody knew where I was or who I was with. Dog was MIA, but that was pretty normal. He tended to disappear whenever Ozzy dropped by. I just wish he'd have given me a heads-up so I could have avoided the grumpy vamp too.

"So, why are we visiting a spooky vampire house in the middle of the night?" I asked.

"Would you have preferred a lunch date?" he

snarked back at me.

"Works for me." Not all of us kept a nocturnal schedule to avoid fatal sunburns. "I meant, why are we going at all? I thought the case was closed."

After my escape from Marissa's brood, Ozzy had interrogated me, but I'd gotten away with only divulging a small handful of facts. I had a feeling he'd have known if I'd lied, so I'd kept everything strictly truthful while leaving out certain parts that suited me. I may have implied that I was the one to kill Will, but it had actually been Marissa's hand that wielded the blade.

"The cases for any missing women that could be traced back to your husband are closed, but there's still the matter of the five vampires that were slaughtered to address. Not to mention that their sire, Marissa, hasn't been seen since your abduction, as well as the fledgling that attacked you."

I could feel his eyes on my neck, where the scar from Merrick's second attack was hidden beneath my heavy winter clothing. It was an ugly jagged reminder of what I'd survived.

With that thought, the cab of my truck suddenly felt less ominous. I'd been strong enough to live through three different vampire attacks—one by Will and two by Merrick, Marissa's insane fledgling. There was no reason for my heart to be beating as fast as it was; I was perfectly capable of taking care of myself.

"His body was never turned in. All we have is your word that he's dead. And since you were the last person to talk to Merrick, you're still a witness in an active investigation. Maybe seeing the crime scene will help jog your memory."

I doubted he was hoping to find Merrick's body; he hadn't even inquired about its location the last time I'd seen him.

No, I had a feeling that he wasn't dragging me out into the middle of nowhere to help refresh my memory since, as far as he knew, I'd never been there before. It was more likely that he was hoping to poke a few holes in my story. I'd have to watch every word I said so I didn't set off his built-in magical lie detector.

"Maybe," I said half-heartedly.

It took three hours, and a hell of a lot more kilometers than I was comfortable putting on my old truck, before we reached the abandoned house. I hoped Ozzy planned on returning it with a full tank.

After living like a hermit for more than a year, my social skills were questionable at best. Ozzy deflected my awkward attempt at small talk, so I was happy to let the creaking of the antiquated vehicle lull me to sleep.

****

"—*Christ*, woman! Would you quit with that racket, already!"

The sound of Ozzy's irritated voice startled me out of a bizarre dream. I blinked owlishly for the few seconds it took to disperse the images of the mystery woman in Farranen's cabin from my vision.

"Huh? Where—" I sat up and looked around as my truck rattled down a small overgrown trail before finally spitting us into a familiar clearing. Marissa's abandoned nest loomed against the clear sky, magnificent and terrible all at once as starlight reflected off the snow to highlight the momentous state of disrepair it had fallen into.

The navy-blue house was two stories tall with a

third-floor attic and stone chimney that leaned so far to the left it would probably topple over the next time the wind reached more than twenty kilometers an hour. All of the windows were boarded over, aside from the top floor. A handful of moldy shingles blemished the pristine white drifts of snow, probably from the massive winds that had blown in from the north three nights earlier.

Ozzy shifted into park and shut off the engine before pocketing my keys. I shrugged off the last traces of sleep from my addled brain and followed him out into the cold night air.

"No tracks; doesn't look like anyone's home." He started toward the empty house with a smooth stride that shouldn't have been possible in two feet of snow. "If there was anyone here, they're long gone thanks to you."

"*Me?* What did *I* do?" It was hard to sound offended as I struggled through the knee-deep drifts.

"Anyone in a two-mile radius heard us coming with the way you were sawing logs."

"I do not *snore!*" I huffed.

"Like a chainsaw." He grinned at me over his shoulder, clearly enjoying my indignant sputtering. "A sweet little baby chainsaw with a sinus infection."

I did *not* snore. And even if I did, it would sound like an adorable little kitten purring, *not* a gas-guzzling small engine designed to take down trees. Besides, vampires had hyper-sensitive hearing, so even the tiniest little sound was probably blown way out of perspective. I harrumphed one last time and let the subject die.

We reached the front porch; someone had

attempted to shut the broken front door, but a small drift of snow had still accumulated across the tiles of the foyer. Ozzy reached into his coat pocket and pulled out a flashlight before extending it in my direction.

"No, thanks," I told him as I pulled out my own. I'd been caught in the woods at night too many times, so now I carried a flashlight everywhere with me.

Ozzy raised an eyebrow in surprise but tucked his light back into the depths of his leather jacket. He had no idea that this old dog had learned a few new tricks.

While Ozzy had never hurt me, he'd caught me by surprise too many times to count, so I'd started taking my personal security at lot more seriously. Along with the flashlight, I now carried a pocketknife as well as a hunting knife that I kept in a hidden holster on my calf. I still had an old shotgun at my cabin, but it was a pain in the butt to carry around, and I knew firsthand that it wasn't made for close-contact situations. And I was just as likely to shoot myself as I was an assailant, so it was more of a last resort in my line of defense.

Our boots made muffled crunching sounds as we crossed the large space. There was a dark stain on the black and white checkered tiles that hadn't been there the last time I'd been here.

"Is that…?" I gulped but didn't look away from the dried puddle.

"Vampire blood. One of the fledglings bled out here," Ozzy supplied in a gruff tone.

I was no expert, but shouldn't there be a chalk outline or some tiny orange pylons to mark this as a crime scene? The cold air had chased away any odors associated with a dead body—unless dead vampires didn't decompose the same way humans did? I wanted to ask Ozzy, but my curiosity took a backseat to my need to not sound like an idiot.

"What happened to the body?" I asked as I followed him deeper into the house. My stress levels decreased slightly as we headed away from the room where Marissa had slit Will's throat. I wasn't really the nostalgic type, but I knew there was a good chance I'd lose my shit if I went in there. Will and I hadn't been on good terms by the time he'd been killed, but no girl should have to watch her husband bleed out at her feet.

"The agency took it."

The Paranormal Intelligence Maintaining Peace Agency, or PIMP Agency as I liked to call them, was still a big mystery to me. I knew Ozzy worked for them, but I hadn't figured out if they were part of the Canadian government or, like most supernaturals, flew under any official radar.

"What exactly were you hoping to accomplish by dragging me here?" I asked.

Instead of answering my question, he led me into a large dining room where another grim stain waited for us. This time, the blood was smeared across the hardwood floor with large hand-sized streaks, like someone had crawled through it.

"The second fledgling died here. Three shots to the chest, and one more point-blank to the head when he tried to get away." His tone was matter-of-fact, but I could sense an underlying anger. I wondered if he'd known these vampires personally, or if he was just pissed that he still hadn't closed the case.

The beam from my flashlight caught a line of dimples in the wainscoting at chest height. Skirting the dried blood, I leaned in closer until I could see the small holes that had splintered the old wood.

"Bullet holes. We already dug the slugs out and sent them to forensics."

I jumped when Ozzy's voice came from directly behind me. Damn, I hated when he snuck up on me.

"Fourteen shots that missed their target from less than twenty feet away. That's fourteen shots more than any agent would need."

"You think someone else did this?"

Merrick, the only witness to the massacre that had happened here, had personally informed me that the men responsible had identified themselves as PIMP agents before killing everyone and kidnapping Marissa.

"I *know* someone else did this."

I wasn't about to argue with the conviction I could feel rolling off his words. "Who? Who else knows about vampires and hates them enough to murder an entire nest? Is there some sort of anti-vampire supremacists' group in Saskatchewan?" The thought of an anti-fae KKK was kind of terrifying. I didn't want to know what they'd think about someone like me, a human with fae magic. Not to mention the shot of vampire mojo thrown in the mix.

"It's possible." He didn't sound entirely convinced. "Come on, their living quarters were downstairs."

The large wooden door to the basement had been blown off its hinges and lay in broken pieces that had been pushed to either side of the hallway. The stairs were completely encompassed in darkness, and I suppressed a shudder at the thought of going down there.

"The last two were in the dressing room downstairs. There was nowhere for them to go. They were cornered, but it looks like they put up a fight." He paused on the first step when he realized I'd stopped in the middle of the hallway like my boots had grown roots into the hardwood.

"I am *not* following you into that creepy-ass basement." This was where I drew the line. If Ozzy decided to force the issue, we'd both get to find out how sharp my new pocketknife was.

After a tense pause, he nodded and said, "Suit yourself. I'm going to take another look while we're here." He disappeared into the shadows, and some of the tension left my shoulders. "Have a look around and don't worry about contaminating the crime scene." His disembodied voice floated up to me, even more disturbing than the darkness that shrouded him.

Silence settled around me, heavier than the silence I was used to at my own cabin. The magic in my blood tingled, and I felt a flare of panic. Now was not a good time for the unpredictable energy to rear its ugly head. Somehow, it had sensed all the death and suffering that surrounded me. I closed my eyes and forced myself to ignore the itch of magic as it started to churn beneath my skin. I dug my fingers into my palms, hoping the pain would distract me.

"*Go away*," I whispered.

I didn't know how to deal with the pressure as it started to grow. It had nowhere to go, and I had no way to let it out without another fae to share it with.

"*Please, just stop.*"

The magic had always reacted when I was around Farranen; it had been pleasurable and felt like a part of me. But now it burned like a fire out of control, consuming me from the inside out. My legs shook, and

I gripped the wall as I fell to my knees. I tried to call out to Ozzy; maybe he'd know how to control the tidal wave of magic before it killed me, but my lungs seized in my chest, strangling the words before I could force them out.

The air in front of me started to bend and warp, until the shimmering outline of something vaguely human-shaped took form. I squinted; it was like looking at a disco ball through a kaleidoscope, and my magic leaped in response to its presence. I was a giant tuning fork that had suddenly found the right note, and without any conscious thought on my part, the magic shot down my arms and exploded out of my outstretched hands.

I regained enough control of my muscles to draw in a ragged gasp as a woman materialized in front of me. Her small hands clasped mine, and I fell into her arms as a wave of dizziness overcame me.

"*Oof!*" She struggled under my weight, and we both fell to the cold floor in a tangle of limbs.

My vision went dark, and I think I might have passed out at that point. Or maybe I just wanted to. When I was finally able to open my eyes, some very unladylike cursing punctuated the harsh crack of flesh on flesh.

"Damn it! Wake up!"

Another sharp slap resounded, and my face let me know that it was on the receiving end of someone's hand.

"*Ow...*" I protested as I batted at whoever was leaning over me.

"It's about time!"

I wiped a hand across my teary vision and focused on the angry woman glaring down at me.

"Vanessa?" I croaked, disbelief making my voice crack.

Vanessa had been a waitress at a local cowboy bar and was the last in a long line of woman that Will had abducted and murdered.

"Hi, Theo." The woman in question quirked a slight smile at me before climbing to her feet and brushing off the pale pink sundress she wore. Her chestnut-brown hair hung in perfect waves around her shoulders, and I could see her blond highlights even with the dim lighting.

"But I thought you were dead." I sounded like a small child confronting the possibility that the tooth fairy wasn't real.

"I am." She smirked.

I doubtfully eyed her; everything from her generous double Ds down to the jewel in her flower-shaped toe ring that matched her perfectly polished toenails looked pretty damn alive to me.

"You look pretty good for a dead woman," I observed.

"Thanks." She flipped a lock of hair over her shoulder. The creamy pale skin on her neck was smooth and unblemished by any of the vampire bites that she'd had the last time I'd seen her. How was that even possible? I still had scars from when Will had kidnapped me and used my carotid artery as his own personal liquid buffet, and Vanessa should too. Then again, she shouldn't have been walking around in a pretty sundress at the scene of multiple murders either. A lot of weird stuff seemed to happen around Tamarac; I really needed to learn to roll with it.

"What just happened?" I clambered to my feet like

a drunk wrestler and leaned against the wall for support.

"Don't know. You said you'd come back, so I waited." She shrugged again and leaned against the opposite wall.

"But you're *dead.*"

"Mm-hmm." She sure didn't sound too concerned. If we'd been discussing my supposed demise, I'd have a hell of a lot to say on the subject. "It's like when you came, I was sleeping, and as soon as you got close, I woke up. I tried to get your attention, but you couldn't see me until I touched you."

I looked down at my hands and remembered the way my magic had shot out of them.

"Can I touch you?" I took a step closer to Vanessa and reached out with all the hesitancy of someone reaching for a live wire.

"Honey, I've heard a lot of lame pickup lines in my day, but that is probably the saddest yet."

I rolled my eyes and gave her a dirty look before I poked her in the arm with my finger. She felt cold but entirely solid to the touch.

After a few more pokes, she slapped my hand away with an irritated huff. "Stop it. I'm not a fucking piñata."

I had to agree with her; piñatas were cheerful and full of sweet things. This frigid bitch was neither.

"So, what are you then? A ghost? A zombie?"

"Dunno."

"Can you walk through walls? Do you have any weird cravings for human flesh?"

"No, and, *ew!* No!"

"Can you levitate things with your mind? We need to narrow down the possibilities if we're going to figure out what you are."

"Calm down, detective—"

"Who's your friend, Theo?"

I shrieked and spun around at the sound of Ozzy's voice. The damn vampire was always sneaking up on me. I should put a bell around his neck. "God, Ozzy! Don't *do* that!" One of these days I was going to have a heart attack.

"Theo?" The wariness in Ozzy's tone made me pause, and my annoyance at Vanessa's flippant attitude found a new target.

"What?" I asked in irritation.

"Who're you talking to?"

"Vanessa." I waved a hand in the general direction of the pretty brunette.

He narrowed his gray eyes at me, like a predator that had caught the scent of something tasty on the wind. "Vanessa, the waitress that Will murdered?"

"Yes, that Vanessa," I growled. God, did he have to remind her that it had been *my* husband's fault that she was dead? *Ex-husband*, I reminded myself. I glanced over at her, but she didn't seem too bothered by Ozzy's impromptu stroll down memory lane.

"I knew it!" Ozzy crowed, and I jumped at the amount of triumph in his voice. "You can talk to the dead!"

I gave him a *duh* look. Hadn't we already established that she was dead?

"Ask her why she's here."

"Ask her yourself," I told him.

"I don't have fae magic that lets me talk to the dead—but *you* do."

"You can't see her? She's right there." I pointed at

22

the bored-looking woman in question.

Ozzy ran a hand through his messy hair and slowly shook his head. "There's nothing there as far as I can see, Theo."

What the hell was going on? How could I be seeing a dead woman, while the all-powerful vampire couldn't? Had I finally reached the tipping point into crazyland?

"Did the guardian tell you anything about the ankou fae that attacked you?"

I bristled at the mention of Farranen but made an effort to keep my discomfort from showing on my face. "Not really, just that he went crazy from something called psychogenic atrophy."

"The ankou are the only ones that can grave reap, the only fae that can bring someone back from beyond the veil."

I shook my head in denial; I did *not* want my messed-up magic interfering in my attempts to be normal. And communing with the dead sounded like the exact opposite of normal.

"Wait—is that why you brought me here? To test your Theo-can-see-dead-people theory?"

He shrugged one of his big shoulders. "Maybe."

What a jerk. I turned to stomp away, but my self-righteous exit was ruined when my knees gave out and I fell to the floor. I'm pretty sure I heard Vanessa snicker from behind me.

"Careful, Theo. You used a lot of energy bringing her into our plane of existence." He grabbed me by my armpits and hoisted me to my feet. "It felt like a damn atomic bomb went off up here."

"You felt it?" I didn't want to admit that he might

be right, but I was starting to feel like I had a semitruck strapped to my back. I was drained and just wanted to get back to my cabin and crawl into bed.

"Every creature from here to Vancouver probably felt it. As far as I know, there aren't many fae on this side of the gate, and none with that kind of power. We should probably get going before anyone comes to investigate."

I nodded tiredly and didn't protest when Ozzy wrapped a thick arm around my waist and dragged me down the hall.

Chapter Three

Ghosts made terrible backseat drivers.

Well, technically, Vanessa was riding shotgun since my truck didn't have a backseat. But still, the three-hour ride home was no picnic.

Ozzy insisted on driving, and that was fine with me since I was exhausted and afraid I'd fall asleep behind the wheel. Vanessa refused to sit next to the vampire, and really, I couldn't blame her, seeing as she'd met her end because my selfish ex-husband couldn't keep his fangs to himself.

So that's how I ended up wedged between a vampire and a ghost for the world's most awkward road trip in history. If I'd have known this was how I'd be spending my night, I'd have stashed a cake in the glovebox.

"What's she saying?" Ozzy asked for the fifth time.

"She thinks you need a haircut. And to stop buying your clothes from the discount-store clearance racks."

"*What!*" Ozzy speared me with an incredulous look.

I rolled my eyes. "She's not saying anything. She's just sitting here."

"Ask her if she knows anything about the vamps that were murdered or Marissa's kidnapping."

"She can hear you; you know," I grumbled, as I twisted the truck's heater knob even higher. As far as I was concerned, spring couldn't come soon enough. And sitting next to a ghost wasn't helping; my thigh was practically numb where it was pressed against Vanessa's.

"Could you put on a coat? I'm cold just looking at you. It's December. Why are you wearing a freaking dress anyway?" I asked the woman who didn't look the least bit chilled.

Vanessa looked down at the simple pink dress covered with tiny white daisies and shrugged. "It was my favorite dress; I haven't worn it in years. It was just here when I woke up."

"Well, I feel like I'm sitting next to an ice cube," I informed her grumpily. I really needed to get some sleep; I was a real bear when I was tired.

"The dead vampires?" Ozzy reminded me.

"Yeah, I saw them," Vanessa said.

"You did? What did you see?" I asked in surprise. "And I thought you were 'asleep' until tonight?"

"What's she saying?" Ozzy demanded.

"Shhh! Stop interrupting," I told him.

"When you were locked in the bedroom with me, I was aware of what was going on around me. You could even hear and see me. It's like I could soak up the magic you were putting out. Then you left, so I followed you downstairs, but you were already gone. I lingered for a few days before I just sort of faded away."

"Sorry," I told her quietly. I hadn't known she was a ghost, and I hadn't wanted to leave her behind. "So, if you hung around for a few days, then you would have been there during the shooting."

"Yeah, I was there. A bunch of men broke in, all

dressed in black. They started shooting the vampires, and you know what? More power to them. Those damn bloodsuckers deserved it."

"She saw the vampires get shot," I told Ozzy.

"What about Marissa?" he asked.

"They tied her up and dragged her out," Vanessa said.

"Where did they take her?" I asked.

"I don't know. I couldn't get past the front door, and it's not like I was going to follow them even if I could."

"You got past the front door tonight," I pointed out.

She shrugged. "I'm new to this whole being-dead thing. Don't ask me."

"Did she get a description of the men?" Ozzy broke through our metaphysical pondering, bringing us back to the topic of Marissa's abduction.

"They had their faces covered, but the she-vamp fought with one of the men and got his mask off. Let me tell you, he was a real piece of work. It was the closest I've ever come to seeing a real Greek god." She mimed fanning herself. "Long dark hair, eyes an inky charcoal—they were almost black. Shoulders wide enough to eclipse the sun."

"Okay, we get the point—he was attractive."

"I'll say. Can we crack a window in here? I'm getting hot just thinking about him."

"No!" My teeth were close to chattering already. There was no way I was opening the window just because Vanessa was getting hot flashes from reliving Marissa's abduction.

"Was he a vampire?" Ozzy asked.

"Dunno. I didn't see any fangs, but then again, he

had a semiautomatic, so why would he need them?"

"He had a what?" I asked.

"A *semiautomatic*. You know—a handgun."

"Oh, right." I didn't actually know, but I figured it was easier to fake it than highlight my ignorance regarding things that shot metal projectiles at high speeds. When I'd first moved to Tamarac, I was shocked to find out that most residents of rural Saskatchewan considered a firearm a necessity. I think it had something to do with the large population of bears, coyotes, and raccoons that were more common than stray dogs and cats in the bigger cities. Thankfully, I hadn't had to deal with any of the dumpster-diving raccoons that Mrs. Swazle warned me of. Probably because I lived with a werewolf.

"She couldn't see their faces, except for one guy. No fangs, but that doesn't mean he wasn't a vamp since you guys don't always walk around with them hanging out. He had long dark hair, dark eyes, big shoulders, and a semiautomatic gun," I told Ozzy.

"PIMP agents are only issued automatics. We don't use semis. Too slow against supernatural law breakers." His voice was a mix of thoughtful and smug as he tapped his fingers on the steering wheel. "And judging by the number of shots that missed, I'd say whoever did this wasn't trained to use it."

"Why would anyone impersonate a PIMP agent to wipe out an entire brood? And kidnap Marissa, when they could have just killed her?" I mused aloud, willing to give his theory some honest consideration now that I had a better picture of what had happened.

"In case any of the vamps escaped, they would have wanted a scapegoat for the attack," Ozzy pointed out. I could see the merit in his theory, since that's exactly what had happened when Merrick had gotten away unharmed.

****

Apparently, using magic to pull a ghost into this realm came at a cost. Within minutes of hitting the blacktop, I was out like a light. A snoring, drooling light.

I woke up in the cab of my truck with my face smooshed against Ozzy's shoulder and a kink in my neck. His leather coat made a loud squelching sound as I peeled my cheek free from the fabric so I could sit up.

"Ugh, what time is it?" I asked sleepily.

"Time for you to get some sleep in your own bed." Ozzy pulled the keys from the ignition and slid out of the truck.

"Hey, where did Vanessa go?" I asked when I discovered the passenger seat was now vacant.

"She's gone?" he asked in surprise.

"Yeah." Well, that was kind of rude of her to leave without saying goodbye.

I shifted myself across the drivers' seat and out of the truck. My knees immediately buckled, and Ozzy caught me before I could hit the ground.

"Thanks," I mumbled, mortified that the big bad vamp was seeing me so weak.

"Don't worry about it," he said before swinging me up into his arms. "That was some pretty powerful magic you expended tonight. It's normal to crash afterward."

God, it was like getting hit by a train after indulging in at least four bottles of cheap wine. If this is what it was like to use magic, then I was never using magic again. Not to mention that I was still pretty freaked out about seeing Vanessa's ghost. Yep, no more magic for this girl.

Ozzy let us in through the front door, which wasn't really a surprise since I didn't bother with locks anymore.

"Next time won't be so bad—" Ozzy was saying before he came to an abrupt halt.

I opened my mouth to tell him there wouldn't be a next time, but the words froze in my throat. We weren't alone.

Two grim-looking fae stood in my dining room.

"Lief?" I tried to push my hair out of my face, but my hand was like lead and I didn't have the strength to lift it.

"Release her."

Uh-oh. Oakenlief, the dark prince of Fairie, was using his I'm-an-entitled-jerk voice, and Ozzy bristled in response. I did not have it in me to deal with another male pissing contest.

"What are you doing here?" I asked.

"I felt a surge of magic and came to see if you were all right."

"I'm fine, just need some sleep is all," I told him.

"She's not fine. She used every drop of magic she had to pull a ghost into this realm. She's completely drained," Ozzy informed him.

"What? That's not possible—she's human," Lief protested.

Have I mentioned how much I hate when people talk about me like I'm not here?

Ozzy shrugged, startling a gasp out of me when I thought he might drop me. "Have you ever known Theo to do what's expected?"

"No, I suppose not." The chuckle rumbled in Lief's voice.

As soon as I could lift my hand again, I was going to smack him.

Ozzy deposited me on the couch, and I finally got a good look at one of my unannounced visitors.

Dressed in a black shirt and pants, Lief returned the sword he'd been holding to its place on his back. His dark hair had grown since the last time I'd seen him and was long enough to graze his shoulders. He strode across my small living room and knelt in front of me.

"What trouble have you gotten yourself into this time, my dear Theo?" His words were teasing, but apprehension clouded his pale eyes. I told myself not to stare, but the way the blue fragmented, like facets of a diamond, was mesmerizing.

"No trouble; just a ghost. Nothing I couldn't handle." And wasn't that a sad reflection on the normalcy in my life?

"May I?" Lief held out his hand, and I knew what he was asking for. The fae were able to sense each other's magic but needed a tangible connection to share it. After a brief hesitation, I put my hand in his. I hadn't forgotten how intimate the experience could be, and I needed the few seconds to prepare myself mentally.

The dark prince's magic slammed into me in a powerful wave that made both of us cry out in surprise. Lief's grip on my fingers tightened until it was painful, but I didn't try to pull away. His magic rushed through me, filling places that had been empty and starting to wither even before I'd brought Vanessa's ghost back to life. It was like trying to fill a teacup from a garden hose.

31

His magic was clean and crisp and tasted like a cold glass of water on a hot day. I shuddered as it teased its way through my limbs and brought my own back to life.

"*Stop!*" The bubble of privacy that had surrounded Lief and me was suddenly shattered by a woman's voice, reminding me that we had an audience. "You're draining him!"

I dropped Lief's hand like he'd developed a deadly case of hand-foot-and-mouth disease, and scooted as far back on the sofa as I could. My eyes shot to the woman standing behind Lief, and I briefly thought about climbing right off the couch to get even farther away from the angry fae.

Hair that varied in shades of red from dark auburn to carrot orange was pulled into a severe bun, and I immediately recognized her luminescent green eyes from that morning in Farranen's window. Her snug black pants, tall boots, and pale gray shirt with gold buttons identified her as one of the queen's soldiers. Her hand rested on the hilt of the dagger that hung from her waist, and her tense expression suggested she was debating using it. Most likely on me, since I tended to piss people off.

"My lord?" She spared a glance to where Lief knelt with his forearm braced on my old couch.

"I'm fine, Celesta." He shot me a quick look full of self-recrimination and humor, but I didn't miss the fine lines around his eyes that hadn't been there a minute ago.

"I'm sorry…" I didn't even know exactly what to apologize for. I'd clearly taken some of his energy to bolster my own, but how big a faux pas had I committed? Judging from Celesta's disapproving glare, it was a pretty big one.

"It's nothing to fret over, my dear. You just caught me off guard; it's been a while since I've felt anything like that." He rose to his feet, lacking the usual grace that I'd always seen him use.

"What the hell was *that?*" Ozzy demanded from the other side of the room.

"It would seem that our dear Theo has inherited another ankou trait: the ability to pull magic from other fae," Lief told him, sounding every bit like a proud parent after their kid's first soccer goal in second grade.

"Well...fuck." I buried my face in my hands. I did not need any more magical bullshit in my life. I was damn sick of having the supernatural spotlight on me all the time.

"I thought her transition failed? She still feels human," Celesta mused, as if we were discussing an interesting complex math equation rather than my messed-up life.

"Yes, well, our Theo has always been a bit of an anomaly," Lief told her. The jerk. Even if I was an anomaly, I didn't want everyone in the nonhuman grapevine to hear about it.

"I'm going to bed," I announced. Lief's borrowed magic was more potent that I'd thought, because I didn't even fall on my face when I stood up. Actually, I felt great considering I'd been too weak to walk from the truck to my cabin.

As I shuffled toward the bathroom, Celesta said, "We need to tell her—"

"No." Lief cut her off. "She's had enough to deal with tonight. She needs to sleep—"

"Oh, for fuck's sake!" I turned and stormed back into the living room. "How am I supposed to sleep knowing there's *more* fae drama waiting to hit the fan? You can't say things like that and expect me to pretend I didn't hear!"

"Theo, this can wait until you're rested and—"

Lief's protest was cut short as Celesta announced, "Farranen has been imprisoned in the queen's dungeons."

My ire deflated in a heartbeat, and I sank onto an armchair as the world tilted around me.

"What?" I asked, hoping I'd heard her wrong.

"The guardian refused the queen's orders and was sent to the dungeons."

I looked over at Lief, and the regret etched into his face was all the confirmation I needed to know Celesta was telling the truth.

"But...but...why?" Why on earth would Farranen disobey the queen? He was a real stickler for the law, definitely not the kind of guy that went around breaking the rules for shits and giggles.

"There's been some political upheaval in the court since the last time you were there, Theo," Lief said in a resigned tone.

"Political upheaval? Like an election?" I asked.

"A rebellion."

I could feel the tension in his simple words. "What? Who would rebel against the queen?" She was a damn scary bitch and not someone I would ever want to cross.

"Me," Lief stated flatly.

I stared into his crystalline eyes, hoping for a sign that he was jesting, but there was nothing but conviction and a hint of weariness.

With a sigh, I stood up and went to the kitchen to put on a pot of coffee and find the half a cinnamon swirl cake I'd stashed in the fridge. It looked like I wasn't going to be getting any sleep tonight, but there was no reason I had to be sleep-deprived on an empty stomach.

****

Ozzy left sometime before the sun came up, promising to return the next night. Although, it sounded more like a threat than a promise to my suspicious ears.

Dog finally slunk in ten minutes after the vampire's departure. His knack for avoiding Ozzy was uncanny. Giving Celesta a wide berth, he padded over to where I sat on the couch and flopped down at my feet.

Lief and Celesta had filled me in on the turmoil that was brewing in Fairie. I can't say that I was able to completely wrap my head around everything that had happened in the last few weeks, but I grasped the basics.

After learning of my possible transition, the queen had latched onto the idea of creating more changelings with all the morbid enthusiasm and madness of an evil scientist. But instead of using the somewhat predictable method of infecting fragile humans, she'd taken to kidnapping nymphs, shifters, and yep, you guessed it— vampires. When Lief had dropped that little nugget of information, Ozzy had nearly lost it. It turned out his mouth was even more foul than his temper. My ears were still burning from the inventive streak of curse words he'd unleashed.

Unsurprisingly, the fae were somewhat divided on

the subject of abducting supernaturals from this realm to bring back to Fairie. The queen had a lot of supporters, but a growing group feared her actions would lead to retribution once the missing females were traced back to the fae realm.

"There are roughly three thousand fae living in Fairie. Eighteen hundred of the Dark Court and twelve hundred of the Light. Some fae live in the wild lands and are ignorant of the queen's recent pursuits, but of the ones that do know, many don't agree with her methods. There are fifty that I know to be trustworthy to the rebellion, while the queen has at least a hundred loyal followers involved in this ridiculous attempt to repopulate her court." Lief absently drummed his fingers on the back of my couch as he relayed Fairie's predicament to me. His normally relaxed demeanor had been replaced by a tension so thick I could practically see it winding through him. Seeing him like this put me on edge. If the mighty dark prince was worried, then we should all be worried.

"So, what's the end goal here? Dethrone the queen? Who would take her place?" I asked. I didn't know much about uprisings in this world and even less about fae politics.

"Whoever takes her head takes the throne," Celesta told me.

"*What?* You want to *assassinate* her?" I said, disbelief making my words loud in the small cabin.

"The queen will never willingly surrender her crown; it must be removed by force."

If I'd ever doubted this woman was a hardened soldier, I had no such misconceptions anymore. Her casual talk of murdering her people's leader was downright chilling. Realistically, something had to be done to stop the kidnappings in this world, but I would have preferred a less lethal method. Wasn't there some kind of Fairie jail they could lock the queen in? As guardian of the gate, Farranen had returned the fae that crossed unlawfully into this realm back to Fairie to stand trial. That had to mean they had some sort of legal structure, right?

Gah, I was far too tired to grasp the full extent of the fae's justice system. I'd been up since yesterday morning; my brain was no longer firing on all cylinders.

"I'm heading to bed," I told them as I stretched my tired muscles and shuffled toward my bedroom with Dog slinking along in my wake.

"I could use some rest myself," Lief remarked, and I instantly felt guilty for stealing all his energy. "We'll return this evening and hopefully come up with a strategy."

I stopped and turned around. "A strategy for what? And why am I involved in this?" I wasn't fae; technically, none of this was my problem.

"To rescue Farranen." Lief's eyebrows slanted down in confusion, like he was talking to a particularly dumb animal. "He is your true mate, is he not?"

I slowly shook my head while my mouth hung open in surprise. "*Noooo...*"

My feet needed to get their act together and take me to bed. I'd avoided asking about Farranen since Celesta dropped the bombshell about him being locked in the dungeons. I didn't want to talk about him. Even thinking about him was painful, and no way in hell would I have an emotional breakdown in front of Lief and Celesta.

"He didn't tell you what the mark meant?"

"What mark?"

"Your mating mark."

"What are you talking about?" I demanded, sounding angrier than I meant to. Lief wasn't the only one to look confused now, and not knowing what the hell was going on always made me cranky.

"The mark appears when true mates consummate their bond. It's different in each bloodline; Farranen is from the Luminess line, and I can't actually recall the last time there was a mated pair in that family."

"I don't have a mark!" I sounded hysterical, but I couldn't keep the panic out of my voice. "There was no bonding thing! And we sure as hell didn't *consummate* anything!"

"You didn't—"

"No!" At the time, I'd definitely been on board with spending some time between the sheets with my guardian, and I'd even thought he might be interested too. Boy, had I been wrong. We'd come close, since the queen had essentially ordered him to impregnate me. Thankfully, Farranen had found a loophole in her royal decree, and we'd followed it down to the letter— meaning, I'd shared my bed and he'd fulfilled his duty to share his seed, but we'd never actually had sex.

Humiliation rushed through me, and my magic stirred in response.

I took a deep breath to calm my churning emotions before I started to cry. I didn't want these two warriors to see me at my weakest.

"Theo—" Lief reached for me, but I backstepped closer to the safety of my bedroom.

"Don't," I told him. "Just don't. I hope your

rebellion is successful and you stop all the kidnappings, but I can't help you."

I turned and fled until my bedroom door was between us with the flimsy lock engaged.

I wanted to help, I truly did, but I couldn't stomach the thought of facing Farranen again. Yeah, I was taking the coward's way out, but if I was forced to look into his beautiful green eyes again, I didn't know that I'd be able to walk away with my righteous anger still intact. His betrayal had cut deep, but I wasn't too proud to admit that some small part of me still hoped it had all been a misunderstanding. That maybe he'd wanted me after all.

I threw the brakes on that particular train of thought before it could carry me away. I was going to get into my coziest pajamas, climb into bed, and forget all about the man that had walked out on me.

And as for all the other complications popping up in my life—well, I'd just deal with them one ghost at a time.

Chapter Four

My sleep was fitful and full of memories that I wished I could forget. And not nearly long enough.

Celesta strode into my bedroom less than four hours after I'd walked out of Lief's let's-pull-Theo-even-deeper-into-the-world-of-supernatural-bullshit meeting. She flung my curtains wide open, nearly blinding me with sunlight before rummaging through my closet like a homeless woman hunting for bottles in a dumpster.

"Here, get dressed." She flung a pair of jeans and sweater on the bed, then proceeded to paw through the underwear in my dresser.

"Hey!" I was going for an affronted bitch tone, but ended up sounding like a scandalized librarian.

"Hurry up; we need to get moving." She crossed her arms impatiently. "The dark prince left to meet with an informant, and we need to be gone before he returns."

"Gone where?" I stupidly looked at the clothes until it hit me that she expected me to change with her in the room. Honestly, the fae had absolutely no sense of propriety. Big girls don't strip down in front of other women they just met. Especially tall, beautiful women that put swimsuit models to shame.

"Fairie."

"What? No. *No*. I'm *not* going to Fairie." No way

in hell was I going anywhere near the magical realm. Who knows how my magic would react? It was less predictable and more volatile than a teenage girl with PMS.

Celesta rolled her eyes in exasperation and lowered herself onto the end of my bed with something that was too graceful to be called a flounce, but too elegant to simply say she sat down. "The dark prince said you were stubborn. I can see why."

Lief had told her I was stubborn? The jerk.

"He is fond of you, so I can see why he wished to spare your delicate human sensibilities."

He was fond of me? Maybe he wasn't such a jerk after all.

"However, you have a right to know the things he failed to tell you."

"What things?" Okay, now I was curious. Lief had already given me more information than I knew what to do with, so what could he have possibly left out? My imagination was happy to supply a few possibilities until I told it to shut the hell up.

"The dark prince's magic is especially strong in seeing prospective events to come."

"Prospective events to come?" I asked in confusion.

"He can see the future."

"Lief can *see* the *future*?" My mouth literally fell open. I knew the fae had some pretty amazing talents, but seeing the future was something straight out of a fantasy novel.

"Yes, he doesn't speak of it often because it's not entirely accurate. His visions show him the most likely outcome, but nothing is set in stone." She eyed me thoughtfully, like she was trying to decide how much to say. Or maybe, how much I would understand with my tiny little human brain. "You were in one of his visions."

Of course I was. I held my breath, waiting to hear what new metaphysical hell hole was waiting to open up and swallow me. If Lief's vision had been of me winning the lottery or anything good, she would have just told me. No, she was definitely building up to something that I wasn't going to like.

"In his vision, he saw you die in Fairie before you could reach your true mate to receive his mark. He assumed that you and the guardian had already completed the bond, so there was no way his vision could come to fruition."

"But we didn't…" I gestured with my hand vaguely, hoping she'd interpret it as a reference to sex.

"And that's why he doesn't want you involved anymore. The possibility of the vision coming true is real, and he doesn't want to put you in unnecessary danger."

Oh. Good. Right? I didn't want to be a part of this insane rescue mission. Did I?

As if she'd been waiting for a sign of my inner doubts to present themselves, she opened her mouth and played the one card that was guaranteed to get my attention. "He also neglected to tell you how your guardian came to be chained up and tortured in the queen's dungeons."

Wait—*tortured?* Farranen was being *tortured?* My stomach dropped down into my toes, and I thought I might be sick. I distinctly remember Celesta saying he'd been imprisoned in the dungeon. There had been no mention of any bodily harm. Until now, my naïve human brain had pictured the dungeons in Fairie as someplace better than a kid's summer camp, but a step down from a luxury motel. Images of clean sheets, three meals a day, and cable TV were replaced with thumbscrews and the rack.

"Tortured?" I asked weakly. It's a good thing I was already sitting down, because my limbs felt all tingly, and I doubted my legs had the strength to hold me up.

Celesta nodded, and something close to pity flashed across her face. "Farranen was appointed to guard the gate almost four hundred years ago. I don't know what happened to the former guardian...It doesn't really matter. Anyway, he marched into the throne room, bowed to the queen, and proceeded to tell her that he wouldn't fulfill her royal decree. Not that he *can't* fulfill it, just that he *won't*."

I could hear the admiration in her voice. I had to assume the queen didn't hear the word no very often. It was totally morbid, but I wish I'd been there to see her face.

"She ordered her soldiers to take him to the dungeons, and it took seven men to subdue him. *Seven*." Respect crackled through her words. "For the first couple weeks she waited, expecting him to come around. When that didn't happen, she attempted to remove the mantle of guardianship from him." Her lips twisted into a cruel smile. "But he refused to relinquish it."

I opened my mouth to ask what that meant, but she must have sensed my confusion and continued with, "As queen, she should have been able to strip his title and some of his powers. But somehow, Farranen's magic has grown and now rivals hers."

I remembered Farranen saying something about his powers increasing since he'd been appointed to guardian.

"She will continue to have him tortured until he gives up control of the gate."

"Why doesn't he just give it to her?" My voice was thick with emotions I'd rather not name. Why the hell wouldn't he just give her what she wanted? The thought of what he'd been enduring for weeks made me want to punch the queen right in her fae lady parts.

"He must have learned of the queen's attempts to create more changelings. Without access to his gate, it will be harder for her to bring females back to Fairie. And even if he did step down as guardian, she'd still punish him for trying to defy her orders. She wants to make an example of his disobedience."

I shouldn't ask, but I pushed the words past my numb lips anyway. I know, I'm a sucker for punishment. "What exactly did he refuse to do?" I had my suspicions, but I was hoping that I was wrong.

"The edict she tasked him with regarding you. He demanded she retract it and release you from any further rulings." She smirked. "He didn't *ask*, he *demanded*. I never knew the guardian had such big balls."

That sounded exactly like something Farranen would have done. I was grateful and a little touched that he'd thought to have me released from the queen's tyrannical influence. Yes, I was still angry at the way he'd ended things between us, but that anger no longer had the sharp jagged edges that it previously had. Now it was more of a slow-burning resentment. And while I knew he had no romantic interest in me, on some level, he must still care.

"So how do we get him out?" I asked with a growl.

Celesta blinked once before a slow grin lit up her face. "You are even more stubborn than the dark prince gives you credit for."

****

My body was still tired, but the cold fresh air of the woods slapped away most of my aches and pains.

After getting dressed and wolfing down a bowl of cereal, I followed Celesta through my backyard and into the trees. I assumed we were headed for the gate, since there wasn't anything else out here but miles of rugged boreal forest.

"So, what's the plan?" I asked, hoping to God that she had a plan. Farranen, Lief, and even Ozzy seemed to have a very loose definition of the word. Their plans usually had a bring-lots-of-sharp-pointy-weapons-and-if-anyone-gets-in-our-way-we'll-kick-their-ass-until-they're-out-of-our-way feel to them.

"If the gate is open, we'll cross into Fairie. If it's not, then we'll wait until it opens."

I waited for her to continue, and when she didn't, I realized with a sinking feeling that I was heading into another life-threatening situation with nothing but two knives and a fae soldier for backup.

"Once we cross, I'll take you to one of the rebels. She'll be able to get you to the dungeons."

"But you're coming too, right?"

"The dark prince requires my presence here. My unexplained disappearance would be questioned."

"So once we get there, I'm on my own?" Horror filled me at the prospect of being alone in Fairie. "But I need you! I can't do this by myself!" It wouldn't be a rescue mission without a badass warrior like her. How was I supposed to navigate my way through a foreign land that I'd only been to twice before? I couldn't even speak the fae language. This trip was doomed to fail.

"Mary will be there to guide you through the wild lands. She is one of Lief's strongest supporters, and you can trust her." Celesta spoke with the confidence of someone used to delegating tasks and having her orders followed. Too bad for her that I didn't like being told what to do.

I opened my mouth to poke some holes in her drafty plan, but the toe of my boot caught on an exposed root and I went ass over teakettle onto the snowy ground. Celesta grabbed my elbow and hauled me back to my feet before giving my outfit a scrutinizing gaze. "I told you to dress for traveling on foot."

I looked down at my jeans and black boots. They were the closest thing I owned that qualified for a rugged trek in the winter woods. Definitely more rugged than the pile of yoga pants in my dresser. Not only did the low-riding cut look amazing on my big hips, but they made me feel like an ass-kicking warrior woman. My sweater was made out of the softest wool I'd ever felt, and I hoped the dark forest-green color would hide any dirt or blood that I was likely to get on it. I knew firsthand that the boots wouldn't give me blisters.

I shrugged at Celesta; if she had a problem with my outfit, then she could run to the nearest outdoors store and find something more appropriate.

It took longer than usual to reach the clearing with

the hawthorn tree, partly due to my clumsiness and partly because nobody had been clearing the path of fallen branches and logs for the last few months. There were footprints in the snow, evidence that it was being used, probably by Celesta and Lief, but some of the prints didn't look human and I glanced around the woods uneasily. Who—or what—had come through the gate lately? I didn't really want to know.

Before we attempted to cross through the gate, Celesta glamoured my winter jacket into a cloak so I'd be able to blend in easier. Her forehead wrinkled in concentration as she held onto the fabric; apparently using glamour required more effort for her than it did for Farranen or Lief. Interesting. Was it because their magic was more powerful than hers? It would probably be rude to ask, so I kept my curiosity to myself.

I pulled the hood up until my face was hidden in its black depths. It completely covered everything above my boots, and I was grateful she didn't try to change my clothes too; I'd been wearing them the last time I'd seen Farranen, and my stupid heart wasn't ready to give them up. Maybe I did have a streak of sentimentality in me after all.

"You should be able to pass for fae, but don't let anyone touch you. Any physical contact and they'll sense your magic is…off."

That was fine with me; I had no desire to get close to anyone in Fairie.

I wanted to ask how she knew what my magic felt like, since I didn't remember ever touching her, but before I could, she took my hand and pulled me toward the gate.

"We may have to wait. The gate is tied directly to

its guardian and has become unstable since his imprisonment. If he's unconscious or too weak, it won't open."

Something in my chest clenched at the thought of what could bring my big strong fae low enough that he lost control over the gate. If I ever came face to face with the queen bitch, I was going to tear her apart.

Celesta extended her hand and tentatively stepped forward until she disappeared into the tree, pulling me with her.

There was a bright flash of light, and then we were walking through a warm curtain of magic that parted as we passed through it. It only lasted for a few seconds, but my magic continued to buzz and tingle long after we stepped into the clearing in Fairie. And I could be wrong, but the magic of the gate felt weaker than the last time I'd crossed it. Then again, maybe I was just looking for problems where there were none. Either way, I couldn't shake the uneasy feeling that something was wrong as I glanced around.

The hawthorn clearing had an abundance of tall, graceful trees with twisted limbs that met overhead to create a soaring canopy of leaves just starting to turn yellow and orange. The beautiful flowers and fragrant fruit that used to hang from them were gone. A glittering backdrop made up of thousands of stars peeked out from behind the leaves. Even without any visible moon, it was bright enough to light up the clearing and paths that led away from the gate.

I peeked out from beneath the hood of my cloak and followed Celesta when she strode down the path straight ahead of us. It wasn't a path that would lead us to either of the castles, and I wondered where we were going. I'd just assumed that the dungeons would be under the queen's castle. Stupid me—you'd think that by now I'd know not to make any assumptions about the fae.

"Where are we going?" I asked, trying not to sound too suspicious.

"To meet Mary."

Oh, right. I'd forgotten about her.

We traveled in silence, and that was fine since I had no idea what to say to the warrior woman. I doubted we had much in common; we were as different as night and day. I obviously didn't share any of her beauty or confidence with weapons. I wondered if she watched movies when she was visiting my realm. Comparing opinions on movies seemed like a safe topic of conversation. What was the last movie I'd seen? I didn't want to come off sounding racist and should probably avoid anything supernatural. Nothing came to mind; these days, I usually let Dog choose, and he had a thing for werewolves, witches, and the fae. I'd seen enough zombie movies in the last few months to last me a lifetime. God help me if he ever found out about the superhero convention every spring in Saskatoon.

The narrow path through the woods had widened into a real road about a mile back, and the woods had thinned to reveal wide swathes of fields hidden past the large clusters of trees. Beyond the fields, I caught glimpses of gently sloped hills that blotted out the stars. The air was still, like it was watching us. But this was Fairie, so it was entirely possible that it was indeed watching us.

Movement in the trees caught my eye, and I peered out from under the fabric of my cloak just in time to see a small figure scamper up the branches and disappear into the dense foliage.

"A tree nigma." Celesta informed me without breaking her swift stride. "They harvest the genda fruit of the manga trees. They're relatively harmless."

I grunted a sound of acknowledgement and focused on keeping up to the female fae.

Being in a new realm was fascinating. *And potentially deadly*, I reminded myself.

Celesta set a brisk pace, and I spent the next hour trying to keep up to the nimble fae. Finally, just when I thought I'd have to suck up my pride and ask for a reprieve from her brutal march, she halted next to a pile of moss-covered boulders. I flopped down onto one of the smaller ones and struggled to catch my breath. When I got home, I was going to increase my morning runs to five kilometers because this was just embarrassing. If Celesta noticed my wheezing, she gave no indication.

"Where are we?" I asked, hoping like hell we'd reached our final destination. Everything in Fairie was saturated with magic, and the constant awareness was making me antsy; I wanted to find Farranen and get the heck back home.

Another thought struck me—what was I supposed to do with my guardian if I was able to break him out? I doubted he could stay in Fairie, since he'd essentially be a fugitive. How was I supposed to get him back to the gate? Was he even in any condition to travel? Maybe Lief could send some of the fae that had joined his secret rebellion. Wait—Lief didn't know I was here. Damn it.

Before I could address the mounting list of doubts

about our flimsy plan, a tall dark figure peeled away from the shadows, and I let out a startled shriek.

Celesta shot me an annoyed glance before addressing the newcomer. "Merry meet."

"Merry meet," a woman's voice answered. I couldn't see her face beneath the black hood, but I instantly recognized her towering height and stooped posture for what it was—she was an ankou fae.

I surged to my feet, tripping in my haste to get farther away from the dark fae. Memories of Lebolus's attack were still fresh, and I wasn't going to give the bitch a chance to sink her claws into me. I fumbled past the long fabric of my cloak until my hunting knife was gripped in my shaking hand.

"Theo!" Celesta walked toward me with her hands out in a placating gesture. Didn't she see the murderous fae? Why didn't she have her sword out?

I pointed to where the dark fae lurked and made some sort of incoherent jangle of syllables that didn't make much sense.

"*Theo!*" Celesta sounded exasperated as she continued to try to get my attention. "This is Mary."

I halted my backward shuffle and looked over at her in disbelief. "*What?*" was the only thing I could think to say.

"She'll be your guide," Celesta informed me, speaking in that too-slow tone that adults use to explain complex concepts to small children.

"But she's...she's...ankou." My brain struggled to sort through what it knew to be true, and what Celesta was saying.

Something foreign crossed Celesta's face, and it took me a minute to identify it as pity. Which only pissed me off.

"Mary is one of the dark prince's most trusted followers. I wouldn't have brought her here if I thought she was a threat."

I peeled back the sleeve of my cloak and waved my scarred arm in the air. "I know exactly what she can do!" The dark purple lines had faded slightly in the last few months, but it was still easy to see where Lebolus had gripped me with his razor-sharp claws.

"Mary didn't attack you, Theo. Not all dark fae would hurt a human if they were given the chance. Assuming Mary is a killer is like saying all Germans are genocide supporters."

"How do you know about our wars?" I asked. Yes, I was still freaked out, but my curiosity got the better of me.

"We've been using Farranen's residence as a home base while in your realm; he has an impressive assortment of books."

"Oh."

Our conversation lapsed into silence, and my fingers throbbed from holding the knife so tightly.

"We should get going." Mary's gravelly voice sounded as if it had been conjured straight out of my nightmares to go along with her Grim Reaper wannabe appearance. "The longer we wait, the likelier we are to be spotted together."

Celesta nodded and stepped closer to me. "Theo, I must return to the Earth realm. Mary will get you to the dungeons and help you free the guardian."

I started to protest, but she silenced me with a look.

"The dark prince is working to initiate the first stages of his coup. When the queen learns that there is more to Farranen's disobedience than just his infatuation with one human, she will kill him as an example to any who would dare oppose her."

I flinched.

"I don't have to tell you that the ankou are inherently stealthy, as well as deadly. She is your best chance at getting him out alive."

I couldn't keep the distrust off my face as I glanced over to where Mary waited demurely, as if we didn't all know exactly how dangerous she was. Like a sleeping viper that could wake at any time to strike.

God, I wished Dog was here. Why hadn't I thought to bring him?

Oh, right. Because I'd foregone all rational thoughts at the mention of someone torturing Farranen and gone running off to Fairie with a half-assed plan that was likely to get me killed. I hadn't even thought to stock the fridge before I left. Poor Dog was going to have to go back to eating rabbits and squirrels again, like he'd been doing before I found him.

Since going after Farranen on my own wasn't an option, and I wasn't leaving without him, it looked like I was stuck with Mary.

"This is the stupidest thing I've ever done," I muttered to myself as I lowered my knife and took a tentative step toward the other women.

Celesta turned and soundlessly disappeared back the way we'd come from, leaving me with a fae that may or may not decide to rip my head off and drink from my neck like a giant juice box. This was turning out to be a seriously crappy night. Not even cake would have made this bearable.

Chapter Five

Going from twenty-four inches of snow in minus twenty-degree weather to a balmy autumn evening was like turning on the hot tap after your bath water has gone tepid. Not that I'd actually know, since my hot water heater was a piece of garbage. But still, you get the idea. It was glorious.

I wanted to take off my cloak to feel the light breeze on my skin, but I couldn't risk any Fairie inhabitants catching sight of my face, in case word got back to the queen.

After my red-headed chaperone had departed without so much as a goodbye, Mary pulled a pack from beneath her cloak and wordlessly handed it to me. A cursory glance showed that it held a skin of water and enough bread, cheese, and a weird purple fruit to last at least a night or two. Following her lead, I strapped it to my back under my cloak, giving me a hunchback appearance. The irony of looking like a mini version of the ankou wasn't lost on me.

Beneath my hood, I scowled as I followed Mary off the road into the woods. This was probably the last thing a victim of a serial killer would see before they were buried in a shallow grave.

"Aren't there any roads that will take us to the dungeons?" I groused.

"It's easier to remain undetected if we avoid the

roads," Mary explained in an annoyingly patient tone.

The trees were spaced far enough apart that walking was a relatively smooth endeavor, and I only tripped twice. It also allowed us to be on the lookout for other fae. And though I occasionally heard the rustle of movement in the foliage, I never actually saw anyone.

Unused to small talk and unwilling to play nice with my escort, I let the silence of the forest settle over me. It was tranquil, and my anger and resentment slowly melted away under the calming buzz of magic from the plants and trees.

We walked for longer than I thought I'd be capable of, climbing occasional inclines and skirting small creeks that burbled happily over time-worn pebbles.

"We can make camp here."

I jumped at the sound of Mary's voice when it cut through my daydreaming. I didn't bother with a reply, I just set to work building a makeshift bed out of my cloak while Mary started a small fire.

When she urged me to try the rations in my bag, my suspicion skyrocketed. During my first trip to Fairie, Farranen had warned me that fae food could have an unpredictable outcome on humans, and it would be a risk to eat anything. At the time, it hadn't been a problem since I'd only stayed for a few hours.

My stomach chose that moment to let out an embarrassingly large growl, reminding me that I hadn't eaten since the cereal that morning. After traveling for the better part of the day, I was starving.

I pulled the fabric-wrapped bundle out of my pack and sniffed the small white lump of cheese. The sweet nutty smell reminded me of swiss or aged cheddar. The hard disc of bread was dark, like pumpernickel, and I picked up mouth-watering hints of molasses. I gave the meal one last suspicious look, and then with my fingers crossed that I wouldn't turn into a hedgehog, I took a bite. It was surprisingly normal tasting, and my tastebuds approved.

"We should get some sleep and head out in the morning," Mary stated as she tucked our leftovers back into our bags.

I looked at the starry sky and gave her a mistrustful look. "How can you tell what time it is? It's been dark since I got here."

Her shoulders moved in a parody of a shrug. "Fairie has no sun or moon like your Earth does. Our diurnal cycle is regulated by the queen and prince's magic. The fact that she has lost control of such a simple task is just another sign that the Light Court is ready for a new monarch." The conviction in her voice dispelled any doubts I had about her playing for Team Lief.

I thought about letting it go, but eventually I ended up asking, "So what happens when the queen is no longer in charge?"

"Someone new will ascend to the throne."

I didn't say anything out loud, but what if the new king or queen was even worse than the current one?

I lay awake in the semidarkness long after the fire had died down to embers, contemplating the possible outcomes of tomorrow.

Death was the likeliest. My death. Farranen's death. Probably even Mary's death. It was my least favorite scenario, but the most likely. Sneaking our way into the dungeon, only to get caught and imprisoned was also a real possibility. Two women trying to outwit an entire army of magical beings—the odds were seriously stacked against us.

Riding off into the sunset with Farranen was probably the least likely thing to happen. But, hey—a girl could dream. With that last thought, I let the soft sounds of the forest wash over me as my exhaustion dragged me into a welcome sleep.

****

I hadn't been sure what to expect the queen's dungeons to look like—but a cozy cottage in the middle of the woods wasn't it.

The quaint little building was made entirely of smooth stones, with shuttered windows on either side of the front door. A lazy tendril of smoke curled from the chimney, drifting upward until it disappeared into the sky. It was straight out of Hansel and Gretel, minus the gingerbread and gumdrops.

Mary and I knelt in the bushes as we surveyed the property.

"I don't see any guards," I stage whispered. Somebody better call a movie director, because I was a shoo-in to join the cast for the next *Expendables* movie. I could play the girl that busted in and rescued Sylvester Stallone after he'd been imprisoned by our common enemy, using only my stealth and wits. Yeah, probably not.

Mary made a noncommittal noise that grated on my ears as she studied the small cottage for weaknesses. "Stay here," she told me, disappearing without a sound into the forest behind us before I could protest being left alone.

After several minutes, Mary still hadn't returned, so I mentally prepared for a combat situation.

Annnnnnd…Yeah, I actually had no idea how to prepare for any sort of upcoming physical conflict. But it kept my mind off my inevitable reunion with Farranen.

I was terrible at hiding my emotions. That was one of the biggest reasons I'd bought a cabin in the middle of nowhere—so I wouldn't have to hide what I was feeling from anyone. I forced my face into a cold mask of indifference, but it probably looked more like I'd taken a bite of something sour while wearing pants that were three sizes too small.

I looked up just in time to see Mary stroll down the cobblestone path and wave me forward.

"What's wrong?" she asked when I joined her.

"Nothing." I looked around but didn't see anything amiss.

"You look like you just ate an unripe gojio fruit."

I shot her a dirty look and rearranged my face back into its normal suspicious lines. "Is that *blood?*" I asked when I caught sight of a wet spot on her cloak.

"Yes. There were more guards than I anticipated. They must have been expecting us."

"How could they know we were coming?"

"There is likely a traitor among the dark prince's followers."

That didn't sound good, especially since most of the fae didn't know that Lief was amassing his own army.

"Come, we need to be gone before the next shift arrives and finds these guards incapacitated."

The way she said *incapacitated* sent a shiver down my back. I doubted her idea of incapacitated meant she'd distracted them with tea and cookies.

I followed her through the front door and into the simple three-room building. The main room held a table with two chairs, a small kitchen, and two fae sprawled on the floor. A bedroom with neatly made beds was along the far wall, and the only other door in the room revealed a crude bathroom.

I breathed a little easier when I saw the fae were both still alive.

In the center of the floor, a wide staircase had been cut into the stone, with its steps leading straight down into what I assumed was the dungeon. Or possibly hell. Metal sconces were mounted on the walls at regular intervals to hold torches that burned far too brightly to be normal flames.

"We're going down there, aren't we?" I asked, even though I already knew the answer. Of course we were going down into the pit of death.

Mary didn't bother with words, and after a heartbeat, I straightened my spine and followed her down the scary stairs. The smell of mold and rot combined with unwashed bodies assaulted my nose immediately. I nearly gagged on the disgusting air and had to hold a hand over my nose. Dog after eating cabbage soup had nothing on the foulness of what waited for us below.

Ahead of me, there was a small cry of surprise, followed by a few grunts. By the time I reached the bottom of the stairs and caught up to Mary, she was standing over two fae soldiers. Beneath their unmoving bodies, a puddle of blood was slowly soaking into their gray uniforms and the dirt floor.

I took a tentative step into the room, and it was exactly what I imagined a dungeon should look like.

The ground was hard-packed dirt, and the walls looked like someone had chiseled them straight out of the rock without a single seam or break. Dull metal bars divided the space into four separate cells. They were probably iron; Farranen carried a set of magical handcuffs made of iron because the fae were susceptible to the stuff.

"Are they dead?" I hesitated, not wanting to get any closer in case they were just playing possum and planned to grab me.

"Incapacitated," Mary supplied unhelpfully. I still didn't know if that was code for dead or not dead.

Movement in the farthest cell caught my attention, and I inched closer. A pile of rags shifted, and I realized it was a person. A soft sigh of breath echoed off the stone walls, and my heart stopped. I knew that sound.

"Farranen?" My voice cracked, making my whisper barely intelligible. But he must have heard me because he shifted again.

I didn't remember moving, but suddenly I was up against the bars, tugging at the door. The damn thing wouldn't open, and I let out a frustrated growl that sounded a tad desperate, even to my own ears.

"Here," Mary called from behind me. I turned and caught the keys she'd liberated from one of the guards. It took several tries, but I finally found the right key and turned it in the lock with a shaking hand.

The door swung open, and I took a single step, only to freeze when two green eyes blinked open across the cell. My breath caught in my chest, and my knees gave out. I crawled the rest of the way, uncaring of the dirt and filth that clung to my cloak.

"Farranen?" I asked, even though I knew exactly who those pain-filled eyes belonged to.

"*Theo?*" He blinked again, and some measure of alertness returned to his face.

"Shhh…it's me."

His shirt hung in tatters from one shoulder, black with dirt and sweat and blood. Cuts of varying ages crisscrossed his chest and arms, some still oozing blood. The fact that he hadn't been able to heal himself was a testament to how badly he'd been injured. I blinked back tears at the sight of his ravaged skin. The damage was spread across his entire body, like someone had inflicted as much pain as possible. I'd already known the queen was one sadistic bitch, but this…this was worse than anything my imagination could have come up with. I quickly removed my cloak and draped it across his cold body, the same way he'd wrapped me in his cloak when I'd been attacked by Lebolus.

"My lady…" He lifted a hand and weakly caressed my cheek.

I couldn't help it. I let out a hiccuping sob that refused to stay bottled up any longer. And my magic, already sparking anxiously under my skin, erupted with all the finesse of a dump truck plowing into a cement wall. It soared toward my injured guardian, pulling a startled gasp past my lips as it burrowed into his broken body.

Farranen tensed, making his back bow off the floor and his eyes slide shut. I pulled away, terrified that I was hurting him, but he grabbed my hand with surprising strength. It took a handful of heartbeats until my magic settled and Farranen relaxed enough to fall back to the floor breathing hard.

"Sorry…" I murmured. God, I really needed to get

a hold of my magic, I was likely to kill someone if I kept losing control like this.

Those beautiful green eyes opened again, pinning me with the same mixture of affection and awe that I remembered him having every time he looked at me. Something painful took up residence in my chest, and I had to look away. He could read me like a book, and I didn't want him to see how badly I'd missed him.

"Are you really here?" He spoke softly, as if he was talking to himself. Like he was afraid I really was just a figment of his imagination.

"I'm here." I squeezed his hand for emphasis and gave him a small smile.

Before he could say anything else, a woman's voice called out in alarm, "They're coming!"

My head shot up because it wasn't Mary's scratchy voice that continued to shout, "There's four of them! Move your ass, Theo!"

Vanessa flew down the stairs, looking like a wraith with her hair trailing behind her as she came to an abrupt halt in the center of the room. Farranen must have sensed my sudden tension and pulled himself up to a sitting position.

"Theo!" Vanessa looked at me in exasperation and pointed toward the stairs. "You gotta get out!"

"What is it?" Mary asked in confusion, and I remembered she couldn't see the hysterical ghost that was screaming two feet in front of her. There would be time to explain later; right now, we needed to get the heck out of here.

"Guards—four of them. We need to move."

If Mary was freaked out by my sudden announcement, she didn't let on. With military precision, she pulled two large swords from beneath her cloak. I was surprised I hadn't noticed them before. The metal gleamed in the torchlight, their curved blades reminding me of the fabled scythe that Grim Reapers were always associated with.

I slid my arm around Farranen and hauled him to his feet. He was taller and heavier than me, so it required some grunting and maneuvering, but I finally got him standing. And even though the circumstances were pretty dire, it felt amazing to have his body pressed up against mine again. And yeah, I was completely aware just how pathetic and selfish I'd become.

Together we shuffled across the cell until we joined Mary in the center of the room. I pulled my hunting knife out, grateful that I'd strapped the sheath to the outside of my jeans. The tramp of boots on the stone steps sounded like nails being driven into our foreseeable coffins.

"Theo, it's him!" Vanessa shrieked. "*He* kidnapped the vampire and shot the others!"

I had half a second to wonder what the hell she was talking about before four of the queen's soldiers marched into the room. Two of them were blond and fair-skinned, while the third would never pass for human with his reptilian skin and yellow eyes. The fourth was built like a mountain and had long dark hair and even darker eyes. It took a few seconds for my brain to conclude that he was a perfect match to Vanessa's description of Marissa's abductor.

"Gus." I narrowed my eyes at the queen's Gray Knight. So, Augustus of the Light Court had been the one to shoot down innocent vampires in cold blood. I wasn't actually surprised, since he'd always had a slimeball vibe.

I'd had the misfortune of meeting him once before, during my first visit to Fairie. He'd been sent to escort me (aka force me) to see the queen once she'd heard rumors about a human with fae magic. Gus had attempted to weasel in on attending me during my transition, but Farranen had claimed guardianship over me since he'd been indirectly responsible for exposing me to the fae realm.

With a cocky grin, Gus unsheathed a giant sword from his hip. Waves of aggression and anticipation rolled off his wide shoulders as he gave the blade a few test swings.

"I knew there was more to this than a paltry human." His smirk grew as he stared down Mary while ignoring Farranen and I. "Her Majesty refused to believe the rumors about a rebellion, but I figured if there was any truth to them, the *guardian* was likely involved." He practically spat Farranen's title out like it was curse.

In my experience, that level of animosity was usually fueled by unacknowledged jealousy. And maybe just a touch of crazy.

"I was counting on the fact that someone would eventually come for him." Gus turned his angry gaze over to me, and I tried not to flinch. "I just didn't think it would be a piddly human."

Piddly? Seriously? That was pretty lame as far as insults went. And who even used that word anymore? I opened my mouth to tell him that I'd been called a lot worse before, but that's when all hell broke loose.

The room wasn't big enough for a full-out brawl,

so when Mary launched herself at Gus, the other soldiers were forced to wait their turn before they could engage Farranen and I. Which was a really, really good thing, since I was only armed with my stupid knife.

"I don't suppose you have your sword with you?" I asked hopefully.

"Regretfully, no," he answered, dashing any possibility that it was glamoured and he just hadn't gotten it out yet. Damn.

I handed him my knife with an apologetic grin and fished my smaller knife out of my pocket.

"I don't suppose you brought your shotgun?" he asked.

I snorted in response. I hadn't actually thought there would be any physical fighting; or if there was, I had assumed Mary would take care of it. *Stupid, Theo. Real stupid.* I'd been so concerned with getting to Farranen, I hadn't thought twice about putting my safety in someone else's hands.

I turned my attention back to where Mary and Gus were locked in a deadly dance of blades. Even though Gus was clearly bigger and stronger, Mary held her own, using her height and long limbs to stay one step ahead of the knight. Her black robe swirled around her with a fluidity that had to be magical, and I caught a few flashes of her skeletal triple-jointed fingers as they gripped the handles of her swords. Remind me never to get on her bad side. The girl could handle herself like nobody's business. There was a certain beauty to the way the combatants moved; it reminded me of waves lapping on the beach. Really deadly waves.

I stifled my shriek when Gus landed a blow to Mary's bicep. Blood splattered across the stone wall, and one of her swords fell from her limp hand. I lunged forward, but Farranen pulled me back with a strong arm around my shoulders.

Gus continued to press Mary backward, using both hands on his giant sword, until she was close enough for me to touch. Vanessa leapt out of the way, jumping through the bars and into an empty cell. Apparently, ghosts had no problem with iron.

Farranen pushed me behind him, silencing my protests with a look. The three guards waited on the other side of the room, content to let Gus have all the fun. And the Gray Knight looked like he was enjoying every second of it. With a masculine grunt, he brought his sword down in an overhand motion, forcing Mary to block the blow with her own. He lifted his booted foot, and with a sickening crunch, he brought it down on Mary's knee. She dropped like a sack of potatoes, and her remaining sword went skittering through the dirt in the opposite direction from where I stood.

"No!" I shrieked, and Gus looked up at me with a triumphant grin. *That bastard!* I might not be Mary's biggest fan, but I wasn't going to let him get away with hurting her.

Farranen kept his arm out, blocking me from charging to where Gus continued to leer at me. I flung obscenities at him like they were bread, and I was feeding a hungry flock of pigeons. A demonic inbred flock of pigeons that took a dump on my truck windshield.

Gus had the gall to crook his fingers in a come-hither type of motion, trying to bait Farranen closer. On a good day, Farranen could wipe the floor with this asshat, but today wasn't a good day. Today, Farranen was weak and injured from weeks of torture, some of it probably received at Gus's hands, and he had nothing but a hunting knife to defend himself with. A girly hunting knife at that.

I knew the exact moment that Gus was going to attack, because Farranen's body tensed in response. The Gray Knight took a single step forward, thrusting his sword at my guardian's chest. Farranen slid to the side, neatly evading the blade while bringing his knife down on Gus's forearm. It was a smooth move, considering he'd been laying prostrate on the floor minutes earlier.

Gus's sword fell to the floor, and I had a moment of confusion at the wicked grin on his face, until he slid his other hand out from beneath his cloak.

"No!" I shrieked, as he drove the dagger he held toward Farranen's unprotected side.

With no time to think, I dove between the men, intent on keeping the blade from reaching my fae. I heard the fabric of my cloak split as the knife slid into me. Unlike the first time I'd been stabbed, I was aware it was happening. I felt every agonizing inch as the blade buried itself in my stomach, like it was trying to reach my backbone through my bellybutton. I had thought it would feel cold, like being pierced with a splinter of death, but it was more like red-hot flames that spread from the wound to the rest of my body.

"*Theodora!*" Farranen's shout brought tears to my eyes, and his arms closed around me. His heart, thudding too fast next to my ear, joined the chorus of his anguished cries. God, I'd missed this. Not the panicked way he was yelling at me, but the way he held me. Like I was something he never wanted to let go of. It's too bad something so enjoyable came at the cost of me dying.

And there was no denying it—I was dying. The part of my magic that perceived Vanessa as dead immediately recognized my impending mortality. It was as inescapable as falling in love with someone that didn't love you back. You could fight it all you wanted, talk yourself out of believing it was happening, but in the end, you didn't have a choice.

Guilt swamped me; I really should have told Farranen that I loved him. Even though it wasn't mutual, he deserved to know that he was loved. That he mattered. I'd been too damn cowardly to tell him before, and now I'd never get the chance.

I struggled to suck in more of the oxygen that my lungs were burning for. Maybe, if I just tried a little harder, then I could get the words out.

But, no. My stubborn chest refused to cooperate.

I hoped my eyes conveyed the words that I wanted him to hear. The pain in his eyes deepened, and I prayed that maybe he had heard my unspoken admission. Or maybe I was just too big for his fractured body to support.

I hoped they served cake at my funeral.

No, actually, I hoped they served steak. Dog was probably the only one that would go, and he loved steak.

Okay, maybe cake *and* steak.

That sounded like a pretty damn good way to go.

Chapter Six

Shakespeare was full of crap.

There was absolutely nothing romantic about dying in your lover's arms, as Romeo and Juliet would have had you believe. Good old William forgot to mention the tears—not tiny dainty ones that caressed your cheeks, but big fat ugly ones that left you with a red nose and snotty lip. And the *pain*—God, the pain was like being eviscerated with a dull spade that'd been dipped in acid while crocodiles played tug of war with your intestines. And the regrets—they were the worst part of dying. Knowing that there was no chance to go back and fix all the things that you didn't get right the first time. That was where the true agony lay.

If I ever got a chance to use my magic again, I was going to resurrect Shakespeare's ghost just so I could tell him how wrong he'd been. Then again, he'd probably already know since he'd gone through his own death. Though, if he'd met a mundane end, like dying in his sleep, I'd be happy to educate him on how it felt to bleed out while you held your guts in your hand.

Being dead was exactly like Vanessa had described it, like I'd been asleep until a few vague images intruded on the darkness. They were hazy and didn't make much sense since they had no context to them.

Clear skies with a billion stars shining overhead.

Tiny eyes in the dark. Dozens of them, all watching

me.

I smelled, rather than saw, trees covered in snow. I clung to the unique scent of a brisk winter wind, the smell reminding me of home, even when I knew I'd probably never see my cabin again. I was grateful for the comfort it provided. It reminded me of Lief, and I hoped it didn't mean he was dead too. The fae needed him to stand up to the queen, and someday lead them toward a better future.

The soft edges of a blanket were wrapped around my shoulders, and I was insanely grateful for the added warmth it provided. It sounded stupid, but I was touched that someone had taken the time to see to my comfort, even if I was dead.

I had no idea death would be so...dark. I couldn't see a damn thing, so I sat up and immediately smacked my head on something solid.

"Ow!" I yelped. Good to know I could still feel things, even in the afterlife.

Rubbing the lump on my head with one hand, I carefully felt around with my other hand. The floor was smooth and cold beneath my fingertips. I traced them as far as I could, until I found walls on all four sides of me. It felt like I was in a small room, about three feet by five feet. The only sliver of light was on the opposite side of the room, so I crawled closer until it was obvious that the strip of light was coming from beneath a door.

My heart churned in my chest; was this some kind of test? Had I gone to hell, and now I would have to prove my worthiness by puzzling my way out of an escape room?

I set aside my fear and brushed my hands across

the door until I found the doorknob. It turned without a fuss—which was probably the only easy thing that had happened since I'd arrived in Fairie. Silently, I opened the door.

After a minute of blinking and shielding my eyes, I was finally able to make out the large bedroom that waited outside the room. A king-size bed dominated the far wall; its four posts looked to be hand carved, and it had enough black fabric draped across it to clothe an entire emo dance troupe. Minus the sequins.

There was a table that would seat six with carvings that matched the ones on the bed. Framed art in monochromatic tones decorated the walls. Thick drapes hid an entire wall of tall narrow windows, and I tugged a corner of the black fabric aside. Three stories below was a large courtyard with walking paths and stone benches nestled among the varied plants. It looked more like a rainforest than a garden in Fairie. Past all the foliage, a thick gray wall loomed that was unmistakably part of a castle. I only knew of two castles in Fairie…and judging by the pale gray color of this one, I was in the queen's castle. Although, Fairie was a big place, so maybe there was more than one gothic-looking palace made of hand-cut gray stone with tall arched windows. But with my luck? It was probably safe to assume I was back at the queen's castle.

The sky outside was light, so I opened the curtains a little more to let some of the brightness pool on the cold floor. Dust motes drifted past looking as lost as I felt. I waved a hand to disperse them, the motion highlighting the scars on my arm. It was a good reminder of the dangers that lurked in Fairie.

I needed to get the hell out of there—although, I'd

already died once and, apparently, hadn't suffered any permanent damage. I mean, what was the worst that could happen if I lingered?

I wasn't brave enough to find out. I needed to find Farranen and Mary and get back to the gate. I was so done with all the drama and dying. But first, I should probably find a weapon in case things got crazy again. Oh, who was I kidding? *Of course*, things were going to get crazy again.

I dug through the two nightstands, but both were empty. The dresser wasn't much better—it had an impressive selection of racy lingerie and sex toys but no weapons. I suppose some of the dildos were big enough to bash someone over the head with…I settled for a whip that made my stomach turn when I realized that Farranen's wounds were probably created by a similar device. I hoped I'd get to use it on whoever had tortured him. Poetic justice and all that.

"What the hell are you *doing?*"

The irate shriek startled me, and I threw up my hands to ward off whatever attack was coming.

Vanessa stood by the door with her hands planted on her lean hips.

"I…" I couldn't remember what I'd been doing so my answer petered out.

"We've got to get out of here—what the hell are you doing with *those?*" She raised a perfectly sculpted eyebrow and glanced at the dildo and whip in my hands.

I blushed and shoved the hot pink sex toy back in the dresser. "Nothing. What are you doing here?"

"Where else was I supposed to go? Nobody else can see or hear me."

She had a good point. I thought about telling her she should go into the light, but it seemed like a poor time for a joke.

"Where are we?" I asked instead.

"Some big castle. After the big guy ran you through with his knife, he hauled away the Grim Reaper girl and the hot guy in chains."

"Mary and Farranen are still alive?" I had to steady myself with a hand on the dresser at the sudden relief of knowing they hadn't been killed too.

She shrugged. "They were when they left."

"So how did we get here?"

"The next day, a man came and carried you here. He was real stealthy about it, like he didn't want anyone to know he'd taken you."

"Who was it?" I only got another shrug in response.

"We should get moving. The soldiers are searching the castle, and they're headed this way."

"Right." I took a step toward the door. Getting out of here sounded like a great plan.

"Not like *that!*" Vanessa laughed.

I looked around in confusion; maybe there was another door that would provide a more subtle exit.

"Get dressed first!" she crowed.

I looked down; the blanket wrapped around my shoulders was actually a cloak—and under it, I was naked. Like, butt naked. How had I missed *that?*

****

There was a foreseeably awkward conversation in my future, if I ever came face to face with the owner of the bedroom that I had woke up in. And I mean *seriously* awkward.

73

A quick search of the dresser and closet revealed an obscene amount of lingerie: teddies, thongs, corsets, bustiers, garter belts, stockings, G-strings, sheer baby dolls, and some items that I didn't even recognize. But despite the heaps of silk and lace, I had trouble finding anything remotely decent to wear. I mean, seriously— was I supposed to wander around the drafty castle in a push-up bra and crotch-less panties?

Vanessa helped me layer two pairs of fishnet stockings with a black leather corset and silky bikini bottoms beneath a sheer black robe that didn't even cover the top half of my thighs. I rejected the shelf of spikey stilettos and instead selected a pair of knee-high boots made of the same leather as the corset. They were surprisingly heavy, with thick rubber soles and a row of giant silver clasps from the ankle to the top that took forever to buckle up. The finished outfit was embarrassingly revealing, but it covered the essential parts of my anatomy and I was just grateful not to be naked anymore. The cloak must have belonged to someone tall, because it dragged across the ground behind me like a bridal train made out of melted coal. But there was no way I was going to run around Fairie without it. I settled the heavy fabric back in place around my shoulders, shielding any curious eyes from my embarrassing state of undress.

"You look like a dominatrix blow-up doll with a big butt," Vanessa informed me.

"Stop staring at my butt."

"Are you sure you don't want the studded dog collar?" she asked.

I shot her a dirty look and attempted unsuccessfully to tug my corset up higher so my boobs wouldn't be in danger of falling out.

"It was just a suggestion." She rolled her eyes. "I'll check if the coast is clear," she announced before walking out into the hall through the door. And I mean she literally walked *through* the door without opening it. Seeing her disappear through solid objects was going to take some serious getting used to.

I stifled a scream when she popped her head back through the door less than a foot from where I stood. "The coast is clear!" she told me cheerfully.

Mustering my nerves and as much dignity as I could find, I opened the heavy wooden door and peered up and down the hallway.

"This way," Vanessa whispered.

I followed her as she took off down the hall. I sprinted to keep up. The rubber soles of my boots muffled my footsteps on the stone floor—probably. It was hard to say for sure, since I couldn't hear anything over the pounding of my heart.

When Vanessa came to a stop at the end of the hall, she held up a hand for me to stop and I gladly obliged. She peered around the corner, then waved me forward. "Come on," she whispered.

"You don't have to whisper; I'm the only one that can hear you," I reminded her.

"It's a good thing, since you're loud enough for the both of us," she snarked back, still whispering.

I followed her down a few more hallways, all of them lined with wooden doors similar to the room we'd come from. The halls here were narrower and less ornate than the ones we'd used when I'd been summoned for an audience with the queen, so I had to assume this part of the castle was mostly bedrooms or residences. I wasn't brave enough to actually check.

Just when I was beginning to wheeze like I'd been smoking a pack a day since I was twelve years old, Vanessa came to an abrupt halt and I ran into her. After peeking around the next corner, she turned and pushed me backward.

"Back up! They're coming this way!" I stumbled as she continued shoving me until we reached the closest door. "Open it!" she ordered, and I caught the sharp edge of worry in her normally bossy tone.

My hands were sweaty, and I fumbled with the knob before swinging the door open and diving into the dark room. I held my breath until the approaching sound of footsteps reached the door and then continued past. Vanessa stuck her head through the door—which is exactly as freaky as it sounds—and let me know once they were gone.

After a few more close calls, we finally found a staircase that led down to the first floor. Judging by how narrow and boring it was, I suspected it was intended for servants rather than any of the more important fae. At the bottom, we discovered a large kitchen that was mostly deserted. Nobody paid any attention to me as I slunk past, covered head to toe in my black cloak. We discovered two large food pantries before finally finding a door that led outside.

Once we were free of the castle, we headed for the closest available cover, which happened to be the surrounding woods. Since this particular castle was more of an eighty-thousand-square-foot cathedral rather than a stereotypical castle, there were no battlements with soldiers keeping vigil. But this was Fairie, so anything was possible; they might have some sort of magical security system that would alert them to our escape. Seeing as everyone thought I was dead, I hoped they wouldn't look twice at a woman who was out for a stroll; dead women didn't typically stroll. Especially when they were dressed like a chubby hooker.

****

While most people would have taken the opportunity to commune with nature and appreciate the exotic beauty that Fairie had to offer, I used our cross-country trek through the forest to do something much less productive. I fretted. The ground was surprisingly smooth, without much in the way of deadfall or exposed tree roots, so my mind was free to wander as my feet led the way.

Who was the mysterious man who had carried my heavy carcass all the way back to the queen's castle? If it was one of Lief's supporters, why not take me to Lief's castle? I owed them a huge thanks, followed by a smack upside the head for leaving me naked. Seriously, what was the reasoning behind that bizarre decision? And stuffed into the back of a closet? Maybe the fae took the phrase "skeletons in your closet" more literally than people in my realm did.

And what had happened to Farranen? Vanessa had said he'd been taken away in chains, so he was likely still alive. He had to be alive. I couldn't live with any other possibility.

My stomach growled, and nausea clawed its way through my belly. He *had* to be alive. But even if he was still alive, there was a very real possibility that he'd be on the receiving end of more of the queen's generous hospitality—the kind that involved sharp blades and whips.

I stopped to lean against a tree as my stomach clenched painfully.

He *had* to be okay.

"We should keep moving," Vanessa told me. I nodded and took a few shaky steps away from the tree.

"There should be a road soon." I did my best to sound confident, but the dubious look she shot me said that she knew I was bluffing.

We traveled in silence for a few minutes before she asked, "So, what happens to me if you die?"

That was a darn good question; I'd been pondering the same thing.

"Uh, I don't know. I'm pretty sure I died once already, and you're still fine." I mean, she was still a ghost, but she didn't fade away into nothing, so as far as I was concerned, she still fit the definition of fine. She looked thoughtful but didn't continue with any more hypothetical metaphysical inquiries. Which was probably for the best, since I didn't have any answers to give her. I was just trying my best to figure this out as I went.

Once we were out of sight of the castle, I'd planned to circle back toward the front of the building, but without a sun or moon to guide me, I had no idea if I was anywhere close to finding the cobblestone road that would take us back to the hawthorn tree.

Chapter Seven

Cabin, sweet cabin.

Light from the kitchen window spilled across my back porch to welcome me home as I stumbled up the icy steps. My teeth were chattering so hard I was afraid that I'd break a tooth, and I'm sad to say the stolen hooker boots were not cut out for winters in northern Saskatchewan. Which was a shame, because they made my legs look like they were a mile long.

The back door opened on silent hinges, and I lurched into my deliciously warm kitchen. The sound of the door slamming cut off Ozzy's irate voice midsentence.

"…where the hell she is—"

Dog and Ozzy looked to be locked into some sort of staring contest in the middle of my dining room. In an eerily synchronized move, they both turned toward me, their faces shifting into identical masks of shock. It wasn't often I could sneak up on a vampire or a shifter, so I'm not exaggerating when I say I laughed out loud.

Dog was the first to move. He launched himself at me like it was Thanksgiving and I was a juicy roasted turkey with cranberries and mashed potatoes on the side. His lean arms wrapped around me tightly enough to squeeze any remaining air out of my lungs, and something in my spine popped as he lifted me off my feet. I endeavoured to grunt out a protest, but I could feel the tension in his body as he clung to me, and I knew he was just trying to reassure himself that I was really home. And honestly, I had big stupid tears in my eyes that I didn't want anyone to see, so I was okay with keeping my face buried in his chest a little longer.

"Jesus *Christ*, woman! Where in the bloody hell have you been!" Ozzy's livid voice cut through my reunion with Dog.

He lowered me with a warning growl, keeping his body between me and the vampire while I greedily sucked some air back into my starved lungs.

"Aww, did you put on pants just for me?" I asked, hoping to diffuse some of Dog's aggression.

He growled again and cast his yellow eyes angrily toward Ozzy.

"You made him put on pants?" I demanded. Don't get me wrong. I was glad Dog had bothered to cover up his boy parts, but I didn't want Ozzy thinking he had any right to issue orders to my friend. This was my house, so I was the only one entitled to lay down the rules under its roof.

Ozzy shrugged indifferently. "I didn't want to look at his junk."

"Then you should have left." I know, I'm a hypocrite—the first thing I would have done was track down Dog's sweats and throw them at his head. Even before the hug. Actually, *especially* before the hug. I loved him, but I sure as heck didn't want certain parts of him that close to me. "Why are you even here?" I asked. And why hadn't Dog disappeared? He usually took great pains to avoid the PIMP agent.

"We were supposed to meet to discuss the crap going on in Fairie two nights ago, but you weren't here." The accusation in his voice did nothing to conceal the worry he was trying to hide.

Oh, right. I had forgotten all about the meeting. Feeling like a schmuck, I told him, "I'm sorry." I should have sent him a text or something. As soon as I'd heard that Farranen was hurt, every thought in my head had flown out the window. It was embarrassing how fast I'd forgotten about Ozzy and the kidnapped women.

"What the hell is that smell?" Ozzy tilted his head to the side and watched me with narrowed eyes. His confusion was apparent as he continued to sniff the air. And of course, because that wasn't weird enough, Dog lifted his face and inhaled. They both stared at me, their smooth movements reminding me of owls searching for prey.

I glanced down at myself and gave a tentative sniff. It wasn't *terrible.* I mean, obviously I needed a shower, but they were acting like I'd willingly rolled in dog poop. Dog prowled a few inches closer, destroying any illusions I had that he recognized the concept of personal space, and thrust his nose behind my ear.

"Hey!" I protested. No girl wants anyone sniffing her when she hasn't had access to a loofa and body wash for days.

A rumble vibrated out of his chest—it was part growl, part whine, and not a bit pleased.

"Good God, Theo!" Ozzy decided to get in on the party, and I threw up my hands as a buffer as they continued to crowd me. "You smell like a damn vampire."

Well...fuck.

Something had changed since I'd felt myself bleed

out on that dirt floor. I just hadn't thought it would be something so drastic.

Ozzy reached past Dog and yanked at my cloak. It fell, a beautiful, velvety puddle of black against my scarred hardwood floors. The vamp let out an appreciative whistle. "*Damn*, Theo."

Dog and I looked down at the same time—oh shit. One glance reminded me that I was wearing nothing but a leather corset and silky panties. My normally stoic companion looked horrified. Actually, I probably looked horrified too. Mortified, at the very least.

"Just…*damn*—" Ozzy looked a little dazed, like he couldn't process the fact that I was dressed like a hussy.

"Stop it," I hissed to both of them. This was weird enough without them acting like a bunch of immature college frat boys. With as much dignity as I could muster (and it wasn't much), I strode into my bedroom and yanked the housecoat off the back of my closet door. It was bright pink and covered in fat green frogs and it was easily the frumpiest robe I'd ever seen— which was exactly what I needed to cover up my stolen outfit until I had enough privacy to shower and change into something comfy.

I marched back into the dining room and glared at them both. "There. Now you can stop acting like you're afraid my boobs will fall out and bite you on the ass."

They both had the acuity to look ashamed. Ozzy cleared his throat before gruffly broaching the elephant in the room. "Do you want to tell me why you're putting off vamp vibes?"

I took a seat at the table and started unbuckling my boots. "No idea. It probably has something to do with me dying when—"

"You *died?*"

"Yes, I *died*. You'd know that if you let me finish my story."

Ozzy waved for me to continue with such a calm expression I could tell he was faking. He was probably thinking about all the different ways he wanted to strangle me.

"As I was saying before I was so rudely interrupted—" I shot him a pointed look, daring him to interrupt again. When he didn't take the bait, I continued. "Gus stabbed me in the belly."

Dog growled, making the air around us tremble. He glared at me, his fierce eyes seeming to say *You were stabbed? Again!*

I stared right back at him, my own eyes calmly telling him *Yes, I was stabbed again—but I'm fine, so stop being such a worrywart or I'll start calling you Mildred.*

I didn't think his expression could get any darker but—yep, it got darker. His fists were clenched like he wanted to grab me and shake me.

"What the hell is wrong with you two? Stop staring at each other, and tell me what the fuck happened!" Ozzy dragged my attention back to the conversation about my unfortunate end. "Who the fuck is Gus?"

"Augustus of the Light Court, aka the queen's Gray Knight, aka the guy that murdered Marissa's brood and kidnapped her."

Ozzy took a full ten seconds to process what I'd told him before he exploded with "What the *fuck*, Theo!" He paced a short way into my kitchen, then back to where I was still unbuckling my second boot. "Those smarmy fae bastards!"

"Yep, the smarmiest," I absently agreed while fiddling with the smallest (and most difficult) buckle.

"We need to get a hold of the dark prince; do we know where to find him? And where is this Gus guy now? I'll call my guys to make sure we have an iron containment cell ready." I'm pretty sure Ozzy had stopped talking to me and was just thinking aloud at this point, so I didn't interrupt him as he continued with, "Of course, we'll need the iron cuffs…and if he resists—damn, I don't have any iron bullets with me."

I was a little surprised that he was planning on bringing a gun to a sword fight. I'd never seen any of the fae with anything but sharp pointy weapons. Granted, they had lots and *lots* of sharp pointy things, but it still seemed a little unfair to me. Not that I minded Ozzy having the upper hand since he was on my side this time, but still, it felt a little unscrupulous.

I finally succeeded in undoing the last finicky buckle and toed the hooker boots off with a sigh of pleasure. The cold wooden floors had never felt more glorious under my feet.

"Theo!" I jumped and looked up at Ozzy's annoyed face.

"What?"

"You didn't hear a thing I just said!"

I shrugged, since he was probably right. I was exhausted and starving, and I'd tuned him out.

"Where is Gus? I won't be able to mobilize very many agents this close to sunrise."

"I dunno. The last time I saw him was in the dungeon when he killed me."

"Dungeon? What dungeon?"

"The queen's dungeon."

"The queen's—for *fuck's* sake, Theo! You were in *Fairie?*"

Apparently, I wasn't the only one who hadn't been listening. I mean, we were talking about a bunch of fae, so realistically, he shouldn't have been so surprised to find out that I'd been in Fairie. It's not like there were that many of them on this side of the gate.

I opened my mouth to say something snarky, but instead I let out a startled gasp as my stomach tightened painfully. It felt like I was trying to digest broken glass and bleach after getting run through with a dagger—oh wait, the dagger part had actually happened.

I fell to my hands and knees on the floor and bit my lip to keep the whimpering to a minimum.

"Theo, look at me!" Ozzy's voice sounded like he was shouting from down a long tunnel, but when I looked up, he was kneeling right in front of me. His crazy red hair blurred when my eyes squeezed out a few involuntary tears.

"Theo! When did you feed last?" His big hands gripped my shoulders, like he could physically shake an answer out of me.

"Bread and cheese—before I died—"

"What about blood?"

"Uh, no!" I intended to sound horrified, but it came out sounding pitifully like a whine.

"Go get her some blood—anything with a pulse." I could tell he was talking to Dog now, and I wanted to protest. I was *not* going to drink blood. Sure, I was hungry, but a nice juicy steak would do the trick. Hell, even a freakin' salad would be better than what Ozzy was proposing.

"*Now!*"

Dog growled at the demanding vampire, but his pants landed on the floor a second before the back door opened and shut with a bang.

"Don't yell at him…" I wheezed.

"Theo, you should have taken blood as soon as you rose from your first death. How long has it been?" God, he was such a mother hen.

"A day…maybe two." Even breathing hurt; I stopped fighting gravity and let myself collapse completely on the floor. "I don't have…a watch." Not to mention that it was tricky to judge time passing in Fairie without a moon or sun to reference.

"Maybe it's your fae magic…You should be ravenous right now, attacking anything that moves." I didn't bother commenting since he seemed to be thinking out loud again. "Fledglings don't master the bloodlust for at least a month. But you…"

I was saved from his raising-vampires-101 lesson when Dog shot through his doggy-door on all four paws. Clutched in his mouth by the neck was a snow-white rabbit. Its giant back feet scrambled furiously for purchase, and its entire body struggled to wriggle out of Dog's toothy embrace.

Oh, hell no. They did *not* expect me to eat that poor helpless bunny. Sure, Dog had scarfed down a few of the unlucky vermin that had the misfortune of burrowing too close to my property, but I was not Dog. I'd never had the slightest inclination to go hunting or fishing, and I'd certainly never looked at something so cute and cuddly and had the urge to kill it.

My stomach spasmed painfully, and I stifled another whimper.

With his tail wagging, Dog bounded over and

dropped to his belly next to me. The rabbit's dark eyes stared at me, pleading for me to do something to help him avoid the tragic end that he knew was coming.

Ozzy took the quivering animal by the scruff of the neck and held it in front of my nose. Bile rose in my throat, and I wanted to roll away from the musky scent of fur.

"Come on, Theo, just try it," Ozzy cajoled. His tone was surprisingly gentle. "See, just like this."

I looked up and saw him pointing at the two sharp fangs that had descended past his regular teeth. Disgusted by the thought of Ozzy taking a bite out of the poor bunny, I reached out and smacked his hand that held the critter in question, and the vamp lost his grip. The rabbit hit the ground running, his nails scrambling for purchase on the hardwood as he dove for cover under my dining room chairs.

From the corner of my eye, I saw Dog tense up in anticipation of going after his escaped prey. I reached out and wound my fingers into his silky fur. "Don't," I whispered.

Dog whined, but his muscles uncoiled and I knew he'd stay put. He was such a good boy. Most people would have picked the rabbit over me.

"Theo, you need blood; most fledglings don't last more than twenty-four hours without it." I could hear the strain in Ozzy's protests; the poor guy was one step away from freaking out. Which would actually be kind of comical to witness—if I weren't lying on the floor feeling like my stomach was trying to eat itself.

Before I could offer up any number of excuses for why I would not be partaking of an innocent rabbit, the front door flew open hard enough to hit the wall. Since moving hurt, I didn't turn toward the sound; I'd find out soon enough who it was.

My fae magic was already sparking excitedly under my skin, and then I felt the vibrations of footsteps as someone strode across my living room. It wasn't much of a surprise when Lief's bossy voice demanded, "Get your fangs away from her."

Dog whimpered and scooted farther away from the pissed-off fae until he was pressed up against me, and the terrified rabbit took advantage of the open door to make a hasty exit. I can't say I blamed him. I would have gladly made a dash for the door if I'd have been able to move.

Ozzy grumbled something about stubborn females and disappeared from my line of sight.

I tried to look innocent when the dark prince knelt down so we were eye to eye.

"Theo?" I'd been expecting a heavy dose of anger from him, but there was genuine concern. "How are you...alive?" His hands hovered over me as if he wanted to touch me but was too afraid to. It was probably a legitimate concern since I'd stolen so much magic from him the last time he'd touched me.

"Long story," I told him flippantly, trying to lighten the mood. Seeing him so close to speechless was making me uncomfortable.

He must have sensed my unease, because he looked around until he found Ozzy and sent the vamp a dark look. "Why is it that every time I find you with Theo, she is in far worse shape than I left her?"

"Not his fault," I muttered. It wasn't Ozzy's fault that I'd been stabbed. But trying to force the rabbit down my throat—that one was totally on him.

"She needs blood." Ozzy's voice was back to its normal grumpy tone, which weirdly put me more at ease than when he'd sounded like an anxious schoolgirl.

"Why?"

Oh man, now Lief sounded grumpy too. Why were the men in my life always so damn cranky? I needed to make some new friends. I briefly pondered if Tamarac had a musical theater group—people who did musical theater were always in a good mood.

"Fledglings need blood to sustain their magic as soon as they wake from their first death." Ozzy was far braver than I; talking to the dark prince in a tone that implied he was an idiot was akin to learning to juggle using live mines and chainsaws.

"Theo is no fledgling," Lief replied testily.

"Of course, she is! I can feel the vamp magic oozing off her from here!"

I wanted to send him a dirty look, but rolling over required more energy that I could muster. Seriously, I didn't ooze.

"Yes, our Theo's had a touch of vampire in her since she was bitten—"

"She fucking *died!* What more do you need for proof?" Ozzy interrupted.

"I'm perfectly aware of what she's been through."

I shivered as Lief's icy words settled over me. You think an angry dark prince is scary? This level of pissed-off frigidness was even more terrifying.

"I will see to Theo's needs."

Chapter Eight

Lief scooped me off the floor and turned his back to the furious vampire, effectively dismissing him. Before I could protest, he carried me into my bedroom and carefully laid me on my unmade bed. I wanted to high-five him for the awesome exit he'd made, but he didn't exactly look like he was in a high-fiving mood. And then I remembered that he'd told Ozzy he'd "take care of my needs."

"No blood," I told him as forcefully as I could. Just thinking about the poor rabbit made me want to throw up.

He sighed, and I could see him debating his options. He was probably thinking, *Hmmm, should I sneak some blood into her morning coffee? Or would it be easier to hit her over the head with a frying pan and then pour the blood down her throat?* He must have reached a conclusion on his own, because he bent down and tugged off his boots. That had to be a good sign, right? Since there were no small critters hiding under my bed, I had to assume he wouldn't be leaving right away to hunt one down.

Leaving his sword next to his boots, he crawled onto the bed and settled himself next to me. After the smallest of hesitations, he wound his fingers with mine. I'd already braced myself for any kind of magical fallout, but his fae magic seemed to be asking for permission before it moved through me like a smooth wave, caressing my own magic as it filled me. Nothing about it was forced; he simply offered and I accepted.

The gnawing pain in my stomach abated until I was able to take full breaths again.

"Does this mean I'm not a vampire?" I asked tentatively.

"Definitely not a vampire," he confirmed with a half smile.

Oh, thank God. Don't get me wrong; I didn't have anything against vampires, but I certainly didn't want to be one. First of all, I loved being outside in the sunshine way too much to ever give it up. And secondly, the thought of surviving on blood for the rest of my life was too disgusting to even think about. Wait—did vampires still eat real food too? Because there was no way in hell I was ever going to give up cake.

Another disturbing thought struck me; if I wasn't a vampire, then what was I? I wanted to ask, but really, how does one ask something so bizarre and not sound like a crackpot? And if the answer was anything but human, did I even want to know? It's not like there were a lot of different options. Maybe a zombie? Or a ghoul? Yeah, I'd take ignorance and the bliss that came with it, thank you very much.

"What do you remember from when you died?" Lief spoke quietly, still holding me in place with his pale eyes.

I thought back to my botched rescue attempt in the dungeon, and my body involuntarily cringed. Lief tugged me closer, until my head was resting on his chest; the thud of his strong heartbeat beneath my ear was strangely calming, and I relaxed against him.

"There was a cottage in the woods. The queen's dungeon was in the basement." I struggled to get the next words past my lips. "Farr…Farranen was inside, locked in a cell. He was hurt." I was glad my face was buried in Lief's soft shirt so he couldn't see the tears that threatened to fall. "We unlocked the door—"

"We?"

"Mary and I—"

"Mary was there?" He let out a grunt when I smacked him on his ridiculously hard abs so he'd stop cutting me off.

"Stop interrupting. Yes, Mary was there with me."

"And how did you come to be in her company?"

He asked lightly, but I could hear his unspoken speculation. Oh crap—did he know that Celesta was the one to hook me up with my ankou guide? Gah, I was such a terrible liar. There really was no point in trying to keep her out of this; he'd find out eventually anyway.

"Celesta arranged for her to take me to the dungeons." And for that, I was extremely grateful since I never would have gotten that far on my own.

An unhappy noise rumbled out of Lief's chest beneath my cheek. The sound promised that Celesta wasn't going to enjoy their next conversation.

"Before we could escape, Gus and three other soldiers showed up."

"Gus?" He sounded somewhat perplexed, which was weird because with only three thousand fae in Fairie, and hundreds of years living with them, I would have expected that he knew them all.

"The Gray Knight," I explained.

"Ah—Augustus. And you call him Gus?" He chuckled, making my head bob with the motion.

"He looks like a Gus." I shrugged. "Anyway, Mary tried to fight him, but he cut her with his sword. Then he went for Farranen, but I kinda got in the way and ended up, you know—dead."

His arms tightened around me, and a few minutes passed before he spoke. "You were missing for two nights before I thought to check Fairie. I was going out of my mind with worry, and Celesta didn't say a word." He was clenching his jaw, trying to keep his words monotone. Poor Celesta was probably on his shit-list for life. "When I got to the gate, it was closed. It took hours before I was able to cross. Once I got to Fairie, I knew you'd gone to rescue the guardian. Only you would do such a stupid, brave, reckless thing."

Ouch. The stupid and reckless parts were probably true, but I still didn't like to be called out on it.

"I went straight to the queen's dungeon; Farranen was gone and you…you were lying in a puddle of blood in the dirt." His arms tightened around me painfully, but I didn't try to stop him. If I was being honest, it felt good to know that someone would care if I died. "It was only a matter of time before more of her soldiers came to retrieve your body, so I wrapped you up and brought you back to the castle—"

"It *was* you!" I thought back over my hazy memories, trying to remember what had transpired before I woke up naked in a closet. The cloak I'd been wearing had smelled like a fresh winter morning, reminding me of Lief. "Hey! Why was I *naked?*"

He laughed at my scandalized tone and told me, "I sent your clothes with a hobgoblin to create multiple scent trails in case anyone came looking for your body."

"You couldn't have at least left me in my underwear?" I grumped.

"They were covered in blood, Theo. Everything was. You *bled out*." He was being serious now. The grief fractured his voice, and I was glad I couldn't see his face. "I held your dead, lifeless body in my arms and knew you were gone."

It wasn't my fault, but I felt like I should apologize for scaring him. Instead, I settled for wrapping my arms around his middle in a hug. It was probably a pretty crappy hug since I wasn't much of a hugger, but I hoped it would chase some of his sadness away. And after carrying my heavy dead ass around Fairie, the least he deserved was a hug.

"I brought you back to the queen's castle and hid you in one of the consorts' rooms. That seemed safer than bringing you to mine, since that was the first place they searched. That was yesterday; I've been looking for the guardian ever since. The gate is still open, so he's got to be alive. I just can't figure out where they've hidden him."

"Vanessa said the soldiers took him and Mary away after I died."

"Who's Vanessa?"

"A ghost. Apparently, she hitched a ride with me to Fairie when I crossed over."

I took his silence as sign that I'd shocked him speechless. Ha! Score one for me!

****

"*Theodora.*"

Farranen was calling to me, but his voice was weak and sounded like it was coming from underwater.

"*Theodora.*"

Hearing him say my name brought back a torrent of memories; they filled the darkness around me until I thought I might drown in them.

"*My lady.*"

This time it was a plea, and I knew I was dreaming—but not like the dozens of other dreams I'd had about my absent guardian over the last few months. I was asleep, and Farranen was trying to pull me into a shared dreamscape.

I'm here, I thought and hoped he'd hear me.

The darkness faded, and I was standing in the woods. I recognized them as the woods behind my property, but it felt like early autumn rather than the middle of winter. The leaves were still on the trees but had turned yellow and orange.

Farranen stood on the footpath that I used to take to Tamarac Lake for early morning swims. His long blond hair hung loose around his shoulders; it was even longer than I remembered. His simple white shirt and tan leather pants were clean and unripped; I couldn't see any signs of the injuries he'd sustained at the queen's hands. It was a simple mercy that I was grateful for. Seeing him hurting would have been enough to break me.

His anxious green eyes found me, and something akin to pleasure replaced the restlessness that had been lining his face. Holy hell, I'd forgotten how beautiful he was when he smiled. I made a surprised little happy noise that I usually only made around cake. It should have been embarrassing, but I couldn't have cared less.

I wanted to throw my arms around him, but I wasn't sure if he'd accept a hug from me. I didn't know what I'd do if I had to face any more rejection from him, so it was safer not to put myself out there. Instead, I offered an awkward little wave and chose not to get any closer.

"Theodora?" His expression turned solemn as he took in everything from my head down to my toes. "How are you here?"

"You were calling to me in my sleep." I scrunched up my face in confusion. "Weren't you?" Oh damn, maybe this really was just a regular dream; it's not like I hadn't had my fair share of fantasies about him.

"Every night, Theodora. Every single night."

My breath hitched in my chest, but I was saved from finding something coherent to say when he continued.

"You died in my arms...The life drained out of you." He looked away, and I couldn't tell if he was angry or disgusted. "Why?"

"Why what?" I asked in confusion.

"Why would you take the blade that was intended for me?" He met my eyes again.

That wasn't anger or disgust that I was seeing, but anguish. Now it was my turn to look away, knowing my thoughts would be written on my face. I didn't want him to know that for me, it had been a no-brainer. When there's a dagger pointed at someone I care about, then I'm damn well going to get between the two.

He must have accepted that my silence was the only answer he'd get, so he didn't press me to elaborate.

"So, we're dream walking?" I asked, and he nodded. "We should have done this sooner." Then again, we hadn't parted ways on a good note. If he'd shown up in my dreams unannounced, I probably would've had some choice words of the four-letter variety for him.

"I didn't want you pulled any further into the dark affairs of Fairie."

"You mean you didn't want me to know you were being tortured in a dungeon."

He nodded stiffly. "I fear the queen grows tired of trying to force me to surrender my guardianship; soon she will end this, and the gate will be permanently sealed shut."

I was momentarily rendered speechless by his casual admission that the queen was going to kill him. And knowing how much of a bitch she was, it would be a long painful drawn-out death.

"Somebody needs to kill that stupid cow," I told him fiercely.

"You can't. Once the gate is sealed, you will be safe from those who seek to harm you."

"But you'll be *dead*." Did he really think I'd be okay with that? Because I wasn't. Not even a little bit. "And aren't there other gates that they'll use?"

"Yes, there are still three gates that remain open; their guardians have been persuaded to remain loyal to the queen's cause."

I'm pretty sure her methods of persuasion were a lot different from mine. But still, Farranen had stood up to her and said no, so they could have chosen that option as well.

"Wait, I thought there were six other gates?" See, I had been paying attention last fall when he'd filled me in on some of Fairie's history.

"Two guardians were not agreeable to bringing unwilling females over from this realm, and the queen had them killed. Their gates are permanently gone."

"Oh," I said numbly. The fae queen was even more of a tyrannical bitch than I'd previously given her credit for.

"I overheard the guards talking; there is one other guardian being held who still retains his hold over his gate. I suspect he is being kept nearby."

I felt a brief flash of relief that my fae wasn't alone, wherever he was. It was selfish, I know, but seeing Farranen lying broken and alone in that cell had nearly destroyed me.

"Where is she keeping you?" I asked. Lief said he'd spent the day searching, but hadn't been able to figure out where the prisoners were being held.

"Theodora, no." He'd never sounded so serious—and that was saying something. The man took *everything* seriously. His face was literally the visual definition of emotional constipation.

"No? Like, you don't know where you are?" I asked.

"No, I won't tell you where I am."

I frowned at him, already suspecting what he was going to say next.

"I know you, and I know you'll come running to my aid in some misguided, brave, stupid, reckless attempt to rescue me and get yourself killed in the process."

I'm pretty sure there was an unspoken *again* somewhere in there.

"I would *not!*"

I lied. I totally would. I was already calculating how long it would take me to pack a backpack with some clothes and first-aid supplies. And darn it, it was stupid and reckless, but I was going to do it anyway. Self-preservation be damned.

"*No.*" He slanted his pale eyebrows in finality, letting me know he wouldn't budge on the subject.

Seriously, didn't he know who he was talking to? My middle name was stubborn. And my first and last names were, respectively, one and pain in the ass.

We glared at each other, neither of us willing to bend to the other's demands, but both unwilling to walk away. Finally, his expression softened, and he murmured, "I'd almost forgotten how tenaciously loyal you can be."

"Almost?"

"Almost, but not quite," he amended.

I couldn't help it; I smiled. Compliments aimed at me were pretty rare, so I'd take what I could get. And tenaciously loyal didn't sound like such a horrible thing to be.

"I need you to do something for me." Tiny lines of worry framed his eyes, telling me it would be something important. Probably not enjoyable, but important enough that he was worried about asking me.

"Of course," I responded automatically; I already knew Farranen would never ask me to do something that would put me in harm's way.

"I need you to retrieve my sword. It's hidden in your bedroom with your shotgun."

Uh, what? How had I not known there was a magical sword stashed in my cabin? "Sure," I told him. "What am I supposed to do with it?"

"Keep it on you. I must leave the gate open as long as I can for the dark prince and his followers to use, but others will also have access to it. If any should be of a mind to seek you out…" His lips tightened into a grimace. "At least you'll have the sword at your disposal."

He had enough to worry about, so I didn't point out that I had no idea how to use the deadly blade. Or the fact that I might get some odd looks the next time I stopped by the Shop 'n' Save for groceries with a big-ass sword strapped to my back. Maybe I could pass it off as some sort of cosplay prop. I probably still had Lief's black cloak to wear with it.

"How did it end up in my cabin?" Every detail from our night together was seared so deeply in my brain that I'd need a wire brush to physically scrub it out. Including the part where he'd walked out with his clothes and sword clutched firmly in his arms.

"When I returned to Fairie, I caught a hobgoblin attempting to cross through the gate. In exchange for my silence, he was willing to deliver my sword without your knowledge."

A shudder ran through me at the thought of a hobgoblin cavorting through my cabin and rifling through my bedding.

"They will come for me soon." The sadness in his words reflected in his eyes, making the green brighter than it should be.

"Who?" I asked, just to keep the conversation going. I already knew he was talking about the sadistic guards.

"Sleep deprivation is highly effective at slowing my ability to heal. They will find a way to rouse me from my unconscious state before long." God, was there no end to the queen's evil? I could take all my newfound knowledge about inflicting pain and write my own horror novel with it.

"Theodora?"

I forced the grim thoughts out of my head to focus on the beautiful man standing in front of me.

"Sorry, just thinking that the queen's villainousness knows no bounds."

"Villainousness?"

"Her evil underhanded way of doing business."

"Ah, yes. It is how she came to wear the crown."

I shouldn't be so surprised that Earth wasn't the only realm with corrupt political leaders. What a dismal thought.

Farranen pulled me into an embrace, and I went willingly. Despite the way we'd left things, I was still helpless to walk away from him. There was nothing overtly sexual about the hug—other than the fact that the man was pure eye candy and it was hard not to think about sex when I was around him. I wrapped my arms tighter around his waist when I recognized his embrace for what it was: a goodbye.

He whispered something against my hair. It sounded like longing and regret. For a brief second, his body became incorporeal against mine, and I backed up in shock.

"My time is up." He looked so resigned, so forlorn, that I said the first thing that I could think of that would get his attention.

"I'll come for you."

"*No—*"

"You swore a life debt to me—and I am the only one who can release you from it."

"That was before—"

"You can't pick and choose when you decide to

honor it; it's all or nothing." At least, I was pretty sure he couldn't just use it when it was convenient. I was still pretty sketchy on the whole guardianship thing. When the fae queen had wanted to pass me around like a shiny new toy for the men in her court, Farranen had gotten first dibs because he was oath-bound to me as my guardian after saving me from Lebolus's attack.

It was time to pull out the big guns. "I *do not* release you."

"Theodora, don't—"

I was left standing alone on the dirt path when my angry guardian winked out of existence. Good. I hoped he used that anger to stay alive long enough for me to find him. Because I meant every word I'd said.

Chapter Nine

I woke sometime the next day. Or maybe it was a couple days later. It was hard to say; I'd been so freakin' exhausted it was possible that I'd slept for a whole month. Either way, I woke with a startled gasp and flailing limbs that probed every inch of the bed for someone that I already knew wasn't there.

The sun was shining behind my bedroom curtains, and Dog was lightly snoring on the end of my bed; Lief was nowhere in sight. Which was actually a relief, because I'm pretty sure it would have been awkward waking up next to the dark prince when I was so flustered from dreaming of someone else. I tried not to take his absence personally; I'm sure he had all kinds of important things to do, seeing as he was leading a rebellion and all. I just hoped finding Farranen and Mary were at the top of his list.

I took care of the most pressing business at hand first: emptying my bladder and showering until I'd used up every single drop of hot water that my decrepit water heater could squeeze out. Once I was dressed in some warm sweatpants and a tank top, and the hideous dominatrix outfit was sitting at the very bottom of my laundry basket, I mixed ingredients for pancakes in a bowl. I was famished, and Dog had the appetite of a grizzly bear gearing up for hibernation, so I made a triple batch. I also scrambled some eggs. Dog predictably trotted out just as I was setting the table.

"You know, you could help me with the cooking if you ditched the paws for thumbs."

He huffed, telling me that was never going to happen.

While we ate, I filled Dog in on everything that I'd learned in the dreamscape. Afterward, I cleaned up the dishes and planned my next move.

"Do you know where Lief went?"

Dog did a doggy shrug that seemed to say, *Who knows, who cares?*

"Well, you *should* care," I told him crossly. "I'm going after Farranen with or without Lief, but I'll be a hell of a lot more likely to stay alive if he's with me."

Dog growled; it was the same growl he used when he was trying to establish dominance over the many furry critters in the forest.

"Do *not* take that tone with me," I warned him.

He continued to stare me down for another three and a half seconds before looking away. Darn right; this was my house. He didn't get to tell me what I could or couldn't do.

Now that he'd been properly chastised, he belly-crawled over to where I was drying dishes and put his head on my foot. And like the sucker I was, I bent down and gave him a scratch behind the ears so he'd know all was forgiven.

****

I packed enough food and water for a few days, since I didn't know how long I'd be gone. I'd found the missing sword between my mattress and headboard hidden under a layer of glamour, and it had taken some inventive alterations with duct tape to get it strapped to my back. It was awkward, and every time I bent down, I expected it to slide out of its leather sheath and slice one or more of my toes off.

I dressed myself in Lief's borrowed cloak, figuring it was already filthy from my mad dash out of Fairie so a little more dirt wouldn't matter.

Since I'd slept the majority of the daylight hours away, the sun had already slipped beyond the horizon when I stepped outside to head to Farranen's cabin. Dog tagged along, even after I told him to stay home. Stupid loyal mutt. I hoped he didn't end up hurt on account of me.

I'd never been inside the tidy white cabin, so it was a little anticlimactic when I knocked on the door and there was no answer. Dang. I'd really been hoping to get a look inside. And, no, I wasn't planning on doing anything creepy, like pawing through his underpants or sniffing his pillowcase because that's something a pathetic stalker would do. And even I had my limits. But it sure didn't stop me from wondering.

I know, my morbid curiosity would be the death of me some day. Just hopefully not today.

I briefly wondered where Lief and Celesta were, but they were centuries-old fae who carried swords everywhere they went—we had much bigger issues than a rebellion to deal with if they needed a clumsy hermit riding in to save their bacon. I marched back down the gravel road to my cabin and continued through the backyard and onto the path that would take me to the hawthorn tree. Suddenly, a voice cut through the twilight, startling a yelp out of me and a growl from Dog.

"Going somewhere, Theo?" Ozzy materialized out

of the dark shadows on the path behind me. Damn vampires, always prowling where you don't expect them to be. I wonder if they had special shoes that made them so stealthy?

"Don't *do* that, Ozzy! You just about gave me a heart attack!" I scolded, while trying to take deep breaths so my heart rate would go back down.

"Don't call me that," he reminded me from a good ten feet away. Smart vampire; if he'd been closer, I would have smacked him. "You shouldn't be out in the woods alone; it looks like there were at least a dozen fae that came through the gate in the last few days."

"What? Why so many?" My stomach dropped at the thought of more women being kidnapped and hauled back to Fairie.

He shrugged, but his nonchalance was phony. "Haven't been able to ask any of them."

I glanced around at the surrounding trees, searching for hidden fae, but didn't see any. Then again, I doubted I would see them until their teeth were ripping out my throat.

"What are you doing out here, Theo?"

"Just taking an evening stroll," I told him warily. There was no need to advertise the fact that I was planning a solo rescue mission. Wait—with Dog, it would be a duo rescue mission.

"You're going to Fairie to rescue the guardian, aren't you?"

Damn it! Now I was convinced that vamps had secret mind-reading skills.

"I didn't read your mind, Theo."

"Aha! Then how did you know that's what I was thinking?"

"Because it's written all over your face. You're an open book, woman—a damn audiobook, with the volume turned all the way up."

He was wrong. If I was any sort of book, I'd be a stone tablet with ancient hieroglyphics hand-carved on it. As a writer, I'd already given the subject some thought.

Ozzy pulled a gun out of his coat, and I took a step back as Dog took a step forward. His I'm-going-to-rip-your-face-off-and-eat-it-right-before-I-turn-your-dick-into-my-new-favorite-chew-toy growl filled the air, warning the vamp that he was in danger of losing important body parts.

After checking that the gun was loaded (with a series of impressively coordinated moves), Ozzy tucked it back where it belonged. "Just wanted to make sure I had the iron bullets loaded before we head out."

Wait—we? What we? Did he have a mouse in his pocket? Because he sure wasn't referring to me. At least I hoped he wasn't referring to me. He gestured grandly at the path, dispelling any illusions I had about him not crashing my party tonight.

"No," I told him flatly.

"If you're going, then I'm going," he told me just as flatly.

"You need to stay here and tell Lief where I've gone," I pointed out.

"Let's just leave him a note," he countered.

"Damn it, Ozzy! Farranen is being tortured; I've got to find him! Stop wasting my time and get the fuck out of my way!" I shrieked, revealing the inner shrew that only made an appearance when I was feeling super panicky and desperate.

The giant vampire stared down at me for a full five seconds before bursting out laughing. His manly chortle irritated me more than it should have. "You are so cute when you're angry!" He topped off the insult by pinching my cheek as he waltzed by me.

Dog looked back and forth between the two of us until I told him, "If you laugh, I will never cook for you again."

Like the good shifter he was, Dog kept his eyes on the path as he slunk past me.

Smart wolf.

****

I wasn't sure what to expect when we arrived at the gate.

Ozzy had been right about the increase in fae using the gate; the path to the hawthorn tree had seen enough traffic that it was hard-packed and easy to traverse. The only downside was my brain had been free to wander as we made the trek.

My entire plan was pretty basic: cross through the gate, find Farranen, Mary, and any other prisoners that were loyal to Lief, bust them out of whatever horrible place they were being kept, and bring them back through the gate. Easy peasy, right?

My plan didn't address the possibility that some of the prisoners might be injured or unconscious. There was also a high probability of soldiers waiting for us. And how was I supposed to keep Ozzy and Dog safe? The fae queen herself was a real wild card—who knew what that crazy bitch was plotting? Hopefully she'd have her hands full with creating changelings from the kidnapped vampires—

Oh, crap. I'd forgotten all about the kidnapped

females. I couldn't just leave them there. Damn it! I was really good at plotting when it came to laying out a story on paper, but when it came to real life, I flat out sucked. Like, big hairy testicles sucked.

We reached the gate, and I tentatively reached for the tree. The magic of Fairie buzzed beneath my fingertips, welcoming me.

"I think we need to be touching for all of us to get through," I told them.

Ozzy took my left hand, and I wound the fingers on my other hand into Dog's soft fur until I could feel the rough texture of scar tissue around his neck.

Well, here goes nothing, I thought. My foot disappeared into the tree with a flash of light, and I kept walking until I was past the thick waterfall of magic that separated the two realms.

Once we reached the clearing that surrounded the tree, Ozzy dropped my hand and tilted his head back in awe. Even though there were was no sun in Fairie, the sky was a beautiful clear blue, dotted with puffy white clouds that slowly meandered past overhead. Delicate autumn leaves drifted silently from the full branches to the ground. The overall effect was magical. And judging by Ozzy's dumbstruck expression, he would have agreed.

"How is this possible?" he asked, sounding nothing like the cantankerous vampire I was used to.

"We're in Fairie." I shrugged. "It's kind of unpredictable here." In hindsight, I probably should have warned him that nighttime and daytime didn't always line up with what was happening on Earth. In my defense, I had just assumed that as a PIMP agent, he knew what we'd be walking into. I mean, he was a paranormal intelligence agent, so that kind of made him an expert, right?

While I'd been watching the shocked vamp, Dog had wandered the perimeter of the clearing, marking a number of unsuspecting trees along the way. I called him over to me and told him, "This is a dangerous place. You can't run off and chase things." I didn't know if there were any squirrels in Fairie, but there were definitely things that Dog would want to chase. Things with sharp teeth that would bite back if he caught them. He gave me an annoyed eye roll and yawned.

I turned to Ozzy. "We should get going, if you're done with the sky-gazing?"

He shot me a disgruntled look and muttered something about bossy women, but it had none of its usual bite.

I idly wondered if the lack of UV rays in Fairie decreased the faes' likeliness of getting skin cancer.

Four grass-lined paths led into the forest. I knew from my previous trips here that the one leading straight would take us toward the queen's dungeons. The one that went right went to the queen's castle, but first we'd have to get past the guards stationed about five minutes down the road.

The castle seemed like the smartest place to start since she'd probably want her prisoners kept close. When it came to torturing members of her court, I had a feeling that she was a hands-on kind of girl.

"The castle is that way." I pointed. "But there are guards watching the road. There's also a large stone arch with weird fae writing, so I'm thinking it might be some sort of magical security system that we should avoid."

Ozzy nodded, and I was relieved to see his familiar bossy-agent-in-charge expression was back. "How many guards?"

"There were two last time; but the rebellion might have spurred the queen to add more."

"Okay, two or more. So, what's the plan?"

I blinked. "Uh, get past the guards. Then rescue anyone being held prisoner."

Ozzy scowled. "*That's* your plan? That's not a goddamned plan, Theo. It's a wish list written by a three-year-old."

It was my turn to scowl. "If you don't like my plan, feel free to make one of your own."

Running a hand through his thick hair in frustration, Ozzy shook his head. "We need to get a head count on the guards and find out if there's a way around the stone arch. One of us needs to scout ahead. Since you're clumsier than a newborn colt on ice"—he gestured to Dog, sniffing at the base of the hawthorn tree—"and he won't be able to tell us what's waiting for us, I'll check it out."

I sent him an indignant glare for the colt reference but didn't try to contradict his assessment of Dog's or my skills.

"I shouldn't be long; try not to get yourselves killed while I'm gone." And just like that, the giant vampire melted into the shadows of the forest without so much as a goodbye or backward glance.

****

Odd things have been known to happen in Fairie.

Then again, plenty of strange things had happened to me when my feet were firmly on Tamarac soil, so maybe odd things happened everywhere. Either way, I was pretty sure I was about to be sucked into something bizarre.

My magic shifted restlessly as soon as Ozzy disappeared. It rippled up and down my limbs, and I fought the urge to scratch as it dug its claws in a little deeper. Dog watched with concern in his eyes as I paced back and forth in the clearing.

The hair on the back of my neck stood up, and I got a hinky feeling like someone was watching us. I scanned the treeline, but all I saw was the sea of leaves as they swayed in the light breeze. Anyone, or anything, could have been out there.

I'd had the misfortune of accompanying Farranen to retrieve two wayward brownies who had crossed through the gate in September. With skin like tree bark and long knobby limbs, they'd be able to blend into the surrounding forest and I wouldn't be able to see them until their sharp teeth were chewing on my limbs.

Having marked a sufficient amount of the trees with his scent, Dog lounged in the grass while monitoring my pacing and the spot where Ozzy had left. His tail flicked stiffly from side to side; he was obviously picking up on my tension, but it was more of a what-crazy-dangerous-situation-is-Theo-about-to-run-head-first-into-now? vibe, rather than a reaction to an immediate threat. If he wasn't worried, I shouldn't be either. I doubted much could get past his shifter senses.

My magic ratcheted up a notch, becoming more of a burn than a sharp pain. I tried to breath through it. My vision blurred, and my knees trembled.

"Dog—"

Dog bounded over before I could even finish trying

to warn him that something was wrong. I opened my mouth to tell him to stay back, but before I could get the words out, he'd planted his shoulder against my hip to help support me. The instant he touched me, his magic—magic that I'd never really been aware of before—brushed up against mine. There was a harsh *snap!* and the air filled with the smell of ozone, just like after a lightning strike. Dog and I were thrown apart, and my magic recoiled painfully back into my body.

I rolled onto my back, holding my hip and praying that Dog was okay. God, I still couldn't see anything clearly, and there were shadows everywhere. Any one of them could have been Dog.

"Dog?" I croaked, sounding as freaked out as I felt.

The small whine was music to my ears. He sounded scared, but alive.

"What the *fuck,* Theo!" Ozzy's familiar demand, full of exasperation and shock, was a welcome distraction from my panic. "I can't leave you two alone for a damn minute!"

I rolled onto my belly and slowly got my shaking arms under me until I was able to rise to my knees. "Don't come any closer," I warned him.

"You're damn right—I'm not getting anywhere near you until you let go of the bloody fae magic you're holding onto!" he informed me. I could see him checking Dog, and I was insanely grateful when Dog lumbered to his feet and gave the vamp a low growl, warning him to back away.

The magic pulsed through my body, like it was searching for a way out. A low moan snuck past my lips, and my back bowed as the pain doubled.

Someone was calling my name. It was enough to

drag my awareness from the all-encompassing pain to the fae that had just stepped through the gate.

"Theo!" Lief knelt a few feet away from me, crouching low so we were eye to eye. "Let it out! You'll burn out if you hold onto it!"

I wanted to tell him that I didn't know how, that I might hurt someone if I unleashed the raw power, just like I'd already hurt Dog.

"Look for the dead, Theo!"

Look for the dead? Another minute or two of this and I wouldn't have to look far—because I'd be the dead one. But because I had no idea what else to do, I turned my watery gaze away from the dark prince and out toward the woods. At first, there were only trees. Then, something near the treeline caught my eye. A rippling shimmer of movement. I blinked, and the pale kaleidoscoping thing moved again.

Oh, fuck. I'd seen something like that once before—when I'd ripped Vanessa out of whatever state of existence she'd been living in and back into ours. And…damn it; I knew what was happening. My ankou magic had recognized that there was a ghost nearby and was literally straining to get over to where it was hovering.

A drop of sweat rolled down the back of my neck. I was close to passing out. If I was going to do something, it needed to be soon. I carefully lifted a shaking hand toward the figure and crooked my fingers. I wish I could say I did it gracefully, like a seductive movie actress, but it was probably closer to something a black widow spider would have done to a fly.

At first, I didn't think anything would happen, but then…the ghost tentatively came closer. Inch by painfully slow inch, it worked its way across the clearing. I kept my hand out, holding my breath until the damn thing was standing right in front of me. It hesitated, and I thought I might throw up if I didn't let the magic *out*. It felt like a bomb about to go off, trapped under my skin.

The ghost extended its hand, and the second that our fingers met, my magic leapt away from me like rats abandoning a sinking ship. My entire body seemed to deflate as the magic exploded outward and tunneled into the ghost.

The forest tilted around me as I fell sideways into the thick grass, and the sights and sounds of the clearing faded into a distant buzz.

Chapter Ten

I let out a small gasp when I was able to move again.

Strong arms held me firmly against a hard body, and I had a brief moment of panic when I thought Merrick had me pinned beneath him on the floor of my cabin.

"Breathe, Theo, just breathe. I've got you." Lief's deep voice whispered next to my ear, and I realized I was in the hawthorn clearing in Fairie, not lying on my blood-stained hardwood floors with an unhinged vamp trying to kill me. Again. Thank God.

Blinking tears out of my vision, I saw Dog lying next to me with his head pillowed on my feet. His worried amber eyes watched me with an intensity that would have been comical if I hadn't been too darn tired to laugh.

"She did it again! I knew it!" Ozzy smugly announced. "Felt like a bloody nuclear charge going off!"

"Did I…" I intended to ask if I'd done the ankou thing again, but if I had, I wasn't sure I actually wanted to know about it.

"A release of that magnitude won't go unnoticed. We need to get you out of here before anyone comes to investigate. Theo, can you walk?" The concern in Lief's voice snapped me out of my stupor faster than anything else could have.

"I'm good," I told him. I was bone tired, but stopping to take a nap was out of the question. I accepted the hand that Ozzy offered me, and once I was back on my own two feet, I realized we had a visitor.

A tall slim male stood a few feet away, watching me warily. He had to be fae because his skin was a pale blue with a metallic shimmer. Dark blue hair teased the collar of his gray shirt, and he studied me with eyes that were a shocking neon blue bordering on indigo.

"Hello…" I gave him a dubious look when he didn't say anything back. Why did fae men always have to be so intense? Just once, I'd like to meet one that didn't look like he was contemplating advanced physics at a world-saving level.

"Theo?" Lief glanced between me and the blue-skinned male in confusion.

"Yeah, we should go," I agreed. Taking care to give the stranger a wide berth, I took a few steps toward the forest. If Lief was worried about being discovered, then the trees would provide some cover until we could get farther away.

"Where's the ghost? With that amount of magic, there should be a ghost." Lief slowly scanned the clearing.

I glanced at the stranger suspiciously. He couldn't be—could he?

The male dipped his chin in a brief nod.

"You're a ghost?" I asked.

Another nod.

"Can you talk?" Maybe some ghosts were mute? Or maybe my temperamental magic had screwed up and made a broken ghost.

After a brief glance at the dark prince, the male cleared his throat. "I can talk." He spoke quietly, and I had to lean forward to hear him.

"Theo?" Lief stepped in front of me and I had to tilt my head back to meet his eyes. "Who are you talking to?"

"The ghost." I did my best not to sound snarky, but I thought we'd already established that I'd accidentally created another ghost.

"You can see a ghost?" His one eyebrow climbed a little higher on his perfect forehead.

"Yes, I can see a ghost." I spoke slowly, trying again not to come across as snarky. I was less successful this time.

"I don't see anything." Oh man, why did he have to use the Theo's-seeing-things-so-somebody-better-call-a-shrink tone? It was so condescending. And irritating.

I stopped trying to keep my snarkiness under wraps and rolled it out like a red carpet. "I'm the only one that can see Vanessa, so statistically speaking, there's a good chance I'm the only one that can see *him*." I jerked my chin toward the wide-eyed ghost. "And you wouldn't see him unless you had a pair of eyes growing out of your ass, because he's *behind* you."

Ozzy let out a whoop of laughter that made it hard to keep a straight face. The dark prince spun around and surveyed the clearing before turning back to me.

"I assume he's fae?"

He sounded less grouchy than I'd expected so I reined in my sarcastic response and just nodded.

"While only the ankou can bring over a ghost, they are visible to all with fae magic. The more powerful the ankou, the stronger the ghost. You just used ten times more power than you needed to open the veil, so I should be able to detect at least a glimmer of anyone you pulled through."

I shrugged. "Well, tough beans. Maybe you could inform my magic that it keeps doing the ghost thing wrong, since it sure isn't inclined to listen to me."

I glanced over to where the ghost was watching our exchange with a horrified expression.

"You should not talk to the dark prince like that." His nervous gaze darted to Lief before returning to me.

"Eh, he's a big boy, he can handle it."

The ghost looked even more aghast at my flippant remark.

"What's he saying?" Ozzy demanded.

"He's got his panties in a knot because he thinks I hurt Lief's feelings." The ghost's face paled—which wasn't a very good look for an already pale ghost. I was going to say he looked like he'd seen a ghost, but that might be in poor taste with the company I was keeping these days. "Uh-oh. Can a ghost have a stroke? I don't think he likes me talking about his panties."

Ozzy snickered, but Lief just rolled his eyes. At least one of them appreciated my honesty.

"You can tell him that my feelings are undamaged by your candor," Lief told me with the barest hint of a smile.

I caught myself smiling back and quickly looked away. "We should get going before someone sees us and tattles to the queen."

The men must have agreed, because Lief silently led us into the trees on the left side of the clearing. Which totally dispelled my assumption that the prisoners would be somewhere near the castle. It's a darn good thing Lief had shown up, or we'd be wandering around Fairie like a bunch of tourists without a map.

****

I was hungry and exhausted and cranky. And maybe a little whiney.

I would have literally cut off my left foot and traded it for a piece of cherry cheesecake right then.

Twenty feet ahead of me, Ozzy and Lief led the way through the forest, speaking to each other in hushed tones. Once in a while, they'd glance back and give me a why-am-I-not-surprised-that-Theo's-at-the-center-of-this-giant-clusterfuck? look. If we all survived this, I was never going to hear the end of it.

The ghost's name was Harvalin, but he looked more like a Harvey. He seemed to relax a little with every step that Ozzy and Lief pulled ahead of us, so it was easy to blame my slow pace on him. Despite my exhaustion, I attempted to weasel some info out of the tight-lipped ghost.

So far, all I'd been able to glean, besides his name, was the fact that he was a merdain fae of the Light Court. Judging by the pale gray shirt with gold buttons and his black pants and boots, he'd been a member of the queen's soldiers. He didn't have the expected sword or dagger at his hip, but maybe my magic could only reanimate clothing and not weapons. I should have asked Mary if there was a manual for rookies. Actually, I should have asked Mary a lot of things. I'd been stupid to let my prejudice and fear keep me from getting answers.

"So, how did you die?" I did my best to sound conversational even though I was dead on my feet.

Harvey sent me a wary look and shrugged. Okay, then. My first ghost had been a sassy bitch, and my second was antisocial enough to make me look like a party girl. I sure could pick 'em.

Dog nudged my hand with his head, and I smiled down at him. He seemed fine after the large jolt of magic I'd accidentally zapped him with, but I still felt responsible. We were going to be eating steak for an entire week once we got home—just so I could appease my guilty conscience.

"So, if Lief is the dark prince, does that mean the queen is his mother?" I asked Harvey. At this point, I think I was asking questions just to annoy him since his attitude was annoying me.

"No!" His blue eyebrows rose even higher. "Fae royalty earn their titles through their actions, not through bloodlines."

I'd already guessed as much; Celesta had mentioned something along the lines of *whoever takes the head, takes the crown.*

"Is there a king? Or a princess?" I persisted.

"No. There is only one ruler for each court. Our monarchs sometimes choose to take consorts, but none have ever found their true mates, so they have always held the sole title for each court." Now Harvey looked confused, like he couldn't figure out how someone with ankou magic didn't know such basic facts.

"Then why isn't Lief called the dark king?"

"I don't know!" I was sensing some ghostly frustration from Harvey.

"So, what happens if he kills the queen? Does he become the boss of both courts?"

"The Light Court can only be ruled by one of its

own members. Why do you ask such questions?"

"I'm new to the whole magic thing," I told him absently, while pondering the question of who would replace the queen. I'd assumed it would be Lief, but he was from the Dark Court. Maybe Celesta? I didn't know enough of the players in this game to even take an educated guess. Most of the fae I'd met had been from the Dark Court.

And I'm pretty sure my subconscious was focusing so hard on understanding the mechanics of the rebellion as a way to distract the rest of my brain from why I'd really come to Fairie: my guardian.

****

The terrain had gone from flat and treed to rocky hills without me really noticing. I'd stumbled a few times, not on a rock or branch underfoot, but because I'd fallen asleep on my feet. At some point, Lief and Ozzy had waited for Dog and I to catch up, and we traveled single file in silence.

When we reached the top of another rounded hill, I stopped to stare at something off in the distance.

"What is that?" I asked, gesturing to the dark shadows that seemed to be leaking between the hills and off into the horizon.

"The dead lands." Lief joined me, sounding pensive. "They're growing." He looked down at me with a small frown. "Our world used to be as large as yours, but hundreds of years ago, when our magic started to fade, our lands did too. The land itself is still there, but it's not alive anymore. It's just...dead."

"Oh." I had nothing helpful to add, nothing to say that would erase that worried look from his face. The fae had been struggling for the last few centuries; they were no longer able to make changelings or have babies. I hadn't known their land was failing too.

"Don't fret, my lady." He gave me a small smile. "There aren't many of us left, so a little lost land is not a problem. My only concern is that the dead space has changed direction; it's only a few miles from the gate now."

It took me a few seconds to envision what would happen if the dead lands reached the gate—the hawthorn tree would be swallowed up by the darkness. And while I wholly supported the idea of most of the queen's subjects no longer waltzing through my backyard, I didn't love the fact that I wouldn't be able to see Lief anymore. Or my guardian.

"Where are the other gates?" I asked, to distract myself from any further thoughts of Farranen.

"Two of the remaining gates are a few hundred miles to the north, one is fifty miles west of here, and the last is to the southeast."

"Wow, nothing closer?" I guess that excluded the possibility of day trips.

"There were originally forty gates, all scattered across the planet. Now there are five." He didn't bother to tell me that two of the five guardians were being held prisoner by the queen and their gates were in danger of closing permanently. Or maybe he just didn't know about them.

I glanced back at Ozzy as we continued our somber procession down the hill. He looked like he was trying to commit every single detail of Fairie to memory. With his heightened vamp senses, it was probably even more spectacular than what I was able to see.

"Camp is just behind the next hill," Lief called

over his shoulder.

Thank God. Because I was about to fall on my face. Having my magic torn out when I'd brought Harvey across the veil had seriously drained me. Any first-grade schoolyard bully would be able to kick my butt with zero effort required.

"Theo." Lief offered me his arm, and I wasn't too proud to take it. I held my breath until I was sure my greedy magic wouldn't try to steal from him without my permission. "Your existence has become common knowledge among both courts, as well as the fact that your transition failed. When we arrive and they sense you possess a hefty bit of ankou magic, there will be questions."

"Is there any way to hide it?" I asked wearily.

"I'm afraid not; you radiate with it."

I...what? That sounded like a compliment.

"They won't mistake you for fae, or even a changeling, which will only add to their curiosity."

"Damn." I was too tired for this.

"I have a solution; a way that will allow you a modicum of privacy." His normally open expression was closed off, and it set off my bullshit radar.

"Do not even try to pull any of the half-truths-and-pretty-words crap with me. Just tell me whatever plan you've cooked up that you already know I'm not going to like." I jabbed him in the arm for emphasis.

To my surprise, Lief smirked. "All right, I'll admit it's not ideal; but if you were to pose as my consort, the other males would know you're off limits."

I gaped at him. "You can't be serious."

"It's not unheard of for me to travel with a female companion," he argued.

Yeah, I'd sure believe that. I'd even bet good money on it.

"You're saying they'd believe that this—" I gestured down the length of my body before continuing. "—that *this* is the body of a consort?" Most of the fae I'd met were the very definition of beauty, not five foot four and a hundred and sixty pounds of plain and boring. I had a bigger chance of passing for a unicorn than a working girl.

"I assure you, Theo, you are well within the realm of those whom I would willingly share my bed with."

His pale blue eyes sparkled like diamonds as he looked down at me, and I was suddenly aware of how close he was. A little tendril of my magic escaped and wound its way down his arm, and I felt sorry for every teenage boy who sported wood next to the popular girls in gym class. Lief's knowing smile only made me blush harder.

"And we already know that the right corset and bottoms can fit you to perfection." His voice was little more than a husky timbre that sent a shiver down my spine.

"You saw me in them?" I asked in horror. Oh God, my housecoat must have come open when we were sleeping. At least Lief didn't carry a cell phone with him, so I didn't have to worry about Facebook and Instagram blowing up with images of me snoring in naughty lingerie.

His smile widened into a dark wicked thing that both tantalized and terrified me.

****

I didn't see the encampment until we passed through the layer of glamour that concealed it. The

125

magic tingled across my skin like tiny cold raindrops. Dog must have felt it too, because he let out a whine and pressed himself tighter against my hip. If I hadn't been so tired, I probably would have recognized the telltale shimmer of glamour.

Seconds ago, there had been nothing but grassy rolling hills and giant mossy boulders, and suddenly the entire valley was filled with the sights and sounds of a war camp. Tents of varying sizes and colors were set up in neatly organized groupings. Small campfires smoked from the center of each group with a number of fae clustered around them, while others strode purposefully from one tent to another. The two closest males must have been acting as guards, and already had swords pointed at us. Lief raised a hand in greeting, and they lowered the blades.

"My lord." They both spoke at once, and it was creepier than it should have been. They both were tall, probably around six feet, but it was hard for me to be sure since everyone looked tall next to me. Both wore matching brown pants that looked homemade, and simple well-worn black boots. Shirtless, their bare chests were liberally covered in coarse brown hair that continued up to faces that would have looked at home on the shoulders of a wild boar.

"Vestin, Odrin, this is Oscar Alderidge from the Earth realm." Lief gestured to the vampire, who looked more curious than grumpy for once.

"Vampire," one of the fae grated from a throat that wasn't really meant for more than squeals and grunts.

Ozzy acknowledged their deduction with a slight nod.

"And Dog from the Earth realm." The dark prince

swept a hand toward where Dog had stationed himself, directly between me and the fae guards.

The males both sniffed the air efficaciously before one of them grunted, "Shifter?"

"Yes." Lief wrapped an arm around me possessively. "And this is my consort, Theo."

Since the dark prince had sidelined me with his shocking plan just minutes ago, I hadn't had any time to think it over. And apparently, Lief had mistaken my lack of denial as consent and was giving his plan the green light. We were definitely going to have some words about this once we were in private. Really, really ugly words.

I smiled demurely as the warthog boys gave me a once-over. Lief's palm slid a little lower, and I fought to keep from snarling at all of them. Yeah, I can be a real bear when I'm tired. Or hungry. Or feeling helpless. And right now, I was completely at Lief's mercy—which is why I was so pissed off.

"Have someone show Oscar and Dog to the available sleeping quarters," he ordered in a voice that left no room for negotiation. I don't think I comprehended until that very second exactly how haughty Lief could be.

I opened my mouth to tell him that Dog would be sleeping wherever I was, but the dark prince silenced me by squeezing my hip in warning. He pulled me against his body and pressed his lips to my ear in a parody of a kiss. "Shhh," he whispered. "Allowing your friend into my tent would raise some eyebrows. Just follow my lead."

Knowing he was right, I nodded imperceptibly before making a show of running my hands up his chest before fisting them in the fabric of the shirt beneath his cloak. When his pupils dilated, I didn't have to fake the smile that tugged at my lips. Messing with the dark prince was quickly becoming my new favorite hobby.

He leaned down until his breath feathered against the sensitive skin on my neck. In a warm puff of moist air, he whispered, "*Tease.*"

"*Asshole,*" I whispered back.

When he finally pulled back to address the guards, I was glad to see I wasn't the only one breathing erratically.

Chapter Eleven

Dog's eyes held a wealth of uncertainty and unspoken words when we were forced to part ways.

I hated leaving him alone. Logically, it was the best way to avoid raising suspicion, but it still felt wrong. I wanted to remind him not to go chasing after any of Fairie's small furry creatures, but consorts were supposed to keep their mouths shut. Damn it, why hadn't Lief tried to pass me off as a cook or something believable? A consort was the last thing I'd be able to pass for.

Ozzy turned and looked back at me with a look that seemed to say Christ-woman-what-are-you-so-fucking-worried-about?-I'll-watch-the-damn-mutt, and I felt a little better knowing the vampire would keep an eye on my shifter.

Keeping an arm around me, Lief led us through the maze of tents and small clusters of people, who stopped what they were doing to greet their leader. I was surprised to see how well liked and respected he was. He acknowledged every comment and concern his people had with a confident smile, and I found my own respect for him growing. Not that I'd ever share that little epiphany with him. His ego was big enough already.

Aside from a few curious looks, I was mostly ignored. I attempted to sneak little peeks at my surroundings, but Lief had warned me to keep my hood up.

When he was finally able to extract himself from the majority of the gathered fae, I had expected him to head for the biggest tent in the center of the camp, so I was surprised when he tugged me by the hand toward one of the smaller ones. He must have sensed my confusion because he explained with a wink, "I prefer to bunk alone; more privacy that way." God, the jerk was insufferable.

When the tent flaps fell back into place, I was amazed to see glowing balls of light hovering near the ceiling. Feeling like I was standing in a cave full of stars, I reached up to touch one. My fingers slid through as if they were made of air.

"They're made of glamour," Lief told me from where he'd been quietly watching.

"They're beautiful," I replied.

Tearing my eyes from the enchanting orbs, I looked around the small space. It looked no different than a simple trapper's tent. The white fabric walls were held up by a network of wooden poles. A large red rug woven with an intricate gold and black pattern covered most of the lush grass underfoot, and a large queen-size bed was neatly tucked into the corner. Opposite the bed, a small dresser supported a mirror and a basin of water, and next to the door of the tent, a wooden chest served as a seat.

From the outside, the tent had appeared to be about ten feet by twelve feet, but it felt slightly bigger once I was inside. Probably due to the minimal furnishings and the tall ceiling overhead.

"Dog is like a newborn; he needs to eat every few

hours." I crossed my arms across my chest, unconvinced that Lief fully grasped what would be involved with feeding an adolescent shifter. Dog's appetite rivaled that of an entire football team.

"You can rest assured that I have already taken Dog's needs into consideration." There was none of the usual condescension in his voice, and that reassured me more than the actual words did.

"Is the food here safe for him?" The bread and cheese I'd shared with Mary hadn't been a problem, but who knows how Dog would react? I'd be seriously pissed if he ended up sprouting wings or shrinking to the size of a chihuahua.

"Fae food is only a problem for humans. There are no ill-effects for any of the supernatural races." He took a step closer, and I appreciated the way he maintained eye contact, allowing me to see his sincerity, rather than blowing off my concerns.

"I'm human," I pointed out, challenging the only flaw in his argument—but only because I was curious why I hadn't turned into a hedgehog after sampling the local cuisine.

"A human with fae *and* vampire magic." He turned away, effectively ending our discussion as he removed his cloak and sword. He hung them from a hook above the chest, and I grudgingly handed over mine at his insistence.

"That's not going to work," he told me once he saw my yoga pants and blue shirt that said BEAM ME UP next to a tiny cartoon image of an alien. He held out his hand in invitation, and I sighed before lacing my fingers through his. He was going to glamour my clothes into something that he considered more appropriate, but his idea of appropriate wouldn't be the same as mine.

I shut my eyes as his magic teased its way up my arm and across my body. There was a pause when it drifted across my butt, and I bit back a gasp. The bastard was just trying to provoke a response, and I was determined not to give it to him. Once he finally released my hand, I opened my eyes and looked down.

The first thing I saw were my boobs. Lots and lots of boobs. They were impossible to miss since they'd been crammed into a push-up bra. An incredibly tight, low-cut push-up bra. A silky black nightie with spaghetti straps did little to hide the racy red undergarments. And I wasn't going to check now, but I was pretty sure there was a thong clinging to my backside like a wet noodle.

I shot the smiling jerk a look that promised payback.

"This is much more suitable attire for my consort." His eyes were a little too bright, his words a little too honest, as he took in my outfit.

"Call me that again, and I will kick you in the junk so hard that you'll be able to get your prostate checked through your mouth," I warned him.

He laughed. "I thought you'd be more comfortable with this than the alternative."

"Which is?" I asked hopefully, because *anything* had to be better than this.

"Naked."

I waited for the punchline, but when it didn't come, it hit me like a slap in the face that he was serious. "Not going to happen," I told him flatly.

"Our food will arrive soon; you should get into bed." He undid the first few buttons of his shirt with slow deliberate movements that had me backing up.

"Why?" I sounded a little bit hysterical and took a deep breath to calm down. Good Lord, a chest that ripped should be illegal.

"They'll give us long enough to enjoy ourselves, but if we're still standing here arguing when they arrive, it will create gossip. They'll either deduce that you're not who you say you are, or they'll question my ability to please you." He tossed his shirt onto the rug, and I forced myself to focus on it instead of the half-naked man in front of me. "And I'd like to avoid having that particular rumor spread around."

"But I'm the consort. Wouldn't they assume that I'm the one who couldn't please you?"

"That's not how it works here, Theo. Sex among the fae is mutually enjoyable. Consorts act as consorts because they want to, not because they have to." He slid back the covers and scooted under them. After adjusting the pillows to his liking, he held the covers open in invitation.

I gave him a suspicious look, but I didn't have any other options and I was starting to shiver in the skimpy costume, so I sucked up my pride and crawled under the blankets.

It was warm enough to thaw my bones, and I gratefully sank into the plush mattress. I didn't even protest when Lief pulled me against his chest; I was just grateful for his heat. The smattering of dark hairs on his chest tickled against my cheek, and a small giggle escaped my lips.

Sleep pulled at me, reminding me that I'd expended a huge amount of magic today.

"Hey, how come my magic isn't trying to steal all

of yours right now?" I asked. The last time I'd created a ghost, I'd nearly drained Lief as soon as we'd touched. I could feel my magic sliding across his; it was a liquid caress that made me want to melt in a way that had nothing to do with heat.

"I suspect your magic has started to settle in so you're able to control it better." His voice sounded sleepy, reminding me that I wasn't the only one who'd had a long day. The five o'clock shadow on his chin rasped across my hair.

"What are you doing?" I asked, when he continued down to my ear.

"Combining our scents. To avoid suspicion." Right, to avoid suspicion.

I could have poked a few holes in his logic, but I was too damn tired. And lying there in his arms wasn't as dreadful as I'd assumed it would be. It was actually kind of nice.

Dreadful would have been easier to deal with.

****

I awoke to a delightful surprise.

The embarrassing lingerie was gone, and in its place was the comfiest pair of pajamas I'd ever worn. They were pale yellow with electric-blue lightning bolts and tiny cartoon characters. Upon closer inspection, the little men were dressed in all black with matching black capes. It took me a full thirty seconds of examining the army plastered over my pjs to realize they were supposed to be the dark prince. It was actually the tiny, barely visible sword handle that clued me in. I snorted in amusement at the stupid territorial things men did. It was really no different from Dog peeing on everything to mark it as his property.

Lief was gone—and thank goodness, because one surprise in my bed was more than enough.

Someone had left a tray of food on the foot of the bed, so I hauled it over and dug in. I was freakin' starved. I needed to carry snacks in my pockets for days like today. Halfway into my meal of bread, butter, cheese, fruit, and some kind of meat that was tasty but unidentifiable, Lief returned.

"So, did they buy our story?" I asked when he took a seat next to me.

"Yes. The food took longer to arrive than I anticipated, so I was able to tell them you were sleeping soundly due to the rigorous activities we engaged in."

I rolled my eyes. "I thought the fae couldn't lie?"

"We can't. Every word I said was true; you were tired from the rigorous amount of travel it took to get here—which we did together."

Huh. Sneaky fae maneuvering.

"We've discovered where the missing females are being kept." He helped himself to some of the mystery meat.

"That's great! Does Ozzy know?" I wondered if Marissa would be one of them.

"I sent him with a team of my best men to liberate the women. Having him there will be a big help if there are any vampires among the females we rescue. Most of my men are unfamiliar with the other supernatural races."

I could understand why; most of the Dark Court would never be able to pass for human, so I doubted they spent much time outside of Fairie.

"And…" I bit my lip nervously, wondering if there was any word on Farranen or Mary.

"No word on the guardian yet," Lief said, not unkindly, and I nodded my thanks. "I've known him for a long time, Theo. If anyone is strong enough to endure, it's him."

The bread suddenly tasted like ash in my mouth, and I felt a stab of guilt. Farranen was still being tortured, while I was scarfing down room service in bed. God, I was the worst friend ever. Well, worst non-friend ever, since I didn't think we were actually friends. Gah, I had no idea what we were to each other, but I sure didn't want him suffering for another second.

"What can I do to help?" I asked. Coming to Fairie without any real plan had been stupid, but seeing the level of organization in Lief's encampment was encouraging. Hopefully they'd be able to locate and rescue Farranen and any other fae who had fallen into the queen's clutches.

"You're already doing it, Theo. That faith you hold in your heart is exactly what we need right now." He reached out and caught a tear that was in the process of running down my cheek.

"They tortured him." I held my breath until I was sure I could speak without blubbering. "They whipped him. He looked *defeated*."

I didn't protest when Lief pulled me into his arms. There was none of the sexual undertones from before, just comfort and a shared grief for someone we both cared about.

"We'll get him back, Theo. I promise." Magic snapped into place around the two of us, forging his words into something unbreakable.

My heart stuttered until the sudden jolt softened, soaking into my own magic, becoming a part of it.

"Thank you," I whispered. With one last sniffle, I looked up and realized someone was standing next to the door of the tent.

"Is this a bad time?" Harvey asked nervously.

"Now's good," I told him while subtly trying to wipe my nose.

Lief stiffened at my words and turned to the door. I pushed at his shoulder, trying to see around his massive width.

"Is it true the guardian is being tortured?" Harvey's throat bobbed with his words, but his voice was steady.

"Yes." I could have told him that I'd seen the damage in person, but why bother? Nobody needed the horrid details of what had been done to Farranen.

"And you're planning to rescue him?"

"Him and Mary and the other guardian. And anyone else being held prisoner." Even if they weren't part of the whole uprising situation, I wasn't going to leave anyone in the queen's abusive clutches.

"Theo?" Lief asked, sounding so carefully neutral that I knew something was wrong.

"Yeah?" I looked back to him.

"Did you bring over another ghost?" His eyebrows rose in a way that made him look like an astonished little boy.

"No, it's just Harvey again." I smiled at the ghost in question, hoping to put him at ease.

"Harvey?" Lief asked in confusion.

"Harvalin of the Light Court. He says he's a merdain."

Lief started, like I'd somehow shocked him. "Harvalin is dead?"

I nodded, surprised that Lief must have known

him. "Sorry."

"Did he say how he died?"

"He couldn't remember." Personally, I thought it was a kindness not having to remember your own death.

"And he's the ghost you raised yesterday at the gate?" His dark eyebrows slanted down like he was lost in thought.

"Yeah, he followed us most of the way here. He's not a real chatty guy." Why couldn't my magic have picked a stand-up comedian? That would have made our wilderness adventure a little more bearable.

"Theo, most ghosts only last for a few hours at most. This one is over a day old."

The intense way he was looking at me made me think he was hinting at something. I wished he'd just get to the point; reading between the lines was never my forte. "So, he's decrepit as far as ghosts go. What's the big deal?" Harvey didn't look any different than when I'd seen him yesterday.

Lief's eyebrows furrowed in contemplation. "We should consult with one of the ankou while you're here."

"Fine by me." If I had a paper and pen, I would have made a list of all the questions I had about making ghosts. Most importantly, how not to make them.

"Theo?" Harvey asked, clearly hesitant to interrupt the dark prince and me.

"Hmm?" I looked back at him, mostly so Lief would know who I was talking to.

"I think I know where Farranen and the others are."

****

It turned out that my newest ghostly companion

had been acting like a cryptic weenie because he'd been batting for the wrong team. That's to say, he'd been working for the queen. I was interrupted from telling him all the different ways I was going to kick his ass by Lief's steady arm restraining me.

"Perhaps Harvalin can redeem himself," the dark prince suggested.

Across the room, Harvey was looking more of a mottled gray than his usual pale blue, and he nodded enthusiastically.

"How?" I asked suspiciously.

"He could start by telling us where they're holding the prisoners, as well as information about how many guards we should expect to encounter."

I turned to Harvey expectantly, and he predictably spilled his guts. "There's been talk among the guards; some of us were assigned to the Fallow Woods, but nobody knows why. That was weeks ago. We still haven't heard from those who left. The Gray Knight is in charge of who's chosen."

I repeated the information to Lief who nodded thoughtfully. "The Fallow Woods would be an ideal location if the queen needed the space and privacy to hold a number of fae."

"Will you tell the dark prince that I had no idea the guardian had been imprisoned? Or about the females…" He looked down at his feet, then back to me. "I heard the males outside talking while you were sleeping. I never would have willingly served someone who would do something so heinous."

My ire for the male dimmed a little. It couldn't have been easy to find out he'd unknowingly dedicated himself to someone who turned out to be a selfish bitch.

"I'll tell him," I assured the apprehensive ghost. I admired the way he always maintained eye contact, even when I was giving him shit.

"Thank you," he said, and I could tell he meant it. "Is there anything else I can do to serve you or the dark prince?"

I thought about it for a second before telling him, "If you do any more eavesdropping and think you have information that might help them, come tell me?"

He nodded briskly before disappearing through the tent wall.

"He's gone," I told Lief, who'd been listening to my side of the conversation. "He says he had no idea about the queen's shenanigans."

"I remember him—a good soldier, dependable and eager to rise in the ranks." Lief looked down at me approvingly. "You handled that well, using him to our advantage."

"I didn't really use him," I protested. "He felt bad and wanted some redemption."

Lief stood and headed for the door. "I need to relay this new intel to everyone."

I jumped up to grab my cloak, but he moved to block me. "Sorry, Theo. It's safer if you stay here."

"No way—" I started to tell him exactly what I thought of sitting on my keister while he went off to plan Farranen's rescue, but he cut me off.

"If I take you with me, you'll have to wear the sexy lingerie again."

I sputtered something obscene before parking my butt back on the bed.

****

By the time Lief returned, I'd investigated every

item of clothing in the dresser drawers, as well as every weapon in the wooden chest. Seriously, who needed twenty-two knives? Some looked like they were made for throwing, while some looked like they were made for stabbing. Either way, they were all meticulously clean and wickedly sharp.

Harvey had stopped by twice to check in. When he informed me that three females had been rescued and were being kept in one of the larger tents, I'd sent him back to see if any of them matched Marissa's description. While I had no love for the vampire who had sired my ex-husband and then sentenced him to his final death, I was still curious to see if she'd survived.

The dark prince crossed the room and gathered me into his arms in silence. His haunted expression told me everything I needed to know. Lief needed comfort, and I was content to provide it. I let him hold on as long as he wanted, even after my ribs felt like they were about to crack.

With a sigh, he let go and took a step back. "They brought back three females...I don't know how they're still alive. What was done to them..." I'd never seen Lief like this; I wondered if he was in shock. He didn't resist when I took him by the hand and led him to the bed. It was a testament to his frame of mind that he didn't have any suggestive comments when I crawled under the covers and pulled him with me.

"This is bigger than just one person; there's no way that Safeena orchestrated this on her own. She may have given the orders, but there had to be others to constitute so much...damage."

"Who's Safeena?" I asked.

"The queen."

Huh. I hadn't known the queen had a name, even though I probably should have.

"Their magic, its been *perverted.*" The horror in his voice made me shiver.

"Perverted how?"

He looked at me, almost like he hadn't grasped I was there until that very moment. He raised a hand to my face and cupped my cheek in his hand. Little tendrils of magic slid from his palm, tingling as they spread through me. "Do you feel the fae magic in me, Theo?"

I nodded, unable to break his gaze.

"All supernaturals have their own flavor of magic; vampires, shifters, nymphs, they're all different from each other, but each race is the same."

I understood what he was trying to say; I could already recognize the fae by their magical signature, and Dog and Ozzy had a different feel to them. I could even tell the difference between individual fae just by the way their magic felt.

"Until now, the only exception I've ever come across is you." He softened his words with a slight smile. "Your magic is this beautiful mix of fae and vampire and something I don't even have a name for. It's like sunshine and seduction and sass, all tangled together. And the way you just throw it around, like it's nothing…Just feeling your magic next to mine, Theo, it literally makes it hard to breathe." He let out a self-deprecating laugh that made my heart clench. He couldn't be serious—my pain-in-the-butt magic wasn't beautiful; it was a messed-up train wreck of uncertainty with a mind of its own.

"Those females…Their magic was so tainted, so

wrong." His hand fell away from my face. "What they're doing is an abomination. It has to be stopped." Some of the familiar resolve was back in his voice. "There's been speculation, but nobody's been able to definitively find out why Fairie is dying until now. But *this* is why. This sickness of the mind that the queen is suffering from, this is why the dead lands are growing, why our magic fades. The land is only as strong as its leaders." His hands tightened into fists. "How could I not see this sooner?"

I covered his hands with mine. "Nobody saw it until now."

He studied my face, as if judging my sincerity. "I've given the orders to break camp and head for the Fallow Woods. I'll have a few of my men escort Oscar and the females back through the gate."

"Does that mean I'm done hiding in here?" I asked hopefully. I was getting a little cabin-feverish being stuck in such a small boring space.

"Yes, but everyone will be expecting to see a consort on my arm…" He glanced meaningfully at my yellow pjs.

I sighed in resignation. Damn it, I was going to miss them.

Giving his shoulder a nudge, I followed as he scooted across the mattress and stood. I held out my hand, knowing what would come next.

Lief's familiar magic flowed like a living thing around me, and when I opened my eyes, the flannel was gone. In its place was a pair of stretchy black leather pants that were so comfortable, I had a brief moment of panic when I thought I wasn't wearing anything at all. A soft red sweater covered my top half, and a quick peek beneath confirmed my bra was the same color. Apparently, the dark prince had a thing for the bold color.

"Is there a red thong somewhere under here?" I asked suspiciously.

He shrugged innocently. "I'd be happy to check for you."

"Don't even think about it," I growled.

Lief laughed and donned his cloak in one swift movement. When he held out mine, I accepted it and slung it over my arm.

"You should wear it," he said with a frown.

"It's too hot out." It was probably close to fifteen degrees outside the tent, and I already had a sweater on.

"Yes, but it's mine and anyone who sees you wearing it will know you're spoken for."

I looked down at the black fabric draped across my arm. I wasn't too worried about unwanted advances by any of the males; I wasn't considered desirable on Earth and probably even less so in Fairie unless they found out about my unusual pedigree. Yeah, it would be hot, but it would also help me to blend into the background.

I slid into the fabric that still smelled like fresh snow and looked at Lief expectantly. "Ready?"

"One last thing." He took a step closer, forcing me to tilt my head back in order to see his face.

"What?" I asked, trying (and failing) not to sound suspicious.

He slowly slid one of his hands into my hair, and when he lowered his face to mine, I froze. His lips, which were ridiculously soft, brushed against mine once. Twice. I could see the unspoken question swirling in his eyes, and he must have seen an answer in mine, because he slowly closed the distance again. Using the slightest pressure, he placed a chaste kiss on the corner of my mouth. Then the opposite corner. I held my breath, waiting to see where he'd go next—his lips feathered over the sensitive spot right below my ear, and my toes curled at the exquisite sensations he could coax out of me with barely a touch.

My hands found his chest, and the hard planes beneath my palms left me light-headed. A sigh escaped my lips, and he quickly moved in to steal it.

His tongue slid slowly across mine, demanding and giving at the same time. Something that sounded suspiciously like a plea bubbled out of my chest as I struggled to match his leisurely pace.

Far too soon, he pulled away from me with a groan, and I was glad to see I wasn't the only one having trouble breathing. "There," he panted. "When people see those bedroom eyes and swollen lips, there won't be any question about what we were doing in here."

Before I could even think about composing myself to face an entire camp of soldiers, Lief took my hand and pulled me out of the tent.

Chapter Twelve

The only tent left standing was the one I'd just come out of.

The tiny valley was vacant, with the exception of four fae males and myself.

"Where did everybody go?" I asked in surprise. "And where's Dog?" Something close to panic tightened my chest until it felt like my lungs were being hugged by a body builder. The shadows next to the tent solidified into my missing friend, and I let out an exclamation of happiness as he trotted over to me. He didn't do it often, but when he was feeling threatened, Dog could turn into a seething mass of shadows. It was pretty cool. I could totally picture him as a stealthy ninja wolf that burgled fancy art from stupidly rich people.

I squatted down to wrap my arms around his furry neck. His yellow eyes were anxious as he shoved his wet nose behind both my ears and over any exposed skin he could find. He was such a worrywart. I attempted to sooth his fears by telling him, "See, I'm fine," while scratching behind his ears. When he finally backed off long enough to give me a disgruntled look for making him worry, it hit me that I'd stepped out of character as Lief's consort. *Oh, shit.*

My hood slid off as I tried to sneak a quick peek— yep, the three fae soldiers were staring at me with looks ranging from shock to bewilderment. Lief was merely smiling in amusement.

"Oops." Even to my ears it sounded inadequate. "Sorry."

"Gentlemen, allow me to introduce Theodora Edwards of the Earth realm." With a hand at the small of my back, Lief gestured to the three males that had all schooled their faces into matching neutral expressions. "Theo, these are some of my most trusted allies; Barthus, Colemeelius, and Gavriel."

All three of the males looked like they'd stepped off the covers of cheap paperback romance novels. Two brunettes and one blond, all with well-muscled shoulders and faces that looked to be chiseled from granite. They were every bit as intimidating as the numerous weapons they had strapped to their bodies.

"Hi." I offered an unimpressive little wave to the males.

Two of them exchanged looks and one of them asked, "Is she—"

"Human," Lief answered with a finality that left no room for more questions. Dog bristled and stepped between me and the three fae. Lord save me from overprotective shifters.

Thankfully, the males caught on that my heritage was not up for discussion and moved on to another subject. "My Lord, we sent the others ahead as you requested while you were—"

"Thank you." Lief cut Gavriel off before he could speculate on what we'd been doing. "We should go."

The men stepped forward across the grassy valley, and I made to follow until I remembered my backpack was still in the tent. "I forgot my bag," I told Dog and turned back—but the tent wasn't behind us anymore. "Hey! What happened to our stuff?" I spun in a circle, thinking that maybe I'd misjudged the direction we'd come from, but, nope, there was no sign of the tent. Actually, there was no sign that there had been any tents here recently. The small groupings of skinny trees dotting the hill weren't thick enough to hide a single fae soldier, let alone the canvas shelter that I'd been cooling my heels in all day. There weren't even footprints or scuffs in the dirt to prove an army of dozens of fae had been camped here.

I looked over to where Lief was waiting and raised my eyebrows in a universal gesture of what-the-hell-is-going-on? before slanting my eyes to say and-don't-you-dare-try-to-tell-me-I'm-crazy-and-imagining-things.

"Remival fae can glamour the shape and density of objects so they can be easily transported." Lief's humorless leader mask was firmly back in place, but I caught the twinkle in his eye that said he enjoyed flabbergasting me. "Barthus, would you please retrieve the lady's bag?"

The fae standing closest to me reached into a large pouch hanging from his belt and pulled out a small wooden cube that was no wider than a quarter. He tossed it on the ground before taking a step back, and I quickly followed his example. The small object shimmered, and a heartbeat later, Lief's tent stood between us.

"Whoa. That's pretty handy," I murmured to myself as Bart retrieved my backpack from the tent. How much magic did it take for him to shrink something so big into a tiny parcel that could fit in his pocket? Having such a cool skill would be convenient. Collecting enough firewood last fall to get through the winter wouldn't have taken nearly as long as it had if I could have inherited remival magic instead of the useless ankou magic I had. As far as superpowers went, raising the dead was pretty lame.

I thanked Bart when he handed over my bag, then watched wide-eyed as the tent shrank down to the wooden cube once again. When he picked it up and tossed it in the pouch, the *clink* of it hitting other small wooden objects reached my ears. For all I knew, he could have the whole damn camp stuffed in his fae fanny pack.

"Can you shrink people or animals?" I asked. I know, consorts were supposed to keep their mouths shut—but come on! The possibilities of what he was carrying around were endless, and I wondered what else he had in his little pouch.

"Nothing living." He gave me a tentative smile before joining the waiting males.

"What other crazy things can the fae do with their magic?" I whispered to Dog. He gave me an unimpressed doggy eye roll. "I mean, Lief can see the future, Farranen has super-healing and can control the doorway between realms, so don't tell me you haven't wondered what else is possible." How had I ended up with the least imaginative shifter in the history of the world? It was a good thing I was creative enough for the both of us.

"I can breathe underwater."

Harvey's sudden appearance tore a scream from me. Ahead of us, Lief turned and reached for his sword as I schooled my face into looking like I hadn't just nearly had a heart attack.

"Sorry! I just saw…" I quickly realized I couldn't lie and lamely finished with "…something that surprised me." Nothing about the picturesque landscape was startling enough to have me jumping at shadows. The handful of late-summer blooms that randomly dotted the landscape were actually quite pretty—which was high praise coming from someone who didn't care for flowers.

Lief gave me a look that I couldn't decipher before continuing on. If the other fae thought my sudden outburst was strange, they didn't say anything about it.

"Sorry, I didn't mean to scare you. I just thought you might want to know where my gifts lie." Harvey kept pace beside me, occasionally walking through the odd tree instead of around it.

I faced forward, but it was hard to talk to someone without looking at them. I figured, *screw it*, if everyone thought Lief's consort talked to herself, then so be it. He'd forced me into this charade, so it would serve him right if word got around that he had a thing for crazy women.

"It's fine," I told him. "So, you breathe underwater? That's a nifty trick."

"All merdain can." He unbuttoned his shirt and revealed four long slits that ran diagonally across each of his pecks.

"Are those gills?" I asked in surprise.

"Yes, we're the only fae who can breathe both air and water."

"Cool. Oh—that's where the name comes from, right? You're mermaids!" I didn't know why I hadn't seen it sooner; the blue skin should have clued me in.

"Not mer*maid*, mer*dain*," he corrected me.

"Mermaid, merdain; tomayto, tomahto." I shrugged and then realized Harvey was looking at me like I'd grown a second head. He must not be familiar with the catchphrase. Great, even the ghost thought I was crazy. I really should learn to keep my mouth shut.

****

I kept my mouth shut for all of two minutes.

As we left the grassy rolling land behind and started to climb the rocky hills that should have been called mountains, spruce trees cropped up. Scraggly and twisted, they were probably the only thing strong enough to survive in the rocky soil. Their fresh crisp scent went straight to my heart, squeezing at the useless organ in my chest as it reminded me of my guardian.

Dog and I lagged farther and farther behind the four fae, who were too lost in talk of battle strategies to even notice we'd fallen behind. And since Dog refused to shift, our conversation had become very one-sided. Not that he was ever very chatty in his other form. Thankfully, Harvey was happy to answer my barrage of questions about pretty much anything; I think he still felt guilty about serving the queen.

He'd enthusiastically shared details of which fae had certain superpowers. And apparently, they were called gifts, not superpowers.

He also gave me a broad overview of the courts in Fairie. I already knew that fae either belonged to the Dark Court or the Light Court. Changelings belonged to whichever court their magic originated from. So, technically, I would have been a member of the Dark Court if my transition hadn't failed. I'm not sure I liked the idea of Lief being my boss. Actually, I didn't like the idea of anyone being my boss—that's probably why I worked as a romance writer.

Anyway, the Light Court was ruled by Safeena, while Lief was in charge of the Dark Court. There were no territories or property lines; the fae were free to live wherever they chose, with the less civilized fae residing in the wild lands, and the rest living in large communities spread across the realm. Hundreds of years ago, their world had extended past this continent, but as the fae magic started to fade, South America had slowly turned into dead land. When I asked about the lands overseas, Harvey said there were stories about fae inhabiting the European continent, but they had died out millennia ago. He wasn't even sure if there was any truth to it, or if they'd just been whimsical tales told to small fae children.

I stumbled over another sharp stone hidden by a clump of long grass, and Harvey offered me his hand but I waved him off. If we'd been alone, I might have considered taking it, but I didn't want Lief and the other manly men to think I was weak.

I turned the conversation back to court politics, still confused about why the queen had an entire army of well-dressed soldiers, called the Army of Light, while Lief's seemed to be a mishmash that came from both courts. It was odd that some of his followers, like Celesta, were members of the queen's army. Although, the fae were a crafty bunch, and every war needed secret undercover agents.

"The dark prince gained the throne seven hundred years ago"—Harvey raised his voice to be heard over the rumble of the river below, sounding like a high-school history teacher addressing a large auditorium—

"after overthrowing Sepian, the dark king." I'm pretty sure Lief had to kill his predecessor in order to gain the title of dark prince, but it was sweet of Harvey to coast over that part for my fluffy human emotions.

"He disbanded the previous king's soldiers and set them to work in other ways. He encouraged them to hone their magic in ways that would rebuild the realm rather than tearing it apart again." My respect for Lief grew as Harvey continued. "War is very much a human concept. Queen Safeena was the first to train members of her court for combat, followed by King Sepian. They both feared dethronement by the strongest members of their courts and thought to surround themselves with soldiers."

"That doesn't explain why some of the light fae are helping Lief," I pointed out.

"I can't speak for them personally, but I suspect they wish to follow a leader who puts his people first. Immortality has it challenges, and the dark prince is a visionary in knowing what will benefit the fae long-term."

He paused when I lagged behind. Even Dog had gotten about twenty feet ahead of me. I really needed to work on my endurance once I was back home; getting left in everyone's dust was flat out embarrassing.

"Do you need to rest?" Harvey asked, sounding like he was genuinely concerned.

I met his vivid gaze and smiled. "I'm good—" My words ended on a shriek as the ground beneath me disappeared. Grass and dirt cartwheeled across my vision as I somersaulted down the steep incline we'd been working our way over.

My limbs and back continued to take a beating as I

bounced off rocks and other hard things that I was going too fast to identify. I bit my tongue hard enough to taste blood, and all the spinning was making me dizzy. The terrifying sound of rushing water was close enough that I could hear it past the screaming in my head. I needed to slow my descent before I went over the edge of the cliff, or I was going to end up dying right then—and then I'd be forced to find the nearest ankou fae so they could bring back my ghost. Then I was going to haunt Lief until he did something about this stupidly dangerous hill. I mean, really? Didn't Fairie have some sort of safety board to ensure death traps like this weren't just lying around for dummies like me to fall into?

"*Ooof!*" The air exploded out of my lungs as I crashed into what felt like a brick wall. Maybe I'd been wrong about the cliff of death and there was a guardrail I hadn't noticed until I smashed into it.

Dog's hysterical barking cut through my inner musings about the need to idiot-proof nature. I went to lift my head, but the simple movement sent sharp knives of pain through my neck. And my back. And pretty much everywhere else. Actually, there wasn't a part of me that didn't hurt.

"Don't move, Theo. Help's coming." Harvey spoke slowly and deliberately, the way you would talk to someone in the middle of a traumatic situation. It was surprising I didn't hear that tone more often, because lately my life seemed to be one big series of traumatic situations.

The hard wall behind me was actually Harvey. The rise and fall of his chest from his breathing was noticeably smoother than mine. I must be crushing the poor guy, and I tried to sit up.

"*Don't move!*" he lamented from behind me.

And since I was doubting my ability to move on my own anyway, I resigned myself to treating Harvey as my own personal recliner.

"Theo!" Lief's voice reached me, along with Dog's excited yelps that couldn't have been more than a few feet away. I opened my eyes and discovered Dog anxiously dancing in a circle around me. Lief reached us a few seconds later and fell to his knees in the dirt inches from where I sat.

"I'm okay," I said with a wince. Bruised and embarrassed, but okay.

"How are you...?" Lief tilted his head to the side and gave Harvey a mystified look. "Theo?"

The three other males reached us, and they looked just as worried as Lief. The blond one, Gavriel, addressed Lief uncertainly. "My lord? What should we do?"

The dark prince ignored him, instead staring at me with an intensity that was alarming.

"They can't see me," Harvey told me. "It probably looks like you're floating a few inches off the ground."

"Oh." I smiled. No wonder the men looked so freaked out. "It's just Harvey," I told the agitated fae.

Lief glowered at me. "Explain."

"I tripped and fell. Harvey must have caught me before I could go over the cliff." It made sense to me. "Thanks, Harvey," I added.

"You're very welcome, Theo." There was a weary note in his voice, and I remembered that he'd been holding my heavy butt for a while.

"You can put me down now," I told him, bracing

for the movement.

"Wait," Lief cautioned. "You're injured. Can I...?"

I'd never seen Lief so uncertain before. It was kind of charming. If only I had something witty and teasing to say to commemorate the occasion.

"Tell him he should be able to pick you up," Harvey coached from behind me.

"You can pick me up," I told Lief.

In a move that completely defied the laws of physics, Lief slid his arms around me, and Harvey just sort of dissolved. I'm not going to lie; it was weird. I looked down at the ground where I'd been sitting, but Harvey was gone.

The edge of the cliff was about six feet from where I'd been lying. Thirty feet below, the river rushed past, unaware that I'd come so close to joining it permanently. A tiny shudder racked my body, and Lief's arms tightened around me as his confident stride carried us up the hill.

"Sorry," I told Lief quietly. "Harvey was spilling some juicy gossip, and I forgot to watch where I was going."

"And he caught you."

It wasn't a question, but I nodded at Lief anyway.

"How," he bit out, "*how* was he able to...do what he did?" He exhaled, like he was frustrated or angry, but I wasn't sure if it was directed at me or Harvey. In all likeliness it was at me, since my clumsiness was to blame.

"I don't know. I think he can materialize in and out of existence. I haven't asked where he goes when he's not here; maybe another realm that's completely different from Earth or Fairie?" That would explain a lot. Then again, I was no expert on the subject, so it would be interesting to hear what the ankou thought. Hopefully, I'd get a chance to ask one of them soon. If I didn't accidentally kill myself first.

"My men will assume you have the gift of levitation, and that's what stopped your descent."

I didn't like the idea of lying to anyone, but as far as deceptions went, faking a superpower didn't sound too hard.

"…Even the shifter wasn't able to catch up to her," Bart was saying to the other males behind us. The awe in his voice only served to increase my guilt.

"I can walk," I suggested softly. We'd make better time if I didn't, since Lief was zipping up the hill like he was standing on an escalator I'd overlooked. Larger rocks and spruce trees whipped across my vision, but Lief didn't stumble on the uneven ground.

He didn't acknowledge me other than a slight clenching of his jaw.

"I'm fine, just a little banged up."

"You're not fine. Not even *close* to *fine*." His harsh words were laced with frustration, and his arms tightened to the point of crushing.

I let out a little involuntary whimper, and he immediately stopped walking.

"Fuck—I'm sorry, Theo."

"It's fine," I wheezed. Geez Louise, the man had arms like a bear trap.

"We'll stop here for the night," Lief announced.

I looked up, and sure enough, the sky was beginning to darken. I could even make out the twinkle of a few stars.

"The others are expecting us tonight," Gavriel

noted.

"Theo's injured; we'll continue on in the morning." The other fae must have picked up on the fact that Lief was using his I'm-the-bossy-jerk-in-charge voice, because they wisely didn't push for us to keep going. "Barthus, leave my personal tent as well as some provisions. You three can meet up with the others and tell them we were delayed. Theo and I will be there tomorrow by midmorning."

The males exchanged glances that said they were hesitant to leave their leader alone.

"Don't worry, I'll take care of him." As soon as the words left my mouth, I regretted them. Coming from a friend, it would have been fine, but coming from the lips of a consort—well, it just sounded slutty.

Lief smirked.

It took every single ounce of self-control I had to not smack him. *Consorts don't smack the high and mighty dark lord*, I reminded myself.

"You heard the lady. I'd like to take her up on her offer, so if you wouldn't mind…" Lief gave them a look that said he didn't care whether they minded or not and it was time to get their asses out of there.

Predictably, they didn't waste time with goodbyes. Bert tossed a wooden cube next to an outcrop of rocks, and it quickly poofed into a black tent that was twice as big as the one Lief and I had shared earlier. The wall of rock that jutted behind and above would protect us from the wind and the dark fabric would blend in with the growing shadows.

A second cube landed in the grass, quickly becoming a backpack. By the way Dog's ears perked up, I assumed it was the requested provisions.

I looked over Lief's shoulder and called to my nosy shifter, "Don't eat anything that lives here!" just before Lief ducked through the tent flaps and into the tent.

Chapter Thirteen

The door fell shut behind us, dimming the roar of the river down to a low murmur. The interior of the tent was darker than the inside of a goat. After a few heartbeats, floating lights flared to life above us, and I blinked at the sudden brightness.

The bed sitting against the center of the back wall immediately caught my attention. It was huge, with four thick posts made of dark stained wood, carved to look like twined branches. Mounds of black and red bedding were piled on a mattress that was ridiculously thick. To the right of it was a matching dresser with an oval mirror, and to the left a privacy screen was folded back to reveal a large metal tub and a rack full of fluffy towels. Everything sat on a plush rug the color of blood. I needed one just like it for my cabin; I'd lost count of how many times I've had to clean blood off my hardwood floors.

Lief slowly lowered me to my feet and backed away.

"What's wrong?" I didn't like the look on his face. He wouldn't meet my eyes as he removed his cloak and sword. "Lief?"

After hanging his things by the door, he stalked back to me and carefully unclasped my cloak. I caught his hands with mine, refusing to let go until he looked at me. When he finally looked up, his eyes were like hard chips of broken diamonds. "You shouldn't be here," he told me stiffly. I let go of him in surprise, and he stepped away with my cloak.

"What do you mean, I shouldn't be here?" I didn't like the skepticism in my voice, but there was nothing to be done about it. I was a crappy liar, so there was no point in pretending I wasn't leery of where this conversation was going.

"You shouldn't be in Fairie. This isn't your fight." He spoke with absolute conviction. "You could have died today. I thought that I could protect you, keep you tucked away in my tent and out of harm's way—but then you fell and I couldn't get to you fast enough—" He stopped with his lips pressed into a tight harsh line.

"I'm fine. Harvey was there—"

"Theo! That shouldn't have been possible!" Lief's words exploded around me. "Ghosts aren't corporeal! You can't touch them! They don't poof in and out of existence! They can't hang around for days! And they certainly can't catch you when you're about to go off a fucking cliff!" He clenched his fists like he was fighting the urge to shake me.

"What are you talking about?" A bitchy tone crept into my voice. I welcomed it, embraced it. I loved the way it chased away the ache in my head and ankle from the fall, loved the way I was suddenly bold enough to go toe to toe with the dark prince.

"Ghosts don't do any of those things."

"My ghosts do." For a second, I didn't recognize the pride in my voice for what it was. But I was proud. "Harvey, can you come here please?"

The ghost in question appeared a second later, looking like he'd rather be anywhere else than in the middle of an argument between me and the dark prince. "Harvey, would you please help me settle an argument with this royal pain in the butt?"

Harvey's eyes widened in shock, but he nodded.

I turned around so I was facing the bed. "Lief, do something and Harvey will tell me what it is so I can prove he's real."

"I never implied he wasn't real." Some of his anger had turned to annoyance. I'd say that was a step in the right direction.

"He rolled his eyes," Harvey reported helpfully.

"Stop rolling your eyes and *do* something," I told him.

"He looks angry again," Harvey announced.

"That's not helping—and I don't need Harvey to tell me that you look pissed off," I told Lief.

"Theo! This is ridiculous."

I turned around when it became apparent that the dark prince didn't like my game and wasn't going to play along. Party pooper.

"Fine. Harvey, do you know what a trust exercise is?"

"No." He gulped, like he was afraid of where this was going. Yeah, knowing me, his fear was justified.

"Lief here thinks I can't touch you, so I'm going to fall backward and trust that you'll catch me." I spun so my back was to Harvey, and I crossed my arms across my chest. This was either really brilliant, or really stupid. Considering how sore my body was, I was thinking it was probably really stupid—but only if I turned out to be wrong.

I didn't give Harvey any time to protest. I just tipped backward and let gravity take me. Right as I reached the point of no return, Harvey's strong arms caught me under my arms. I grinned up at him. "See! I knew you'd catch me."

The smile he sent me was a little wobbly but genuine as he set me back on my feet.

"Theo, I never said I didn't believe you—I just said it's not done. Yet here you are, making the impossible possible." A wave of thick black hair covered half of Lief's face as he shook his head in exasperation. "I should know by now to expect the unexpected from you."

I looked back to thank Harvey for his help with the ghostly demonstration, but he was already gone.

"Is this because my magic freaks you out?" If so, he could join the club.

"No! Theo, your magic is an incredible, precious gift. I'm just...frustrated. I'm frustrated with my inability to keep you safe." He stepped closer and held out his hand. My magic leapt in response when my palm slid into his. "Being around you brings out something dark in me; darker than anything I've ever felt before. It's primal and possessive, and sometimes I don't even recognize myself when I'm around you." He let out a humorless laugh that did nothing to dispel the tension that I could feel building between us. "God, Theo...whatever this is, it's killing me, but at the same time, I feel like I'm finally living." He stared down at me, like he was willing me to understand something that I wasn't grasping.

I didn't know what to say. Honestly, as a writer I should have been able to string at least a few coherent words together, but—nope. I had nothing.

He must have sensed the turmoil building in my

aching head, because he pulled me toward the big metal tub. "How about a hot bath? Once you're clean, we can take care of your injuries."

I was profoundly grateful for the change in subject. A hot bath sounded heavenly, but I felt the need to clarify. "Alone?"

"If that's what you'd prefer," he smirked, letting me know he'd be fine with joining me.

A small laugh bubbled out of my throat, mostly because I was relieved Lief was back to his old cocky self-assured ways. Seeing him suddenly so serious and afraid had tilted my world on its axis. I still felt off kilter, like my feet weren't on completely solid ground anymore.

He knelt next to the tub and swirled his fingers through the water.

When steam rose to fill the air, I knelt next to him and stuck my hand in. "It's hot!" I exclaimed gleefully. It was delightfully hot, almost bordering on scalding. Far warmer than anything my crappy hot water heater could have produced.

"It's glamour," Lief explained. Taking a small glass bottle from a side table, he added a few drops to the tub. "Lavender to help you sleep tonight." He added a few more drops from a second bottle. "And peppermint to help with the bruising and swelling." The combination of oils smelled like heaven.

"Thank you," I said softly, surprised how much his thoughtfulness was affecting me. Nobody had ever drawn a bath for me or considered what oils I might benefit from. I studied the hard lines of his back as he returned the tiny bottles to their shelf; I still wasn't sure what to make out of his earlier speech. Had he been joking? Was this part of some elaborate scheme that I hadn't caught on to yet? And what would be the point in making me think he was attracted to me? Sure, Lief like to flirt, but it was just harmless banter; I was pretty sure he did it with everyone. Right?

When was the last time I'd seen him around a female other than myself…Had he made any suggestive comments when he'd been in my cabin with Celesta? I didn't remember anything that was seductive in nature. The healer in Fairie who had patched me up after I was stabbed had been a female, but he'd barely acknowledged her. Actually, I couldn't recall him ever flirting with anyone beside me.

Which didn't make a lot of sense, because let's face it, Lief was the walking definition of a playboy with his incredible body, chiseled jaw, and confident smile. If the advertising agencies on Earth ever got a hold of him, they'd beg him to star in every one of their shampoo, sports car, and underwear ads. I doubted he ever spent a night longing for female companionship. Most nights he probably had to beat the ladies off with a stick.

I smiled sweetly at him. "Out."

He swaggered to the door before pausing to throw me one last hopeful glance over his shoulder. "If you change your mind…"

"I won't."

****

He kept his word and didn't return uninvited.

I soaked until I was squeaky clean, prunier than a raisin, and the water was tepid. Which was kind of confusing, because if it was cold water glamoured to feel like hot water, shouldn't it stay hot until the glamour was removed?

My backpack and Farranen's sword had been lost in my tumble down the hill, so I rummaged through Lief's dresser and borrowed one of his shirts. Like everything else he owned, it was—shock!—black. I had to roll the sleeves up, but it was long enough to cover my generous backside. It was no different from sleeping in a silk nightie.

I didn't bother with boots when I stepped outside; my ankle throbbed like it had its own heartbeat, and I limped across the grass like I was a pirate with a peg-leg. It was thick and tickly between my bare toes, and I sighed in pleasure at the simple luxury.

Lief sat with his back to the wall of rock with Dog near his feet. They both had their faces tilted toward the ocean of stars that blazed overhead. Dog was the first to notice me, and his tail started to swish back and forth in the grass as I made my way to where he waited. The backpack from Bart's magical fanny pack of wooden cubes rested next to him, and judging by the way it lay flat on the ground, its contents had been thoroughly enjoyed by my ravenous shifter.

I flopped down as gracefully as I could with only a shirt on and reclined with my head and shoulders on Dog's warm body. It was incredibly peaceful, and I could almost forget this was a hostile realm full of things determined to kill me. We sat in companionable silence, surrounded by the roar of the river and the wind in the grass, until a snore rumbled out of Dog. I was close to following his example when Lief rose to his feet and offered me a hand.

"Thanks," I said as he pulled me to my feet. "It's beautiful here." I wasn't looking forward to when it would be time to head back to the frozen wonderland of Tamarac and all its wintery goodness.

"It is." His body was relaxed as he gazed up at the sky; he truly cared about this magical place and its inhabitants. "I believe these belong to you."

I looked down and found my backpack and Farranen's sword dangling from his outstretched hand.

"Oh!" I thought they'd been lost for good. I shot him a grateful look and took the proffered goodies. The backpack didn't look any worse for wear; it had been pretty beat-up before I'd brought it along on this particular adventure. Unfortunately, the sword hadn't fared as well. The sheath had a couple of deep scratches in it, but I was pretty sure they were just cosmetic and wouldn't affect the actual blade. The handle part that was made to be gripped had floral vines etched into the metal, and it looked like it had smashed into at least one rock during my tumble down the hill, damaging the beautiful design.

"Dang. Will it still work?" I asked, worried that I'd broken something expensive that I'd been trusted to care for.

Lief carefully pulled it from the sheath and gave it a few test swings. "Yes, I think it fared better than you did in the fall."

I self-consciously rubbed at the knot on the back of my head. It hurt like a bugger, but it would heal; I'd survived a lot worse, so I wasn't too worried.

"I'm starving," I announced, hoping to change the subject from my injuries; I didn't want Lief feeling like he needed to play nursemaid. "I've got some snacks, if you want to share?" It was a good thing Lief had retrieved my backpack since all of Bart's provisions had become collateral damage to Dog's appetite.

Lief smiled and extended his arm to escort me back to the tent. "I'd be delighted; but first, let's wrap your foot."

"Sounds good to me."

Once I was settled on the bed with way too many pillows behind me and nearly as many under my injured ankle, I dumped the backpack upside down. Lief stared at the pile of protein bars, applesauce pouches, trail mix, jerky, and bottles of water. "No cake?" he asked with an arched eyebrow. His tone was serious enough to tell me he had the proper amount of respect for the sugary necessity that I loved.

I shook my head. "I didn't have time to make one."

"That's a shame."

I threw a pouch of applesauce at his head. "Don't make fun of cake."

He laughed, and we dug into the buffet of prepackaged cuisine. I was hungry enough that anything would have tasted gourmet, and Lief made no complains about our makeshift meal. We kept our conversation limited to light banter, both content to keep our worries for whatever the next day held unspoken.

Once our bellies were full, Lief dimmed the floating lights overhead and crawled under the covers next to me. When he reached to pull me closer, I tensed. I didn't mean to, but it would hurt if he banged into my ankle, and I had nothing on beneath the long shirt.

It was stupid, but my prudish tendencies trumped my need for physical comfort. Even though I knew without a doubt that Lief would never take advantage of me that way, I was still a woman without much experience in the bedroom and I just wasn't comfortable with my intimate parts so easily accessible. I had an extra set of clothes in my backpack, but the thought of Lief knowing that I was bothered by being pantiless was too embarrassing to deal with. He'd probably slept next to hundreds of women who wouldn't have batted an eye at sleeping in the buff.

He didn't say anything, but I saw the brief flash of hurt in his eyes before he turned on to his back.

I rolled over with a sigh. I hated that I was screwing everything up so badly. I hated that I had no idea how to fix it. I especially hated that I was lying here worrying about trivial things like my modesty when Farranen was literally being tortured.

"Good night, Theo." Lief's soft words held none of the hurt I'd briefly witnessed.

"Nighty-night," I replied with a yawn.

I'd just about drifted off when Lief gently touched my back. His magic slid around me in a flash before withdrawing. It took me a few seconds to figure out he'd glamoured my shirt into a pair of pajamas. They were warm and cozy and made me smile.

"I thought you might get cold," he whispered.

I ran my fingers over the supple fabric, shocked by the small kindness. Something equally soft cupped my bottom, and I almost snorted out loud at Lief's attention to detail. The man sure knew enough about women to dress them with confidence.

With a sigh, I snuggled up to his side.

Chapter Fourteen

I woke to Dog's yellow eyes staring at me in the dim glow from the floating orbs.

That alone wouldn't have worried me since he spent most nights sleeping across the foot of my bed. But the fact that he was mere inches away from me with his hands gripping my shoulders, that scared me. Hands—not paws. Dog didn't spend much time on two legs, so I immediately knew something must be wrong. He climbed off the bed and dug through my backpack until he pulled out the pair of sweatpants I'd packed for him.

I sat up and shook Lief until he roused. If he was surprised to find Dog and I awake, he didn't let on. "Something's wrong," I whispered.

Dog growled and pointed at the tent doors. Lief nodded before soundlessly pulling on his boots and sliding out of bed. I quickly followed, struggling to get my swollen ankle into my own boots. It took another few precious seconds to get Farranen's sword and my backpack slung across my back.

I could hear something outside the tent; it sounded like stones slowly grinding together and reminded me of arthritic joints. Then came the whisper of metal cutting through air—like someone was warming up their wrists by swinging a blade.

Lief made a series of gestures to Dog that I

interpreted as take-Theo-and-run-like-the-dickens, before drawing his own sword. It was no less deadly than Farranen's, and it moved like an extension of his arm when he lifted it toward the tent door. My stomach tightened painfully as I waited for something to happen. The air around us swirled with pent-up magic, adding to my apprehension. This couldn't be good. Whatever was outside wasn't here to drop off a welcome basket.

The orbs floating above us flickered brighter, bathing us in their soft glow. They would have looked more appropriate if we'd been hosting a fancy dinner party rather than waiting for the impending ambush by whatever was lurking in the darkness outside the tent.

Dog turned toward the side of the tent that held the giant bathtub, his shaggy black hair twisting around his shoulders like it had a life of its own as he moved to put himself in front of me. Immediately, something slashed through the wall of the tent, ripping a hole big enough for someone to walk through. The fae who slid through the gaping hole had an ugly expression on his beautiful face. His long golden-blond hair was pulled back in a tight braid, and he wore the traditional uniform that marked him as belonging to the Army of Light. He dismissed Dog with a flick of his head before setting his gaze on me. His hard brown eyes held the promise of pain to come.

Across the room, the door was blocked by two more guards who were sizing up Lief. His cocky posture and calm demeanor let me know they would be no match for the dark prince.

I slid Farranen's sword free from its sheath. There was a very distinct possibility that I would end up hurting myself with it, but I wasn't going down without a fight. I'd had enough of these pompous assholes trying to hurt the people I cared about.

The blond sidestepped the bathtub and strode toward me with the grace and fluidity of an apex predator. His lips twisted into a cocky sneer; he'd already labeled me as easy prey. Maybe I could use that to my advantage.

The sound of metal on metal rang out from across the room. Lief had his hands full with the two fae currently slashing at him. Dog and I backed farther away from the blond stalking toward us until my back was pressed into the wall of the tent. An angry growl vibrated through Dog's chest, and his tense shoulders seemed to grow even wider until they completely blocked my view of the fae.

"A shifter…" the fae intoned in a low voice. "Let me have the female, and I'll let you leave." He couldn't lie, so the only reason he'd let Dog leave was if someone else was lying in wait outside the tent.

Dog's rumble increased; he must have recognized the fae's words for the trap they were—and he wasn't especially big on sharing. I was glad to see his covetousness had extended beyond pork chops to include me.

It was hard to see past the quivering muscles of Dog's back, and I was just about to sidestep the shifter so I'd have room to maneuver my sword without slicing him in half, when he turned back and shot me a wolfish grin that said, *I'm about to do something really stupid that you won't like, so get ready to run.* I'd only seen that look once before, when Dog had cornered a badger in my woodshed. Needless to say, it hadn't ended well.

"No—"

But my stubborn shifter had already turned back to the smirking fae. The muscles in his back bunched like liquid steel beneath his skin and then, with a snarl that conveyed possessive anger and excitement, he launched himself at the blond bastard.

Knowing I'd only be a liability, I turned and split the tent wall with a swipe of my sword.

****

The air outside the tent was cool against my feverish skin.

I limp-jogged with no thought to the direction I was headed in. I just wanted to give Dog and Lief enough space so that I wouldn't be in the way. And I know what you're thinking, because I was thinking it too.

I shouldn't have left them behind; I should have stayed and done everything in my power to protect them. Running to save my own bacon was cowardly and not something I was particularly proud of. But I wasn't stupid. The best way I could help them was to get out of their way. If I had stayed, I'd only have been a distraction at best, and worst-case scenario, I'd have ended up dead.

There was absolutely no question in my mind that, once Lief and Dog were done with the ass-kicking and name-taking, they'd come find me. So, I just had to keep myself alive until then. Sounded easy, right? Yeah, not exactly. Trouble had a predilection for finding me, even in the most unlikely of places.

The stars overhead were bright enough to see the broad rise of the rocky outcrop to my left and the gentle slope that led to the cliff overlooking the river on my right, but I couldn't make out the individual rocks that littered the ground. My ankle protested venomously as I stumbled on the uneven ground, and I gritted my teeth to keep from swearing out loud. It wouldn't surprise me if more of the queen's soldiers lurked nearby, so I did my best to keep any noise to a minimum. I wasn't sure how good fae hearing was, and even with the roar of the river nearby, I didn't want to risk announcing my location.

Once I'd left the tent, I'd returned the sword to its scabbard on my back, but now I missed the illusion of safety it provided when I held it. The sword had a penchant for glowing in the dark, and I didn't want it acting like a beacon and leading anyone to me.

A cluster of giant boulders appeared on the slope, and I hobbled closer, hoping they might make a good hiding place. Before I could reach them, part of the wall of rock next to me broke away, knocking me over and burying me beneath a crush of stones.

Something in my chest cracked, and I gasped, inhaling dirt and pieces of grass. Before I could claw my way out from under the pile of rocks, they moved, shifting enough that I was no longer smooshed beneath their massive weight. I had just about made it to my hands and knees when the rocks wrapped themselves around my waist and hauled me into the air. I wheezed out my best semblance of a scream as I realized the rocks were alive. Well, they probably weren't even rocks at all. Most likely, I was being held by a fae that looked like he was made of small boulders.

"Let me go!" I shrieked, nearly breaking my toe when it connected with his hard leg.

"You're a feisty one," the rock fae commented in a gravelly voice. Little did he know that my feisty hadn't even gotten warmed up yet. Squealing like a banshee, I flailed my limbs, hoping he'd drop me. After several attempts to break his grip, all I'd succeeded in was bruising myself. My mood soured even further when he let out a huff of laughter that sounded like stones rubbing together.

I reached for the sword on my back, but he squeezed my arms to my sides with a tsk. It was hard to tell since I wasn't fluent in rock fae.

He shuffled across the uneven ground, and I demanded, "Where are you taking me?" I was pretty sure I'd come from the other direction.

"The queen wants this silly uprising to end."

"What does that have to do with me?" I gasped out the last few words; it felt like some of my ribs were broken, and it was harder to breathe with every jarring step we took.

"Kill the rebels, end the rebellion."

He said it so flippantly, that for a second, I thought he was joking. When I finally grasped he was serious, I pounded my fists on his stupidly hard arm. "I'm not a part of that! I'm not even fae!"

He slowed as the ground sloped downward, and his magic rubbed up against mine. It was gritty and dry like sandpaper. Not entirely unpleasant, but definitely not as smooth as some of the fae I'd met. "You're fae..." he told me, but there was no confidence in his words, and I knew he was questioning his own assessment. He was probably confused by the vampire magic that had grown stronger since I'd died.

The rumble from the river below was getting louder, and I could see the edge of the cliff where the ground disappeared. At some point, he was going to have to put me down to kill me—unless he decided to squeeze me to death—so I'd make a run for it. Getting too close to the edge of the cliff was something I'd have to avoid; nearly tumbling into the river once was more than enough. And while I enjoyed a nice leisurely breaststroke in Tamarac Lake now and then, I'd never survive the current of the water down below.

My magic chafed as he continued to probe at it. The overall experience of sharing magic was fairly intimate, and what little of I knew of this asshat wasn't exactly endearing me to him. I tugged at my magic, trying to pull it away from his. It came easily, coiling back into the center of my body like it too was eager to get away from the creepy rock fae. The only problem was, it tugged the rock fae's magic along with it.

He must have felt it, because he stiffened and stopped walking. "What are you—"

What had Lief said when I'd accidentally stolen his magic the night I'd accidentally brought Vanessa's ghost over? It was embarrassing how many accidental things I'd done that night.

It would seem that our dear Theo has inherited another ankou trait: the ability to pull magic from other fae, or something like that.

I gave the magic another experimental tug, and it came eagerly, like a moth to a flame, never suspecting that I was going to burn it to ash. But the rock fae must have known what was coming, because he released his crushing grip, dropping me like a hot potato. My ankle yelped in protest and gave out. I landed on my butt on the hard ground, but I wasn't done with the wanker who wanted to kill me. I scooted closer and latched onto his leg with all four of my limbs, doing my best impression of a barnacle. My magic beckoned, and his answered the call eagerly.

"Stop it! Don't—" He stumbled on the uneven ground and kicked at me with his free leg. His massive foot connected with my thigh, and I screamed but held on. The momentum from the kick tipped him forward, and he fell headfirst down the steep incline.

"Theo! Let go—" Harvey's panicked yell was cut off as the rock fae tumbled over the edge of the cliff with me still clinging to his leg.

****

The shock of free-falling through the air was broken the second we smashed into the raging river.

Every single muscle in my body seized, and I couldn't even gasp because my lungs weren't working. It was cold. And I mean, not just *cold*, but so fucking cold my bones had hypothermia. This was like taking the New Year's Day polar bear plunge sometime during the last ice age.

The rock fae was sinking like—well, like a stone. It took a few seconds for my stiff frozen limbs to cooperate, but they finally let go.

My lungs were burning, and it was only a matter of seconds until I passed out. Something grabbed me by the armpits, and I lashed out with my fists. It took a few swings, but I finally connected with something that was too soft to be the rock fae. Before I could theorize about this new potential threat, my head broke through the water, and I gulped in a delicious lungful of air.

The arms that still hadn't let go now circled around me, and I realized someone had jumped in the river to save me.

"Just breathe, Theo," a calm voice told me. I

twisted around and found Harvey keeping us afloat. God, this was the second time he'd saved me from a certain and painful death. He was easily on his way to being my favorite ghost.

When I'd finally finished hacking up the thirty liters of river water that I'd accidentally swallowed, I gave Harvey a watery smile. "Thanks, Harvey."

"You're very welcome."

There was a bend in the river, and Harvey expertly guided us toward the flat expanse of pebbles on the opposite shore from where I'd fallen in. My mind was a little blown that he could walk through trees but water was tangible enough that he could swim in it. The mysteries of Fairie never ceased to amaze me. Maybe it had something to do with him being merdain and their natural affinity for water.

My arms and legs were shaky as I dragged myself out of the water and crawled as far up the shore as I could before collapsing. Gah, I felt like I'd run a hundred kilometers. I was going to be pissed if I didn't lose at least a pound from all the calories I'd just burnt.

"What happened?" I asked.

Harvey gave me a look that said I'd clearly have to elaborate, since a *lot* of stuff had happened in the last few hours.

I decided to begin with the basics. "How did you know I needed help?"

"I felt your distress; it called to me. If I hadn't been resting, I would have known what was going on sooner."

"Ghosts sleep?" I wondered where he went to take his nap.

"It's not really sleep. It's more like recharging. I

was drained from stopping your earlier fall."

I hadn't known there was a cost for the energy he expended in this realm, but it made sense. "I'm sorry, Harvey." I felt awful that he was tired because he had to keep bailing me out of trouble.

"Don't be; I like helping you, Theo. It's a lot like being in service to the queen, only with a little more excitement." He softened his words with a tired grin. "I have to go soon."

"Okay. Thanks again, Harvey."

He smiled once more and then disappeared.

Like Harvey, I was exhausted and wanted to shut my eyes and sleep. But this was Fairie, so it would be a really, really bad idea to leave myself vulnerable to whatever friendly neighborhood fae were lurking nearby. With a tremendous sigh, I sat up and looked around. The dark sky had faded to a pale navy, and most of the stars had faded out of sight.

A giant stone wall towered above me from across the river, and beyond that rose the gentle slope of a hill. Behind me was a large flat expanse of grass-covered land with small clusters of trees. Since my only choices were braving the river for another swim or chancing whatever might be hiding in the tall grass, I chose the grass.

Dog or Lief would eventually come looking for me, so I followed the curve of the river upstream. I kept my eyes on the top of the cliff across the water; I had no idea how I'd get back over there once we met up, but I'd cross that nonexistent bridge when I got to it.

My ankle was still stiff, but the deep ache from before had vanished, probably from my impromptu dip in the freezing cold water. Or maybe the river had magical healing properties—at this point, I wasn't going to discount any theories. My ribs felt better, and I took an experimental deep breath. There was none of the grinding pain that I expected, so apparently, they were healed too. Maybe the water really was magical—oh, crap. With a little pang of guilt, I figured out why I was feeling so good. It was because of the magic I'd ripped out of the rock fae.

Well...fuck.

I hadn't meant to steal so much from him, but in my defense, he *had* been trying to kill me. I'd just wanted to weaken him so I could get away. The drowning part had been unintentional. Damn it, now I could add "supernatural homicide" to the growing list of things to attribute to my messed-up magic.

A cold breeze swept past me, leaving goose bumps in its wake. I wrapped my arms around myself, but it didn't do much to warm me. I was still wearing the glamoured pjs; this time they were a deep purple with little cartoon ghosts. *Hilarious,* I thought. Lief had a warped sense of humor. And why did I seem to spend all my time running around Fairie in pajamas? At least my backpack and Farranen's sword had survived my involuntary swim.

I trudged on, hoping like hell that I'd see a friendly face soon. How many days had I been in this cursed realm already? Two? Three? And I was still no closer to finding Farranen. God, I was royally fucking up his rescue. Now Lief would have to waste time searching for me when he should be looking for the queen's prisoners. Maybe I should head for home and leave all the heroic extraction efforts to those better suited to the task.

I wiped a tear from my cheek with the wet sleeve of my pjs.

I hated this. Hated that someone I cared about was in trouble, and I couldn't do anything to help him. I hated the horrible overwhelming sense of powerlessness that threatened to crush me. And most of all, I *hated* that I was the one who'd let this happen; that *I* was the one who had allowed another person to get close enough to become emotionally involved with.

I'd already gone done this road once before, when Will had gone missing. Buying my cabin and moving out into the middle of nowhere had been my way of preventing it from ever happening again. Yet, here I was—trapped in a hopeless situation by my own stupid affection for a man who didn't even reciprocate. Gah! If I ever made it out of Fairie alive, Dog and I were moving to Alaska to live off the grid with only the grizzly bears for neighbors.

Something in my chest twanged painfully when I thought of Dog. He was a first-class worrier and must be beside himself not knowing where I was. I picked up my pace a little, to get back to him as soon as possible. How far had the river carried me? The gentle rise and fall of the meadow went on forever. Realistically, I had probably only been in the water for a few minutes, but it was rushing past faster than a rollercoaster fueled by crack.

Something across the field in the gently swaying grass caught the attention of my magic. It shifted excitedly beneath my skin, reminding me of a curious gopher as it sat up and took notice. I stopped walking and scanned the area with trepidation. This was Fairie, so I was fairly certain I hadn't stumbled upon an innocent yard sale. No, with my luck, it would probably be a rabid pack of slaughterous raccoons. Or whatever the fae equivalent of a raccoon was.

My magic had already identified it as fae. Whether it was a friendly fae or a deadly fae remained to be seen.

Chapter Fifteen

I slowly reached over my shoulder and pulled Farranen's sword free. Maybe I could use my disheveled appearance to my advantage; it wouldn't be much of a stretch to pull off my this-crazy-bitch-is-having-a-really-bad-day-and-will-mess-you-up-if-you-get-in-her-way look.

A small pair of pink eyes blinked at me from six feet away. I blinked back, because it was probably just a rabbit. Rabbits had pink eyes, right?

More eyes, this time lavender, appeared next to the first ones. Behind them, another pink set materialized.

The darkness had receded enough to reveal another two dozen tiny eyes. It was super creepy until I was able to make out the small pale faces surrounding them. I'm not sure why, but the idea of disembodied eyes watching me was far scarier than something that had a face.

"Hello?" I ventured.

The first set of pink eyes moved forward, and I was glad to see there was a body attached. The fae was female, only about a foot tall with pale, nearly translucent skin. Her long hair was a few shades darker than her eyes. Full cupid's-bow lips were topped off with a pert nose, and her short dress belonged in a high-class dance club rather than a grassy field.

She tilted her head and studied me like I was a

particularly interesting bug. "You live." Her eyebrows slanted down toward her perfect little nose.

"Uh...yeah."

She must have liked my answer, because her face lost some of its suspicion and she smiled. It was a horrific thing, full of sharp teeth that could probably chew my leg off before I even knew it was happening. Behind her, more of the little fae crept closer.

I had no idea what the proper etiquette was, so I didn't move.

"The dark prince slept next to your dead body," she told me conversationally.

"What?" I asked in confusion.

"In the glade north of the dungeons, with your body wrapped in his cloak, the dark prince slept. We kept watch." Ahh—I understood. She must have seen Lief carrying my dead body to the queen's castle.

"You kept watch over Lief—I mean, the dark prince?"

"Yes," she replied. A few of the curious faces behind her nodded.

"Thank you." I didn't know if she was from the Dark Court or the Light Court, but I appreciated that someone had been watching out for Lief. Actually, one of the strange blurred images I could remember from before I woke up in the closet was of small eyes watching me in the dark. "Who are you?" I asked softly.

"Karista of the Dark Court," she answered primly.

I nodded in acknowledgement and introduced myself, leaving off the part about being from another realm. If she hadn't figured it out by now, I didn't think it would matter.

"I'm trying to get to the Fallow Woods. Can you point me in the right direction?" I asked hopefully.

Karista frowned, and matching expressions appeared on a few of the other fae. "The light fae lurk there," she told me with a sneer.

"I know, but I think my friend is there and needs my help," I told her honestly.

"The queen's soldiers bring pain and destruction to the woods. Its not safe there."

I could tell by the stubborn set of her jaw that she wouldn't be swayed into helping me find Farranen.

I sat down in the grass so I could see her better. "Could you draw me a map? Or even tell me if I'm going in the right direction?" I pleaded.

"Why?" She narrowed her eyes at me, like she was trying to figure out if I was trying to trick her.

"The queen is hurting someone I care about. I don't know for sure where he is, but I have to look somewhere. I told him I'd come for him." A frustrated laugh escaped my lips. "I don't even know what I'll do when I find him—I'm not exactly qualified to be rescuing people—but that's where the dark prince and I were headed before I got lost."

"The dark prince seeks the Fallow Woods?" she asked suspiciously.

"Yeah," I told her glumly.

"Our lord has always treated the pixies with kindness; we will accompany you."

I looked up in surprise. "Really?"

She gave me a toothy smile that sent chills skittering down my spine. "Oh, yes. We leave now."

****

From the branch of a large tree, Farranen dangled

by his wrists, with thick chains, probably made of iron, holding him in place. His tattered shirt was gone, leaving him bare from the waist up so I could see the massive lash marks that bisected his torso. The jagged tears had all healed enough to make me think he'd been here since my failed rescue attempt at the dungeon days ago. His ribs were noticeable beneath his scarred skin, and his jutting hip bones made me mad all over again. In addition to the beatings, he'd clearly been starved.

I glanced at the group of pixies next to me and was glad to see they looked just as outraged as I did. With my new allies leading the way, it hadn't taken us long to reach the Fallow Woods. The trees here were ancient, with massive trunks that rose hundreds of feet into the air. Along the cracks in their gnarled bark, strange fungi grew that I was hesitant to brush up against.

Karista growled something dark and unintelligible before looking up at me. "To torture a guardian is sacrilege," she spat. A few of the tiny fae behind her nodded venomously.

"I don't see a guard." Maybe they'd left him there in the hope that starvation and the elements would finish him off. Which only fueled my rage higher; this was passive-aggressive bullshit at its finest.

"There, I smell him in the tree." She pointed across the clearing, and I followed the delicate arch of her tiny finger with my eyes toward a large tree that already shed most of its leaves. And sure enough, about fifteen feet up, a slight wavering glow identified something hidden by glamour. I'd once pointed out Lief's glamoured sword, and he'd been surprised, so I had to assume most people couldn't see things hidden by glamour. Just one more way I was an anomaly.

"Are there any more?" I asked suspiciously.

Karista carefully scanned the woods before announcing, "Just one." She turned to look at me with her pink eyes full of intensity. "It's a trap." She gestured toward Farranen. "He is the bait."

"I know," I replied morosely. A dozen doll-sized pixies and one sarcastic hermit wouldn't stand a chance against a soldier trained to be in the queen's army. I wondered if it was Gus himself in the tree.

"We need a plan," I announced decisively. My first attempted rescue had been half-cocked at best, and now I was smart enough to recognize the importance of solid planning if I wanted a shot at retrieving my guardian without getting myself or the pixies hurt in the process. "Do you guys have any superpowers—er, I mean, gifts?"

Karista arched a tiny pink eyebrow and planted a hand on her cocked hip. "We can pull the unwilling into the dreamscape."

Farranen had once told me that dream sharing could be incredibly pleasurable or exactly the opposite, depending on who was guiding it. I had a feeling that Karista wasn't talking about making him the star of his own personal erotic daydream.

"Okay, so you're saying you can distract him long enough for me to free Farranen?"

She nodded confidently, and my hopes rose. Maybe we really could pull this off.

****

The small group of pixies assembled into some sort of tactical formation before fluttering their small wings and lifting off into the sky. Karista shot me one last gruesome grin over her shoulder before they disappeared behind a layer of glamour. A faint glow flitted along the outskirts of the clearing. Once they had closed in on the tree, they hovered in place around the unsuspecting guard. I waited, watching for any sign that they'd succeeded in distracting him.

If I hadn't been crouched in the bushes to avoid detection, I would have stretched out my back and shoulders to relieve some of the pent-up tension I was holding onto. Knowing that the next part of the plan rested solely on my shoulders was nerve-racking. Still, this was far better than sitting on my butt like a helpless ninny, waiting for someone else to ride in and save the day.

Across the clearing, the glamour surrounding the guard melted away like someone had doused it with water. With his legs straddling a thick branch and his back resting on the trunk of the tree, he appeared to be sleeping. I'd already expected to see the traditional uniform of black pants and a gray shirt, but I was surprised by how young the male was. In human terms, he was probably no more than twenty, but as a fae, he could be a millennium old and I wouldn't have a clue. Dark brown hair was cut neatly around a round face, and his full lips pursed slightly.

The pixies dropped their glamour, and I wondered how they'd gotten him to go to sleep so fast. Did they have pixie dust? Maybe he'd already been asleep? I giggled at the thought of the queen learning that one of her men was sleeping on the job. Or maybe it was all tied into whatever unique gift the pixies themselves had.

Karista shouted a single syllable, and the entire

pack of tiny fae descended on the sleeping male. I watched in horror as their jaws came unhinged to allow them to take golfball-sized bites out of whatever they wanted. And at that particular moment, they were only interested in the poor sleeping guard. Blood spurted as they ravenously tore chunks of skin and muscle free.

Feeling ill, I looked away before I could figure out if they were swallowing the lumps they removed, or if they were dropping them to the forest floor before darting back in for more.

I rose to my feet. This was my only chance to free Farranen. I stumbled through the bushes, and once in the clearing, I sprinted to where my unconscious guardian waited. Karista had assured me Farranen's sword would be strong enough to cut through the iron chain. I sure hoped she knew what she was talking about.

As I got closer, I could see that the branch the length of chain was draped over was thicker than my waist. The chain continued back down, wrapped multiple times around the base of the tree, and was anchored in place with a giant metal stake. The circumference of the stake alone was bigger than my fist, so it had to be at least a foot in length—and impossible to remove by hand.

When I finally reached the tree that Farranen was tethered to, I had to remind myself to breathe. He was unconscious, but the slow, steady rise and fall of his chest meant he was still alive. I reached up with trembling fingers and touched his arm.

"Farranen?" I whispered. "It's me, Theo."

When he didn't answer, I repeated the words a little louder. There was still no response, and I glanced back at the pixies that were still happily chomping on the light fae. I wasn't sure how long they'd be able to keep up their attack, or if another guard would arrive soon to replace this one. Since there was no way I'd be able to drag Farranen any distance on my own, I needed him to wake up.

"Farranen!" This time I shouted, uncaring who heard.

When nothing happened, I thought, *Fine. If you won't hear my words, then maybe you'll listen to my magic.* I tucked the sword back where it belonged and placed both my hands on his hips where there was the least amount of damaged skin. I let a little trickle of my magic unravel, and it immediately found Farranen's.

His magic was sluggish but didn't resist when I wound my own around it. His magic always felt like safety and today was no different; the familiar feeling brought tears to my eyes. Mindful of when I'd accidentally shocked Dog with my magic, I tentatively pushed more into my fae's broken body.

After a few seconds, the responding tug was every bit as intimate as I remembered. Knowing I was wasting time, I unleashed everything I had. Every ounce of my magic poured out of me, eagerly reuniting with the male in front of me. Farranen had the gift of healing, so I was hoping he'd be able to use my magic to mend the damage that was plaguing him.

Just when I was getting light-headed, the muscles under my hands jerked. I looked up and met his vivid green stare. And for a few seconds, all I could do was stare back. I'm pretty sure his stunned expression matched mine.

"Hey…" I whispered hoarsely, and some of the

confusion faded from his face. I took a step back and let my hands fall away, disrupting the connection between our magic. I swayed on my feet a little, drained from sharing with him.

The chains above clinked as he struggled to put his weight back on his feet.

I pulled his sword from my back and lined it up with the chains above his wrists.

"Don't move..." I told him unnecessarily, because really, he had to have caught on to my plan. Before I could lose my nerve, I swung the blade back and then straight forward. It cleaved through the chain like it had been made of gummy worms instead of iron. Farranen stumbled forward, and I dropped the sword so I could catch him.

"*Oof!*" I struggled to support as much of his weight as I could, but we both ended up on our knees in the grass. I pulled back to give him more space, but his arms were locked around me. I belatedly remembered his wrists were chained together.

"Theodora..." So much grief and uncertainty colored his voice that I refused to look away from the mostly healed scars on his chest. Yeah, it was cowardly. But I just couldn't face the recrimination that was sure to come. This was not a man who would be happy about being rescued by someone like me—someone he viewed as weak. Someone he'd already dismissed.

I bowed my head so he could lift the chains over it, and once we were no longer bound together, I scooted backward to retrieve the sword.

"Theo..." A thread of anger this time let me know he wasn't happy about being ignored.

"Give me your hands," I murmured.

My stomach cramped, reminding me that I needed to eat, and probably sleep, to replenish the magic I'd given away. When Farranen didn't immediately move, I reached out and unwound the loose chain without his cooperation. The skin beneath was an angry purple and rubbed raw in places, but it had probably looked worse before he'd had a chance to heal himself. I tossed the chain aside and, trying not to look shaky, got to my feet.

"My lady…"

I ignored his appeal and focused on unbuckling the sword scabbard from my shoulder. If he noticed the duct tape, he didn't mention it.

"We need to get moving," I told him numbly. A quick glance over my shoulder confirmed that the pixies were gone, and the bloody guard was still sleeping in the tree. He was missing a good chunk (Ha—unintentional pun!) of his body mass, but he still appeared to be breathing. I assumed he'd be fine, since he was immortal; it would take more than a few hungry pixies to outright kill him. Still, I didn't want to be there when he woke up.

I slid the sword back where it belonged one last time, then held it out to where Farranen knelt before me in the grass. When he made no move to take it, I risked a look at his face.

He'd told me not to come, yet here I was, so I was ready for whatever righteous anger or scorn he might throw my way. Maybe even a little embarrassment that he'd needed help from me. Instead, there was only the same regret and longing he'd had in the dreamscape the last time I'd seen him. I wanted to ask what the regret was for, but now wasn't the time. It wasn't really even any of my business.

I held out my hand, and I was stupidly relieved when it didn't tremble. He reached for it like a starving man would reach for cake and rose to his feet with a fluidity that let me know that I'd done the right thing by sharing my magic.

I thrust his sword into his other hand and took a few steps back to put some distance between us. Now that we were face-to-face, I wasn't sure how to hide the hurt or awkwardness that came from being around him. I didn't regret coming to rescue him exactly—I'd do it again in a heartbeat. But I was anxious to find Dog and get back home in one piece. I needed to put all this could've/should've/would've-but-it's-a-moot-point-since-he's-not-interested bullshit behind me.

I'd have to deal with my baggage later, but not until I knew Lief and Dog were safe. So, first things first; I needed to find them. I doubted they would have waited around near the river or its overlooking cliffs—they weren't the type to sit around and wait for things to happen. And since I hadn't seen any sign of Lief's army, I couldn't even be sure that they'd made it to the Fallow Woods yet.

I put myself in Lief's shoes (and Dog's paws). Where would I look for me, if I was them? They'd probably assume I'd head for home—so, logically, I should head for the gate. Farranen should probably get out of Fairie for a while too; the queen was going to be one grumpy bear when she discovered I'd stolen her favorite whipping boy. And as much as he deserved the chance to kick her butt, he wasn't up for the task yet. I schooled my face into a semblance of neutrality and calmly told him, "We're in the Fallow Woods. Do you know how to get to the gate from here?"

Not wanting him to see any of the chinks in my emotional armour, I busied myself by digging a water bottle out of my backpack. By the time I looked up and handed it to him, he had his own cold expressionless mask on. My heartrate slowed in response to my sudden relief. This I could deal with—the frigid guardian who didn't share his emotions. I was glad he wasn't going to make this any more awkward than it had to be. Just a normal day for two people traveling together to reach a mutual destination.

More like, just a normal day for two people traveling together through a hostile realm, avoiding capture by the land's tyrannical leader, while ignoring the huge pink elephant in the room.

I forced myself to hold his gaze; I refused to act like I'd done something wrong.

Farranen wordlessly strapped his sword over his shoulder. I belatedly realized that I could have offered him the shirt in my bag to glamour into something that would cover his wounds. If they bothered him, he didn't let on.

After glancing at the sky, he pointed toward the opposite side of the clearing. "This way. It's a two-day walk from here."

I followed him through the grass, and when we passed the sleeping fae in the tree, I briefly considered climbing up there and stealing some of his magic. I was wiped, and I could use a magical boost. The pixies' magic would wear off sooner or later, and the male would be feeling every single gnaw mark and bite of missing flesh once he woke up. It might actually be a kindness to put him out of his misery.

With an inner sigh, I continued past the tree. I was too damn soft. Draining the rock fae had been unintentional, and I'd carry around a pile of guilt over that for the rest of my life. But I'd never be able to knowingly take another life just to benefit myself.

Stupid morals, I thought.

Chapter Sixteen

We walked in silence, stopping at the few streams we passed to refill our bottles and drink our fill.

Farranen shot perplexed glances at me, but I pretended not to notice. I didn't know what to make of his considering looks. It was like he was trying to figure out a puzzle that he didn't have all the pieces for.

By late afternoon, my stomach was a twisted growling mess, and my attitude was no better.

The fallen leaves muffled our footsteps, so I nearly jumped out of my skin when Farranen cut through the silence. "Theodora—"

"Theo," I interrupted him. "It's just Theo." I know, it was a nitpicky thing to say, and bitchiness had crept into my voice. Him using my full name had never bothered me until now; I'd actually enjoyed the way he was the only one to do it. I hated to admit it, but it had made me feel special.

"Theo," he amended, in a level tone that I was jealous of. "What happened before, when we—"

I knew where he was going with this, knew that he wanted to talk about our night together last fall. So, I stopped him before he could rip the scab off the wound I'd been trying so hard to heal since he left. "*Don't.*" I was too tired to put any real viciousness into the word, but he must have gotten the message because he didn't try to bring it up again.

The trees thinned out, and the land slowly changed from woodland to rocky hills. I didn't know if these were the same hills where Lief's army had camped or if we were closer to where we'd been attacked last night. I couldn't hear any indication of a river, but my weak human ears probably wouldn't have noticed until we were within a half mile of it. I scanned the horizon, hoping to see the dark prince or Dog.

Farranen must have noticed my attention had wandered, because he stopped to scan our surroundings.

"Lief and his army have been looking for you." The words seemed important enough to break my stony silence. He needed to know he hadn't been forgotten, and I wasn't cruel enough to withhold info like that. "He's probably still looking. They were on their way to the Fallow Woods before we ran into some trouble."

He looked over his shoulder at me, the slight rise in his eyebrow inviting me to elaborate, but he wouldn't push if I decided to end the conversation there.

"Lief sent his soldier guys ahead to scout out the woods, and then we fell behind because—well, because I'm a klutz and slowed us down. We stopped for the night and were attacked. I fell in the river and got washed downstream, so I don't know where they are anymore. I don't even know where I am."

Farranen stopped and waited until we could walk side by side before continuing. "The dark prince accompanied you...alone?"

Seriously, *that's* what he wanted to focus on?

"Is that a problem?" My tone implied that it was in fact going to be a problem if he had a problem with me spending time with Lief.

"The dark prince has a target on his back right

now, and if the queen learns of your visit to Fairie, you will have one as well."

Oh—I hadn't looked at it that way. He had a point.

"We weren't completely alone; Dog was there too."

"You brought Dog to Fairie?" His eyebrows flew up.

I shrugged. "He probably thought he could keep me out of trouble if he came." I didn't bother to mention that Dog liked Farranen. Enough not to bite him at least.

"Who attacked you?"

"Soldiers from the Army of Light. There were four of them that I could see." Plus, who knows how many more I hadn't seen.

"Describe them." A muscle ticked in his jaw, a sure sign he was angry.

"The two that came through the door looked human. Dark brown hair, tall, but not as tall as Lief. Sharp swords. They wore gray, so I knew they worked for the queen." I thought back, trying to find something useful to tell Farranen. "The third fae was blond, with his hair in a tight braid. He had hazel eyes, a beautiful face, and a bad attitude; he looked cockier than a rooster."

"And the fourth?"

"He was made out of rock."

Farranen's eyebrows furrowed. "A graveel fae?"

Huh, I liked calling him a rock fae better. "Does it matter?"

"They're from the Dark Court."

I blinked. I don't know why, but I'd never stopped to consider the possibility that some of Lief's court was playing for the wrong team. I already knew some of the light fae were working with the dark prince, so it would make sense that loyalties had shifted on both sides.

The constant changes in the incline had my foot throbbing again, so I gritted my teeth and fought against the urge to limp. To take my mind off the pain, I said the first thing that came to mind. "The pixies thought you'd been chained up as part of an elaborate trap, so how come there was only one fae guarding you?"

"I was to be made an example of. The chances of anyone attempting a rescue were slim, so there was no need to station more than one of the queen's soldiers. I don't believe she's aware of how many oppose her new...endeavors."

"But you do—oppose her, that is." I still had trouble wrapping my head around the idea of my rigid rule-loving guardian having such a dramatic reversal of allegiance.

"Yes. The queen lost my fealty when you became the first casualty in this charade she's set in motion." A hard edge in his words spoke of bitter resentment. It wasn't something I was expecting to hear, and it softened some of my own ire. Until then, I hadn't stopped to consider that I might not be the only one hurt by this convoluted situation.

"We'll stop here for the night," Farranen announced.

I looked around; the sky had darkened enough that the first few stars were just twinkling into sight. With a hearty sigh that I felt all the way down to my bones, I strode into the little thicket of trees and collapsed on the soft bed of leaves. I'd never felt anything so opulent in my life; my aching joints were ecstatic to finally get a break.

In a move that was far more graceful, Farranen lowered himself to a sitting position with his back to one of the bigger trees.

I sat up and tugged my worn backpack off. "Here," I called before tossing my spare shirt at the shirtless male across from me. "It won't fit you, but you can glamour it, right?"

He nodded, and the pale pink shirt morphed into a deep green cloak. "Thank you."

There were two packs of trail mix and a protein bar at the bottom of my bag, so I tossed him half of the bounty and we ate surrounded by the sound of the wind playing with the fall leaves.

"Will you let me look at your ankle?" he asked softly.

I squared my shoulders. "It's fine."

"You've been favoring it all day." His voice was mild, like he was afraid of upsetting me.

"It'll be good to go by morning." It would probably still hurt like a bitch in the morning, but I wasn't going to admit that to him. If he sensed I was lying, he didn't say anything.

After an eye-watering yawn, I lay down on my side with my backpack under my head and stopped fighting the need to sleep.

****

The silence woke me.

"*Shhh.*" A strong arm slid around my waist, and Farranen quietly whispered next to my ear, "We're being watched."

I battled against the urge to sit up and look around; that would only alert our stalker that we were aware of his presence. All I could see while lying on my side was the thick carpet of yellow and orange leaves spread across the ground. The darkness hid the nearby trees in smears of shadows that could conceal any number of threats.

"Don't move." His voice was a puff of warm air, and I dipped my head in a slight nod.

The attack came from the trees to our left. Something big dropped from the branches and shot toward us like a furry missile. Farranen rose to his knees and lifted the sword that he'd been holding. Before the creature could abort its failed ambush, its forward momentum propelled it straight toward the pointy end of the sword. With a squeal that nearly shattered my eardrums, our stalker impaled itself. The force of it knocked Farranen backward and away from me.

I scrambled to my hands and knees as my guardian deftly dodged teeth and claws until the writhing ball of olive-colored fur stopped moving. He pulled his sword from the dead creature and wiped the blade on his pant leg before meeting my eyes. "It's a tibber. It must have caught our scent and followed us from the woods; they don't usually live this far north."

I made a little sound of acknowledgement that I hoped sounded normal.

"There's a stream in the valley on the other side of this hill. You can bathe while I take care of this." He gestured with his sword at the pile of blood and fur. Now that it was wasn't moving, I could see the tibber was the size of a large dog. Its fur was an ugly shade of green with black stripes that would have been good for blending into the trees and brush found in the Fallow

Woods. The claws looked like they could be used for climbing trees as well as eviscerating anyone stupid enough to fall asleep without a sword-wielding fae to watch their back.

"Thank you," I murmured, and his eyes softened a little when he nodded.

I grabbed my pack and walked through the trees in the direction he'd mentioned. Above me the sky was lightening to a beautiful mauve color. Aside from the fact that I'd nearly had heart failure, the tibber's attack wasn't totally without benefit. The early wake-up call meant we'd embark on the last half of our journey sooner and hopefully get back to the gate sooner. Because there was no way I could spend another night out here—not because I was afraid of the animals wanting to eat me or the fae trying to kill me, but because Farranen's company was slowly chipping away at my resolve.

Sometime after I'd fallen asleep, I'd woken to the whisper of leaves and fabric rustling next to me. When he lay down next to me and covered us both with his cloak, I didn't say anything. Instead, I just selfishly accepted the warmth and comfort that he freely gave.

And there was no way in hell I could let that happen again.

****

A beautifully clear stream slowly meandered between the two hills, exactly where Farranen had said it would be.

The sky was still dark enough to provide the illusion of privacy, and I quickly stripped out of my pjs. The ghosts on the fabric looked a lot more gruesome with the tibber's blood splattered across their tiny white bodies. And it was no big surprise to discover my panties were flaming red and made from lavish silk. I grinned despite my annoyance and wondered for the dozenth time what kind of trouble Lief had gotten into since I'd last seen him.

The water was cold, so I cleaned myself off as quickly I could, while keeping one eye out for unexpected company. I'd probably die of embarrassment if anyone caught me frolicking outside in the buff. Once I'd finger combed the leaves and twigs from my hair and every last drop of tibber blood was scrubbed from my face, I redressed in the dirty pajama shirt and clean panties, socks, and jeans from my backpack. My ankle protested at being shoved back into my boot, but I wasn't up for a barefoot hike, so after a few choice words and a lot of grunting, I finally got the stupid thing zipped up.

I quickly braided my hair and filled our empty water bottles before traipsing back up the hill and over to where we'd spent the night.

The aroma of roasting meat hit me as I picked my way through the thicket of trees. Oh my God, when was the last time I'd had a real meal? The smell was divine.

I found Farranen arranging chunks of meat on sharp spikes over a small fire. When he looked up, the hard lines of his face eased into something less harsh. "Hungry?" he asked.

I nodded and took a seat next to him. When he held out some meat on a stick, I accepted it with a thanks. It popped and sizzled from the heat of the fire, and once it was cool enough to touch, I took a tentative bite.

Farranen watched me cautiously, while he sampled his own piece. When he raised his eyebrows, I answered his unspoken question with a smile. "It's better than cake."

We ate in companionable silence, and some of the shakiness faded from my limbs. Partly from the meal, and partly because my magic didn't feel nearly as depleted as it had the day before. I suspected being near another fae had helped recharge it, but I was too embarrassed to ask.

It didn't take long to clean up after ourselves and put out the fire.

"Would you like me to glamour your shirt?" There was a wary note that I wasn't used to in his voice; he was anticipating a brush-off from me. Which was justified, since I'd been pumping out the bitch vibes pretty hard.

I looked down at the sad little ghosts that were now a pale pink instead of white. They didn't exactly fit into traditional fae fashion trends. "Please."

Judging by his expression, he was just as surprised by my answer as I was. But we had a long day ahead of us, and it would only be harder for both of us if I continued to punish him with my bad attitude. Yes, I was hurting because of the way he'd led me to believe he'd cared, when, in fact, he'd only been following orders to be with me. But lashing out at him was petty, and it wouldn't accomplish anything constructive.

With my mind firmly made up on the subject, I held out my hand in invitation. I was done acting like a child, and I was fairly confident I could behave accordingly.

His palm slid against mine, and the magic in me leapt for his like a long-lost lover. Sparks filled my veins, and his cold mask of indifference wavered for a second. I closed my eyes to hide the riot of emotions that he always stirred up. Just because I was trying to forget the pain he'd caused didn't mean it wasn't still there. And I certainly didn't want him to know about it.

****

I struggled to keep my gaze on the beautiful landscape as it rolled past, but my eyes were inevitably drawn back to the fae in front of me.

He'd glamoured himself a pair of tan pants and a white shirt that couldn't hide the deep ridges of muscles beneath. His hair was pulled back into a ponytail, so I could see the sword resting between his shoulder blades. The scars from his imprisonment weren't visible, but I knew they were there.

"How long was I gone?"

Farranen's words startled me from my not-so-subtle ogling, and I met his eyes with a blush.

"The days and nights got harder and harder to keep track of. I'm no longer sure how much time has passed."

I tried to remember when he'd left…There had still been leaves on the trees, so probably late September. And since it was the middle of December, I was guessing that he'd been an unwilling captive for about three months. I told him as much, and he nodded silently. By the set of his shoulders, he was contemplating something else, but it took a few minutes before he asked, "Will you tell me what transpired during my absence?"

It wasn't a trip down memory lane that I was eager to take, but I figured he had a right to know.

"Let's see…After you left, Merrick came back for round two—only this time, he made me drink his blood so he could turn me into a vampire." I glossed over the fact that he'd turned me into his own personal chew toy. Farranen didn't need the gruesome details. "Dog wasn't impressed, and they got into a fight. I killed Merrick." There wasn't an ounce of remorse in my voice; nobody got to hurt my shifter and get away with it.

I looked over to see if he was following along, and his clenched jaw let me know just how much he wasn't enjoying my little tale of magic, mayhem, and murder.

"Then my magic got kind of wonky, and I accidentally brought a ghost through the veil—two, actually. And somewhere in there, I died; but you already knew that." I offered him an apologetic smile, since it was a lot for him to take in. I didn't see any point in telling him that I hadn't yet perfected my ghost-making techniques. Once we reached the gate, we'd part ways, and I doubted we'd run into any more random ghosts on the way. At least I hoped we wouldn't.

"Do you know what happened to Mary and the other guardian?" I'd almost forgotten that Farranen hadn't been the only one to piss off the queen, and I hadn't thought to ask until then.

"I believe they were given similar treatment at different locations so the queen might showcase her displeasure to a greater audience."

"That bitch," I said, but it lacked any real growl. I briefly contemplated turning back toward the woods to find the missing fae, but without a pack of pixies to back me up, I doubted I'd be able to do much for them.

The ground leveled out, allowing the throbbing in my ankle to ease a fraction. The soft carpet of grass provided a cushion that cobblestone wouldn't have, and I was grateful for the reprieve.

We kept walking, and I tried to think if there was anything else Farranen had missed during his hiatus.

"Your sword got banged up when I fell. I'll get you a new one if it can't be fixed." I had no idea how much it would cost to repair a sword, but the damage had been entirely my fault.

He took out the blade in question and turned it from side to side.

I pointed to the handle where the beautifully carved flowering vines had been dinged. "Right there. It hit a rock when I fell."

He studied it for another minute before telling me, "Every weapon has a history; this mark just adds another story to the blade's annals." He slid it back into its holder and gave me a reassuring look. "I would be proud to wield a weapon that can attest to your courage and bravery."

"Oh—no, I wasn't courageous or brave; I just tripped and fell down a hill." It was more like a mountain, but my pride could only take so many hits before I reached my limit.

Farranen stopped walking, and I was forced to stop too, so I wouldn't run into him. "You have more courage and bravery than any fae I know. Journeying to a foreign realm to face unknown dangers, in the pursuit of righting the wrongs that plague my people—*that* is the very definition of courage and bravery. Coming to the rescue of a male that you care not for—*twice*—and then taking the blade meant for him—for *me*—Theodora, I can think of no effort more noble than that."

I could read the sincerity in his face, could tell that he meant every word, and it shocked me. "I just tripped and fell," I told him numbly. How could he possibly think my actions noble, when all I did was mess things up? Maybe I should have told him about the ghosts that didn't behave like normal ghosts, after all.

And as for him being "a male that I cared not for," well, it would be easier to just let him think that was true. Unfortunately, I didn't always do things the easy way.

Chapter Seventeen

"I care," I told him. "I never stopped caring, even after you *fulfilled* your *duties*." I don't know why I was still talking; this wasn't a conversation I was ready to have, but my mouth had a mind of its own. "I wasn't the one that walked away."

His eyebrows rose, and he looked liked he'd been physically slapped. "You think that I left...that I willingly *left?*" Anguish and a hint of anger tightened his face, and I briefly entertained the possibility that being tortured at the queen's hands had done him more damage than I'd previously thought. His memories of our night together were clearly skewed.

"Yes." I crossed my arms defensively. If we were going down this road, I wasn't going to tiptoe. "That's exactly what you did. As soon as we finished..." I made a random gesture so I wouldn't have to go into details about what we'd done that night. "...you informed me that my *duties* were fulfilled for the night, you picked up your clothes, and you walked out." I arched a brow, daring him to contradict even one of the words that I'd said. Images from that night were seared into my brain like a bad movie on repeat, and every night I was forced to relive it.

"Theodora..." I wasn't surprised when his words trailed off; fae couldn't lie so he was unable to deny any of it.

"That's what I thought." I moved to stomp past him, but he grabbed me by the arm and spun me around. I gave him my best glare, because honestly, anger was a welcome reprieve from the bitter hurt that threatened to drown me. If I lost the fury I was nursing, I didn't want him to see the tears that would inevitably fall.

"Let me explain." He loosened his grip, and I knew he'd let me walk away if I wanted to. It was the only reason I didn't. "Whatever was happening between us, I didn't want it to be tainted by the queen's orders. Yes, I very much wanted everything you were offering that night—but not like that. Not with her magic compelling us." His eyes were bright with grief, and I took a step back.

"I returned to Fairie and requested an audience with the queen; I told her the edict was useless, that you were unable to bear children, and your dwindling magic should be cause to release you from any further rulings."

I doubted the queen took the news of her new plaything's infertility very well.

"I had no idea that she'd already placed such importance on your ability to procreate. Her displeasure was swift and considerable."

"She punished you because I'm the one that's broken?" Typical; the crazy bitch had essentially shot the messenger for bringing bad news.

"You are far from broken, my lady."

He'd change his tone once he learned about the broken ghosts I was making, but that was a discussion for another day.

I took a few more steps back until I found a nice

hard boulder to sit on. My head was reeling; I had no idea what to do with Farranen's confession.

Had he really planned to come back? If so, I'd spent the last few months bitter and sullen while he'd been struggling to stay alive. Bile crawled up the back of my throat, tasting a lot like regret.

I looked up and met his gaze, expecting to see recrimination or censure or maybe even some anger. But the only thing I could read in his dark green eyes was wary anticipation. I said the first thing that came to mind, the one thing that had been lingering in my heart since his disappearance. "I *missed* you." I held up a hand when he opened his mouth to speak. "But you *hurt* me." I held his gaze, needing him to see my pain and know I was being completely honest. "I understand that it wasn't entirely your fault—but you could have told me what was going on before you slunk off like a thief in the night." If I'd have known that he was planning to come back, his abrupt exit wouldn't have stung so badly.

"Theo—"

I shook my head and told him, "No, I'm not done yet. What the queen did to you was wrong, and I'm sorry you had to go through that alone." I took a deep breath and struggled to find the right words for what I was about to say. "I can't forget what happened between us, but I'm willing to move past it—if you want to be friends again." Or whatever we'd been.

"And if I desire to be more than 'friends'?"

I probably would have thrown something snarky at him, but I could read the hint of vulnerability in the rigid set of his shoulders.

I looked away, unsure how to answer that

particular question. Yes, once upon a time I'd been eager to see what a relationship with such a brave thoughtful male would be like, but that was before I'd fully comprehended how much I stood to lose. I honestly didn't think I was strong enough to handle anymore heartache.

"Let's just get to the gate; everything else can wait until we find Dog and Lief." We could decide what to do about a hypothetical "us" later. If he was even still interested.

He nodded, and I was relieved the conversation was temporarily resolved. I took the hand he offered me, and when his magic slid up my arm in a slow caress, I didn't protest. It was everything I'd been missing, and the simple familiarity made my breath hitch in my chest. There was just something about way his magic ebbed and flowed around mine that was unique to only us.

"Am I interrupting?" A hesitant voice sliced through the moment, and I leapt away from Farranen like a guilty kid caught with her hand in the cookie jar.

"Harvey!" My words were partly admonishing for scaring the heck out of me, and partly delighted to see him again. "Are you all recharged?" He certainly looked much healthier than the last time I'd seen him; his pale blue skin was practically glowing and his eyes were a deeper indigo that I remembered them being.

"Yes, thank you. I'm glad to see you've freed the guardian." I followed his gaze over to Farranen and nearly laughed out loud at the expression on his face. It was a weird mix of confusion and alarm, and he held his sword pointed in Harvey's direction. I'd forgotten that my ghosts couldn't be seen by anyone else.

"Farranen, this is Harvalin. I'm still getting used to the whole ankou magic thing, so I haven't figured out how to make a ghost that other people can see yet."

My guardian gave me one of those considering looks that I really should be more used to seeing, before asking, "Harvalin is dead?"

"Yeah, sorry...Did you know him?" They were both from the Light Court, so maybe they'd met before. Then again, neither one of them struck me as social butterflies.

"Yes, but not well. He joined the queen's army after I was promoted to guardian of the gate," Farranen explained.

"The guardian is well known in Fairie; we sparred together a number of times. His skill with a blade is legendary." Harvey sounded like a starstruck teenage girl. Minus the training bra and bad hair.

"Let's keep that between us, okay, Harvey? His head is already big enough."

The ghost stood up a little straighter and nodded. "As you wish, my lady."

Farranen regarded me and the spot where Harvey stood with suspicion but didn't comment further.

"Shall we?" I gestured in the direction of the gate, suddenly overcome with the urge to get home.

"The dark prince and his entourage are camped half a mile in that direction." Harvey pointed to a hill off in the distance, and I rounded on him with incredulity.

"You know where Lief is? Why didn't you say something sooner?"

"Sorry. When I arrived, it appeared that you and the guardian needed a moment of privacy, so I took the liberty of scouting the surrounding hills." He looked so stricken I immediately felt bad for sounding like a sullen old woman.

"It's fine, Harvey. Can you take us there please?" I tried to put just the right amount of modesty into my voice. I didn't want to appear ungrateful for his ghostly services.

He must have sensed my chagrin, because he led the way with a slight smile.

****

There is something incredibly rare about a male that can hold his tongue.

Farranen had questions about Harvey, so when it became apparent that he wasn't going to mention it on his own, I told him, "You're wondering why you can't see him, aren't you?"

To his credit, my guardian just dipped his chin in acknowledgement.

"I have no idea why I'm the only one who can see him." My magic was a fickle bitch that I doubted I'd ever completely understand. "He's also corporeal when I touch him, which is supposedly impossible. And he's kinda vintage as far as ghosts go."

"Vintage?" Farranen asked in a carefully neutral voice that let me know he was still trying to decide if I was being honest or making up the whole story. Which ticked me off, because if I was going to pretend I had an imaginary friend, it would have been a kick-ass purple dragon named Blaze. I mean, I was a writer, for goodness' sake! I could come up with a lot better than a blue-skinned ghost mermaid.

Never mind. A blue-skinned ghost mermaid actually sounded pretty cool.

"He's old," I clarified. "Probably three or four days old. I've kind of lost track." I glanced over at the ghost in question, and he shrugged. At least I wasn't the only one too distracted by our grand escapade to keep track. "And he saved my life. *Twice*."

Farranen's eyebrows rose in surprise. Or maybe disbelief.

I opened my mouth to sing Harvey's praises, but a throaty howl cut me off.

Dog! I would know that sound anywhere.

We'd just crested the top of a giant hill, and my furry friend was racing up the other side. His massive paws were a blur as he closed the distance between us. And while most people would have found the sight of a massive black wolf barreling toward them terrifying, it filled me with joy.

He stopped short of knocking me over, but just barely. I let him prance around me a few times, winding his body against mine like a cat, before I knelt and wrapped my arms around his neck.

"Are you okay?" I murmured against his soft fur.

He growled, probably offended that I'd doubted his ability to kick fae butt and remain unscathed. His big yellow eyes darted over every inch of me, and his wet nose poked at the majority of my nooks and crannies—but not quite all. I'd already established a firm stance against the sniffing of any crotches. Especially mine.

Once he'd satisfied himself that I'd incurred minimal damage in his absence, he cast a wary look at Farranen. After a tense pause, he edged closer and butted my guardian in the hip with his furry head. I'm pretty sure he did it in a hey-how-are-ya? way, rather than an I'm-just-tenderizing-my-upcoming-meal sort of way.

"Merry meet, Dog," Farranen told him softly. It was nice to see them getting along. Not that they hadn't gotten along before; it was more like they'd just remained neutral toward each other. And after all the times Dog had seen me weeping over a pint of rocky road ice cream, I'd been prepared for a little resentment on his part. I probably should have been embarrassed that an adolescent wolf had more emotional maturity than I did, but I was too busy feeling grateful to worry about it.

"Theo!" I looked up and saw that Lief had followed Dog. He was dressed all in black, and his cloak flowed behind him like a living shadow as he ran toward us. Anger and trepidation was written on his face, and even Dog backed up at the alarming sight of the dark prince's unconcealed temper.

Without a thought to propriety or whether he'd even want me to touch him, I launched myself at him. It was only a few steps, but he didn't slow down until he caught me and lifted me off my feet. His arms were like thick bands of steel around me; it was almost painful, and yet it still wasn't enough. I buried my face against his neck and didn't bother trying to hide my strangled cry of joy at seeing him again.

The familiar scent of winter mornings wrapped itself around me like a blanket; I hadn't realized until then just how worried I'd been about him.

When he finally pulled back, his pale blue eyes studied me with an intensity that made my tummy fill with butterflies. "What. *Happened.*" The way he growled the words sent a shiver down my spine. "Dog tracked your scent to the edge of the cliff and then—

nothing. *Nothing.*"

"I fell in." I attempted to show a proper amount of shame, but I was still smiling from finding out he and Dog were okay. His glower said he wasn't buying my phony chagrin.

"You fell in." His flat tone managed to convey skepticism and mockery at the same time.

"Yes—well, actually it was more like the guy I was holding onto fell in, and I just went along for the ride." I anticipated Lief's next question and quickly added, "Harvey helped me get to shore. The rock fae wasn't as lucky. He sank like a stone." Nobody laughed at my pun.

The dark prince arched a dark eyebrow in confusion. "The rock fae?"

"He looked like he was made out of rocks…" I looked to Farranen in question, because I couldn't remember what he'd called the fae that had nearly drowned me.

"A graveel?" Harvey supplied helpfully.

"Yes! A graveel. Thanks, Harvey." I'd forgotten he was still here.

"One of the graveel fell into the river?" I was glad to see most of Lief's anger had faded into bewilderment. Then I remembered that the rock fae belonged to the Dark Court—Lief's court.

"He was with the fae that attacked us in your tent. He thought I was fae and said the queen wanted anyone involved in the rebellion dead. 'Kill the rebels, end the rebellion' were his exact words."

Lief and Farranen exchanged a look that I couldn't decipher. The dark prince finally broke the silence by saying, "It would appear that our rescue plans are no longer needed."

Farranen's lips curved into a brief smile. "Thanks to Theodora's efforts."

Lief shot me a look that could only be classified as accusatory.

Ungrateful jerk. I'd saved him the trouble of having to drag Farranen's butt out of the queen's evil clutches himself, and this was the thanks I got? Ungrateful jerk, indeed.

****

Somebody loved me. Maybe it was Lady Luck, maybe a divine higher power, or maybe it was just that the dark prince knew me fairly well. The how and why didn't really matter.

There was cake waiting for me when we reached the bottom of the hill. Honest to God, *cake*.

Six fae males and one female waited for us around a table filled with food. It might have seemed strange finding the table out in the middle of nowhere, but I recognized Bart as one of the fae gathered. With him and his magical bag of goodies, I wouldn't have been surprised to find a cruise ship lying around. The other six were vaguely familiar in a way that told me I'd probably seen them in passing at the larger camp.

"The dark prince assumed you would be hungry when we found you," the remival fae told me with a smile. I smiled back, relieved that Lief hadn't written me off.

Since everyone else had already helped themselves to the buffet, I took one of the mini-cakes to fill my growling belly. There were also an assortment of fruits and meats that I didn't recognize, but I wasn't one to pass up the opportunity for cake.

The breeze picked up, rippling the long grass and filling the air with its fragrance. The absurdity of picnicking with some of the realm's deadliest soldiers in the midst of a civil war wasn't lost on me.

Farranen filled in Lief and the other fae on his imprisonment and subsequent rescue. I ignored the appreciative looks that a few of the males gave me. I hadn't done anything spectacular; as far as traps went, it had been pretty lame. And the pixies had done most of the heavy lifting—with their teeth.

"How did you know there was just one guard?" Bart asked.

I shrugged. "He was the only one I could see."

"He wasn't glamoured?"

"Yeah, but his glamour sucked so I knew where he was." I reached for some of the meat and tossed it to Dog.

"He was glamoured, but you knew where he was?" Now Bart sounded dubious.

"Theo has the ability to see through glamour," Lief interjected. "She spotted my sword almost immediately."

"I can't see *through* glamour; I can just tell when something is being hidden or covered up. The air kind of shimmers." I shrugged again, ready to be done with discussing my many abnormalities.

Thankfully, Lief returned the conversation back to the issue of the continuing rebellion. Now that the queen had essentially decided to squash them like a bug, it was time to quit lurking in the shadows and make a stand against her tyranny.

Until the attack on Lief in the tent, he'd believed the queen wasn't aware of his involvement. That probably wasn't the case anymore.

From what I could gather, the two courts usually kept separate. When someone made a move to overthrow the current monarch of a particular court, the upheaval stayed within that court. This was the first time that fae from both courts had worked together to dethrone a leader. It was also the first time that some of the light fae had professed loyalty to the Dark Court and vice versa. So basically, fae from both sides were working with Lief to prevent the imminent demise of Fairie, due to Safeena's mental instability. I secretly wondered if repairing Fairie's magic would be enough to heal the realm and restore the fae's ability to procreate or make changelings. Which would be really ironic, since the queen's obsession with both was only making the realm's magic weaker.

After a lot of debate that I mostly didn't participate in, it was decided that the gathered fae would leave to find the rest of the army that was currently searching for me. Farranen would escort Dog and me back to the gate, since we were tourists and had no idea how to get there on our own.

"I can be back by midday tomorrow." He brushed the crumbs from his hands, and I took that as a sign that it was time to go.

"No, you'll need to be at full strength before you can finish this," Lief told him. "Stay with Theo until you've regained your strength and magic. We'll handle things here until you're ready."

Farranen's face remained impassive, but I could see his jaw muscle doing that tic, tic, tic thing that meant he wasn't a happy camper. "Theo was able to restore a sufficient amount of my magic." I wasn't even fae, but I could hear the way he was skirting the truth—a "sufficient amount" wasn't the same as fully restored.

"Bullshit. Even with the magic I gave you, you're as weak as a newborn tibber." What? Everybody was thinking it; I was just the one to say it.

Lief studied the grass for a few seconds, and I suspected he was trying not to laugh. "I believe Theo has eloquently summed up everyone's thoughts. You will stay in the Earth realm until you've fully recovered. If the queen learns that she's still alive, that's the first place she'll look."

My guardian clenched his fists, and for a moment, I thought he might challenge the dark prince's authority. Although, if he was from the Light Court, would Lief actually have any sway over him?

When he finally let go of the tension in his body, I let out a relived breath that I hadn't even known I'd been holding onto. Even though he'd lost some weight and his magic wasn't up to par, I had no doubt that a fight between him and Lief would be epic. And not in a good way.

"Very well, I'll safeguard her until I've recovered." He sounded as enthusiastic as a man asked to babysit his neighbor's old incontinent dog. I tried not to take it personally.

****

Our trip back to the gate was uneventful. And I mean that in a really good way.

Nobody attempted to kill me. I didn't fall into any large bodies of water. My ankle was stiff but didn't slow us down. It was glorious.

I had never been so happy to walk into the midst of a raging blizzard before.

Dog bounded ahead of us, stopping occasionally to roll in the snow and catch snowflakes on his tongue. It was reassuring to know that some things, like Saskatchewan winters, were reliable when the rest of my life had been turned upside down.

Once we reached my dark cabin, Farranen set to work lighting a fire in the hearth while I took a tepid shower. Scalding-hot would have been my preference, but beggars couldn't be choosers.

Feeling cleaner than I had in days and dressed in my favorite white pjs with chocolate cupcakes on them, I was ready to crawl into bed and sleep for a week. I stopped short. My bed wasn't empty.

"What are you doing?" It was ridiculous how shocked I sounded, considering how many times Farranen had slept here before.

"Waiting for you," he answered. Yeah, I'd already figured that out.

"Firstly: gross. When was the last time you showered? I just washed those sheets. And secondly: no. You can take the couch." I put my hands on my hips to emphasize my firmness on the subject of co-sleeping.

"Our magic is depleted. We'll both recharge faster if we sleep together."

Dog let out a huff of amusement from where he lay across the foot of the bed. As least one of them recognized the hokey line for what it was.

"I'm only suggesting close physical contact; nothing of an intimate nature."

Well, he was wrong there, because any close physical contact with him was intimate as far as I was concerned.

I studied him with slanted eyes, trying to figure out

if this was a ploy or if he was telling the truth. I finally told him, "Shower first."

Chapter Eighteen

I was going squirrely locked up in my cabin.

For the past week, we'd been stuck inside due to a blustering snowstorm. Over forty-five inches of the white stuff had already fallen; it was thick and wet and stuck to everything it landed on. The occasional *boom* of trees succumbing to the snow's weight echoed through the woods.

Dog and I binge-watched TV until the power went out. It was only a matter of time until the snow downed one of the power lines that supplied my street, so I had plenty of candles and flashlights ready to go. I cooked our meals, as well as heated water for bathing, over the fireplace. I tried to coax Dog into shifting so I could teach him to play cards, but he stubbornly refused.

I kept an old generator in the shed out back, but so far, I'd been enjoying the novelty of living like the Ingalls family in *Little House on the Prairie*. I'd bet Laura Ingalls would have been thrilled to meet Dog.

Farranen disappeared during the day, presumably to his cabin, since he couldn't have gone very far in the whiteout. And like clockwork, he'd show up each night as I was getting ready to crawl into bed.

The lingering awkwardness between us was slowly dissipating, and I was grateful for the sense of security his presence gave me. And his body heat. The guy was like an industrial-grade furnace.

The hurt and resentment I'd been harboring was fading. The fact that he didn't try to address the previous attraction we'd felt for each other gave me enough time to try to work through some of it in my head. It also went a long way toward calming my suspicions.

On the seventh morning of our self-imposed isolation, I woke to silence.

The blustery winds outside had stopped, and I could see the outline of sunshine around my curtains.

I stretched and realized Dog wasn't draped across my feet; he must have ventured outside to investigate. Probably adding a few yellow spots to the snowy white canvas Mother Nature had just finished creating.

Sometime during the night I'd flung my arm across Farranen's chest. The muscles beneath my fingertips had softened in sleep, and I lightly traced the puckered ridges of scars that marked his time spent at the hands of his leader. He'd put on weight since we'd left Fairie, but the dips and hollows around his pecs were still more pronounced than I was used to seeing.

My eyes roamed higher, memorizing the contours of his collarbones and throat, until I found his clear green eyes staring back at me.

"Sorry," I said with a blush, embarrassed to be caught ogling him like a creeper.

He caught me by the hand when I moved to roll away. "Don't be." He laced his fingers through mine, and my magic stirred in response, stretching contently like a cat in a patch of sunlight.

"It stopped snowing," I offered lamely. God, I was making things awkward between us again, but I couldn't stop it from happening. I licked my lips nervously, and he tracked the movement like it was the most interesting thing he'd ever seen.

"My lady…" he whispered, and when he slid his other hand into my hair, I forgot how to breathe.

Forgot pretty much everything, actually. The contemplation of potential morning breath, my fear of rejection, hell, even my own name was forgotten when he looked at me with such intensity. My tummy fluttered in trepidation; I wasn't used to feeling worshipped or desired. Not this way. For my status as a possible changeling, sure; but not just for being *me*.

I couldn't say for sure who closed the distance between us; it could have been either of us, or maybe both. Or maybe it was the way his magic pulled at me, like it was physically trying to draw me in. Our lips met in a soft clash, and assigning blame ceased to matter.

His lips were gentle as he slowly explored my mouth with his, giving me time and opportunity to stop the kiss if I wanted to. I sighed and pulled him closer, loving the way his pulse jumped as I ran my hand up his chest and into his hair. Our magic had already begun its own sensual dance, moving and blending together until I couldn't tell whose was whose.

Farranen let out a small groan and deepened the kiss, chasing away the last of the reservations that had been haunting me. Each mingled breath, every impulsive touch only proved that he wanted this, that he wasn't with me out of some misguided sense of duty or obligation.

He fisted his hand in my hair, tilting my head back even farther, positioning me so he could delve even deeper. I sighed again, and my magic sighed with me.

The harsh sound of *rap, rap, rap* dragged my

attention back to the room around me.

We broke apart, and Farranen let out a harsh curse that I silently echoed. He shot me a dark look filled with heat and the guarantee that he wasn't finished with me. No, his unspoken promise said we weren't even *close* to finished.

Grabbing his sword from next to the nightstand, he silently made his way out of the bedroom and toward the back door. I followed, for no other reason than the sight of my guardian in a pair of black boxer briefs was too good to pass up. The man had an ass you could bounce a quarter off of. Heck, you could probably bounce a car off it.

The polite knock came again, and Farranen threw the door open, nearly ripping it off its hinges.

I already knew it wouldn't be someone delivering a package; people (and I use the term lightly) only used my back door when they were coming from the gate to Fairie. The chances that a random human would come stumbling out of the woods, right after a week-long blizzard, were nonexistent. And knowing my luck, if it ever did happen, it would be someone freshly escaped from a maximum-security prison, looking to take up serial killing again.

"Merry meet, guardian!" a cheery voice called.

*Oh no, I knew that voice…*I craned my neck to see past Farranen's wide shoulders. And—damn it. Two familiar fae stood in the snow that had drifted across my back porch.

I'd first met Daphorus and Elvinian of the Light Court last fall when news of my transition had reached all the eligible bachelors in Fairie. I hadn't been impressed by their salacious attempts to court me then, and time had done little to change that. It probably had something to do with the fact that they'd dropped their pants in the middle of my kitchen to show off their male goods. Uninvited nudity tended to tick me off.

"We come with news of the dark prince's rebellion—" Daph's words were cut short when Farranen grabbed him by the collar of his shirt and pulled him into my kitchen. Elvie quickly followed and shut the door behind him.

"Do *not* discuss the dark prince's business so candidly. The queen has ears everywhere." My guardian didn't have to raise his voice to get the message across to the brothers.

"My sincerest apologies, guardian. I didn't—"

"What news have you?" Farranen demanded.

Uncertainty crossed Daph's face as his gaze went from the sword held in Farranen's hand to the visible bulge that his boxers were doing little to conceal and back to the sword. "It would appear we've come at an inopportune time. Should we wait outside while you and the lady finish indulging yourselves?" He looked over to where I was waiting, and his blue eyes brightened. "Merry meet, Theodora!"

Elvie offered me a half smile and a bow from where he stood.

Deciding it would be a good time to play the gracious hostess and hopefully diffuse the tension before Farranen put his sword to use, I offered to make coffee. Thankfully, the power had come back on sometime during the night, and I coaxed another pot from my ancient percolator.

The T'Holly brothers warily took seats at my small dining room table and accepted the hot mugs while my sullen guardian disappeared into the bedroom to get dressed. Dog remained unaccounted for, but I couldn't blame him since he'd been forced to witness the brothers' lame attempts to woo me last time.

"You're looking as lovely as ever, my lady." Daph smiled, but with an edge of apprehension behind it.

I slanted my eyes and gave him a look that said one-wrong-move-buddy-and-my-friend-with-the-pointy-sword-would-be-happy-to-turn-you-into-a-pincushion. Yeah, forgiveness isn't my strong suit.

I was happy to let a strained silence take over until Farranen arrived. He'd donned his pants and shirt and tied his loose hair back into a ponytail. The sight of his bare feet was oddly endearing. A warm feeling bloomed in my chest; I liked that he felt at home in my cabin enough to forego shoes.

"Has the dark prince summoned me?" If I didn't know better, I'd say the gleam in Farranen's eyes was eagerness.

Daph shook his head. "Not exactly. Gavriel has been acting in the dark prince's stead—"

"Why? What happened to Lief?" I demanded.

Looking a little shocked by my growly tone, Elvie answered. "We were able to discern the location of one of the queen's safe houses where some of the dark prince's followers were being held. Seven from the Dark Court and two from the Light Court were rescued. The dark prince himself handled the interrogation of the four responsible."

I didn't let myself think too hard about what a prince would use for interrogation techniques against fae who doled out torture like a chubby housewife handed out candy on Halloween.

"He was able to glean the location of the Gray Knight."

Daph leaned forward in his chair and took over where his brother had left off. "The next morning, he told Gavriel that he had a personal score to settle with Augustus and left him in charge. That was two days ago; he hasn't been heard from since."

Oh, crap. I hoped Lief's personal score didn't have anything to do with Gus killing me.

"You let the dark prince embark on a journey for vengeance unaccompanied?" My guardian had been deceptively quiet until then, but his barely leashed fury coiled tighter with every word. "He is your *leader*. He is the best chance of survival that Fairie has until the queen can be unseated from her throne."

"He said it was personal and that he'd be back within a day," Elvie insisted.

"Can we play the blame game later? Right now, Lief needs our help." I gave all three males a withering glance.

"Theodora is correct. The dark prince's magic is the only thing sustaining Fairie right now." Farranen stood and strode into my bedroom. A few seconds later, he returned with his boots and cloak firmly back in place like armor. "It is well past time for me to fulfill my role in the dark prince's script."

Alarm bloomed in my chest, hot and suffocating. "What role?" I demanded.

Farranen glanced at the two fae still nursing their coffees at my dining room table. "Wait for me at the gate."

Looking somewhat put out, the T'Holly brothers offered me polite smiles and a quick goodbye with identical words of "Merry meet, my dear!"

I stood up and followed them to the door, making sure they were really plodding their way back through the field of snow behind my house and not eavesdropping on the porch. Once I was satisfied, I rounded on my guardian. "How come you didn't warn me it was them at the door? You had to have felt them come through the gate." As the guardian, Farranen had a connection with the gate that let him know whenever someone crossed though.

"I can no more differentiate between an ally of the dark prince, than those working for the queen. I had to leave the gate open for when word arrived that it was time for me to serve my purpose."

"What purpose? What role in Lief's 'script'? Why are you being so damn mysterious?"

The muscles in his face tightened, clashing with the weariness in his eyes. "Theodora, the dark prince and I have long contemplated what ailment has befallen Fairie. Now that we've discovered the depths of Safeena's deterioration, we need to act. *Before* the damage is permanent."

"Is it the same thing that made Lebolus crazy?"

"Yes, psychogenic atrophy affects us all differently, and I suspect the queen is aware and uses her power to conceal it." He stepped closer, until our toes were touching, but I refused to budge an inch. "I must go."

"You haven't completely recovered yet," I argued.

"The dark prince's life is in jeopardy." Damn him, using the one thing that he knew would get me to move.

"What if Gus already killed him?" The words were like ashes in my mouth. "You'll be putting yourself in danger for nothing."

"Fairie would have already collapsed."

His hands slid around my waist, effectively shutting down any further arguments on my part. When he lowered his face to mine, I pulled away.

"No. Don't turn this into a goodbye. If you think there's any chance of *this*—" I gestured between the two of us. "—working out, you need to come back alive." I planted my hands on my hips and waited for the familiar magic of a sealed deal to snap into place.

But instead of telling me he'd return in one piece, he shook his head sadly. "I can't promise that."

My heart sank down into my toes, and I understood why he'd been so vague about what he was planning to do. He didn't think he'd survive whatever scheme he'd been planning with Lief.

"*No,*" I whispered.

Remorse brightened his eyes, and I didn't protest when he wrapped me in a hug.

Chapter Nineteen

This is bullshit. A big steaming pile of smelly bullshit.

There had to be another way, but it was damn hard to figure out what it was since Farranen had left without sharing any details of the top-secret plan that was sure to get him killed.

My fury at being left in a position where I was helpless to protect the people I cared about was interrupted by a knock on the door. Before I could put down the bowl of cake batter I was holding, Celesta let herself in. Jeez, my backdoor got more traffic than a shopping mall Santa.

"Theo." She nodded a brief greeting.

"They left an hour ago," I told her testily. I was still feeling prickly toward the beautiful redhead; I didn't like that she'd strong-armed me into trying to rescue Farranen, when Lief and his army would have been better qualified. My resulting death only served to increase the ire I was feeling.

"Who left?" she inquired in a tone that made me think her surprise was genuine.

"Farranen and the T'Holly brothers." Now it was my turn to sound confused. If she wasn't looking for the males, then why was she here?

Her eyebrows slanted thoughtfully. "The guardian was here."

Well, shit. I'd forgotten that news of Farranen's escape was supposed to be kept hush-hush.

"You were the one to rescue him."

It wasn't a question, but I nodded anyway.

"Does the dark prince know you're here? It was presumed that you died in the river."

I shrugged. I'd totally forgotten that nobody, aside from Lief and a handful of his soldiers in Fairie, knew I was alive. Gah, I was the worst secret-keeper ever.

"I'm not sure who knows." My non-lie would have made any fae proud. I stirred the batter again, knowing it was overmixed but needing to keep my guilty face averted from Celesta. I was a little surprised that she hadn't talked to Lief since he'd found me. Unless she had, and he just hadn't told her that Farranen and I were holed up at my cabin. Something about the whole situation was niggling at the back of my brain. Why wouldn't Lief tell her something so important? Unless—

A small whisper of sound caught my attention. It was the familiar slide of a well-oiled sword being drawn in one smooth motion. I whirled around and found the tip of Celesta's blade pointed at my throat. It looked equally as sharp and cruel as the smile that slid across her face.

"Lief was furious with you," I said, sounding a little stunned as I realized what had been bothering me earlier. When I'd told Lief about Celesta's plan for me to rescue Farranen, he'd been livid at the absurdity of it. It was sheer stupidity for Celesta to think one lone hermit and an ankou fae could possibly stand a chance in hell of pulling it off. Which was evidenced by my resulting death.

"I was never supposed to save Farranen. You set me up." My magic stirred angrily, swirling beneath my skin like liquid coals.

"You're not as stupid as they said you were." Her words were mocking, but I could see the calculation in her eyes. She pulled out a set of handcuffs with her free hand, and I recognized them to be identical to the ones Farranen used. With a muttered word that I couldn't understand, they clicked open. She tossed them to me, and I fumbled before catching them awkwardly.

"Put them on," she instructed.

I opened my mouth to tell her iron didn't work on humans, but I quickly realized that could be to my benefit. The cuffs were cold and slightly too big. When I snapped them shut, they shrank to accommodate my wrists and a small buzz of magic pulsed through them. The small symbols etched on the sides of them were pretty but unfamiliar.

"So, now what?" I asked in a bored tone. The bitch obviously wasn't going to kill me if she was handcuffing me. I doubted that I'd be impressed with whatever diabolical plan she had in mind; Gus had pretty much set the bar by disembowelling me. Anything she came up with would be peanuts in comparison.

If she was surprised by my lackluster response, she didn't let on. "I will escort you to Fairie for an audience with the queen."

The possibility of seeing the queen chased away most of my bravado. She was terrifying on a level that I hadn't experienced personally—yet. But I'd seen what had been done to my guardian, and the thought of having to endure something so painful, so barbaric, made my hands shake.

****

It usually took ten minutes to walk to the gate; Celesta and I took thirty-five due to the massive drifts of thick snow.

I had no idea where Dog was, and the only footprints I saw once we left my yard were forged by the three fae males that had already left for the gate. I struggled to stay in their tracks, but they obviously had some additional height working in their favor. After I tripped for the hundredth time, Celesta let out a frustrated groan. "You're tripping on purpose," she accused.

"Why would I do that?" I asked incredulously. She hadn't even given me time to put on gloves, did she really think I was enjoying the frostbite on my fingers?

"To piss me off," she growled.

Well, in that case…I fell twice as often until we finally reached the clearing with the hawthorn tree.

Just as she was about to shove me through the gate, I yelled, "Harvey! Vanessa! Dog—"

My call for help was cut off as I tumbled face first through the bright layer of magic that separated the two realms.

I landed on my hands and knees in the grass of Fairie. My wrists were still bound, so I flicked my head back to flip my hair out of my face. I caught sight of a pair of shiny black boots standing next to a pair of strappy white sandals. My face split into a grin when I recognized the small glittery flower-shaped toe-ring on one of the dainty feet.

"What the *fuck*, Theo?" Vanessa demanded.

Harvey turned to her in surprise, and I realized

with no small amount of relief that he could see her. This would have been so much harder if I'd had to play translator between the two ghosts.

Celesta grabbed me by the back of my sweatshirt and hauled me to my feet. Not wanting to let her know that I had brought along some friends, I kept my mouth shut but winked at the ghosts. It was a little odd; I'd never winked at anyone before. Judging by Vanessa's eye roll, I probably wasn't very good at it. Maybe I should have just held up a finger to my lips to let them know I couldn't talk right now.

Since my last visit to Fairie, the leaves had all fallen from the trees and the wind had piled them up in big drifts along the path that led to the castle. The bare tree branches above held none of the beauty or life I was accustomed to seeing; they'd become restless and spooky. The grass underfoot crunched unhappily as it neared the end of its own lifespan.

When we passed through the stone archway that was marked with fae symbols, I didn't feel the subtle hint of magic pulsing across my skin. The two guards were missing from their positions on either side of the arch, so we continued until the path widened out enough to walk side by side.

The air was cool and held the slight tang of decay instead of the usual floral aroma that reminded me of expensive air freshener. Something was definitely wrong with Fairie. The magic pulsing through the realm was subdued and far weaker than it had been before. It felt tainted and prickly and maybe even a bit hostile.

"Fairie is dying." I hadn't meant to say it out loud, but now that I had, the truth of the words rang through the air around us.

Celesta, who'd been doing her best to studiously ignore me up until that point, turned and angrily wagged a finger in my direction. "This is a direct result of the dark bastard's unwanted involvement in the Light Court's affairs!"

I bristled at the way she'd referred to Lief. If I'd had any doubts about her double-crossing him, they were now fully laid to rest. The beautiful redhead was the very definition of a two-faced backstabbing bitch.

"Lief is trying to save Fairie; it's the nutcase queen who's killing it!" Not my smartest move, arguing with someone who was trained to wield a sword with deadly precision.

"Shut your pathetic human mouth! You couldn't possibly understand what's going on here." The look she gave me was rife with contempt and anger; that kind of resentment usually stemmed from jealousy.

"Are you *jealous?*" I asked in disbelief. Her green eyes narrowed; I'd hit a nerve. "Of what?"

"Our magic has dwindled for years, and now, when it finally returns, it's wasted on someone who isn't even fae!" She threw the accusation at me with all the conviction of a true believer. Nothing I could say would matter so I kept my mouth shut.

"You're unworthy of our magic!" she continued, and I wondered how long she'd been keeping the crazy bottled up. "Grave reaping should *only* belong to the ankou! Not some miserable human! To commune with the dead is sacred—"

"Fine, I get it; I'm not worthy, blah, blah, blah…" I turned my back on her and continued down the path toward the castle. I'd had enough of her lecturing me. I hadn't been given a choice when Lebolus had infected me with his magic, and I wasn't going to apologize for it.

Vanessa let out a whoop of support, and both ghosts fell into line behind Celesta and me.

With my hands shackled and my head held high, I marched toward whatever new hell was waiting for me.

****

The sky had dimmed to an ugly gray, like something was slowly leeching the color from it.

The same could be said for the gothic castle built from large blocks of slate. Its normal pale gray looked washed out, like an overexposed black and white photograph. The four, square corner towers, tall narrow windows, and flying buttresses left me feeling dizzy as I craned my neck to take them all in. Four of the six floors held large balconies of different heights and lengths.

Two large wooden doors swung inward, each four stories tall and as wide as my cabin. Beyond them, two guards stood, wearing matching gray shirts with polished gold buttons and shiny black boots that came nearly to the knee.

With a firm hand on my elbow, Celesta nodded to the males as she strode past. I briefly entertained the idea of pleading with them for help, but then I caught the satisfied approval rolling off them at the sight of my handcuffs. No, as far as these guys were concerned, I was exactly where I deserved to be.

The halls were empty of life; the only sound was the echoing slap of my wet sneakers on the tile floors as I toiled to keep up to Celesta's brisk pace.

Somewhere along the way, Harvey and Vanessa had disappeared. I hoped they were just conserving their energy for when I might need them.

She led us deeper and deeper into the castle, allowing enough time for dread to build in my tummy. Once we'd past the third massive staircase, I knew where we were headed: the queen's private chambers. I'd been there once before, when I'd first come to her attention and she decided I would make a good breeding mare for her court. There had been enough magic in me that when she'd issued a royal command to Farranen and I, we'd been compelled to obey. Actually—I stumbled when it hit me that wasn't entirely true.

Farranen had been forced to comply, but I hadn't felt any need to heed her words. Yes, I'd wanted to sleep with him, but that desire was all mine, not something I was coerced into. The attraction I'd felt for him had begun long before the queen's tainted magic had attempted to force us together.

I smiled to myself, knowing that the queen couldn't take away my free will as easily as I'd feared. That didn't mean she couldn't chain me up and whip me, but at least I didn't have to worry about being forced to dance like a chicken or eat dog poop or something equally heinous.

When we arrived at the blank wall, I wiped the grin from my face and did my best stoic-guardian impression. Celesta uttered a word I couldn't understand, and the stones on the wall swirled and spun, blurring into a weird hypnotic oval that looked like a mirror made from mercury.

She pulled a small dagger from her belt and drew blood from her index finger. The crimson drop ran down her finger and slowly pooled in her cupped palm.

Then, like she was making an offering, she slowly reached out and slid her hand into the swirling light.

Magic flared around us, probing and searching until it was satisfied, and the portal on the wall grew to the size of a door and hardened. Celesta stepped through the frosted glass, dragging me with her.

****

The last time I'd been in the queen's private chambers, she'd been alone. This time, I knew she had company by the harsh, rhythmic slapping and gasping cries that filled the air.

My face heated with embarrassment as I realized the queen and her guest were engaged in some very physical activities. Very enjoyable, very intimate activities. Oh God, I'd walked in on the queen having sex.

Safeena was bent over the side of the massive four-poster bed, with her fists clutching the sheets. Her long blonde hair obscured her face, and the sage-green ends brushed across the purple bedding as she rocked back and forth. Behind her, a large male thrust himself into her with single-minded determination. He was tall and well-muscled, and his chest heaved with exertion. They both gleamed with a layer of sweat that attested to the fact that they'd been going at it for a while.

The profile of their joined bodies was going to be burned into my brain for the rest of my life. And, I was ashamed to say, it turned me on. The way his muscles coiled as he drove himself into her was erotic in a way I'd never experienced firsthand.

Celesta forced me down to my knees and then knelt on one knee beside me. When it became apparent that she wasn't going to say anything, I fumbled to think about something else, *anything* else, but all I could hear was the sound of hips slapping against the queen's ass and then, *finally*, her cries reached a crescendo and tapered off. I looked up just in time to see him step away from the bed with the evidence of his enjoyment still firmly jutting out.

Blushing even harder, I looked away from his arousal to his face.

Oh, shit. I recognized those dark eyes and hard jaw. The last time I'd seen them, they'd leered down at me while a dagger was buried in my belly.

I growled in the back of my throat and scowled at Gus. Recognition dawned on his face, followed quickly by confusion. I would have laughed if I wasn't so busy wanting to kill him.

I opened my mouth to say something snarky, but Gus turned back to where the queen was lounging on the rumpled sheets and announced, "Your Highness, can it be? I see a mating mark!" He ran his hand reverently down her back, with a look of awe on his face.

I glanced at Celesta in confusion, but she kept her face arranged indifferently. My gaze scanned the windowless room, skipping from the fancy dressing table in front of us, to the mantle of knickknacks above the fireplace, and finally back to the bookshelf and wardrobe along the far wall, but I didn't see anything that would explain what the hell was going on.

The queen rolled over and rose to her feet, seemingly unaware of her nudity. After peering over both her shoulders unsuccessfully, she told Celesta imperiously, "Rise."

I followed suit when the redhead stood, not sure if

I'd been included in the command, but my knees were aching from kneeling on the stone floor.

The queen spun, putting her back to us. She gracefully pulled the curtain of hair over her shoulder to expose the perfect curve of her pale shoulders. Celesta gasped and brought a shaking hand to her lips. "*A mating mark.*"

I looked back to where the queen's lithe body was on full display, but all I saw was the same porcelain skin that dipped in at her waist, before flaring out to cover the slight curve of her hips. My eyes refused to go any farther south.

"It's beautiful," Celesta whispered.

I squinted and tilted my head to the side. Something shimmered between the queen's shoulder blades. "What is that?" I asked.

"A mating mark." Celesta spoke with a devoutness that was usually reserved for holy objects and miracles.

I looked at the glimmering patch of skin again. It was half the size of my palm, and something about it was familiar.

Celesta dropped to one knee and tilted her head to where Gus was pulling on a pair of pants that had been tossed across one of the two highbacked chairs next to the fireplace. And thank God for that.

"My king," she breathed, holding her right hand over her heart.

With a smug look, he told her, "Rise." He continued, in a voice that was condescending and grated along my nerves, with, "Your timing was fortunate; as you were here to bear witness to our coupling."

Celesta nodded enthusiastically. "It was my honor,

my king."

"Go forth, and tell every fae in my court that our copulation has resulted in a union. The queen wears my mark, and I am now her equal. I shall only be referred to as the light king, ruler of the Light Court." He finished his pretty little speech off with a dismissive wave, and Celesta bowed before disappearing through the portal.

"And you..." Gus turned his sights to me, and I fought the urge to squirm. I'd really been hoping that he'd forgotten about me. "What are you doing here?"

I glanced over to where the queen was preening in front of a large mirror that was resting between the wardrobe and hearth. She angled her body to see her back in its reflection. It didn't look like she'd be much help if Gus decided to get stabby again.

I held up my hands and shook the iron chains. "I didn't exactly have a choice." Skinny-dipping in an active volcano would have been preferable to standing in the queen's private chambers, surrounded by the lingering musk of their furious lovemaking.

"I killed you," he stated flatly.

"You tried to," I corrected him, just as flatly.

His brown eyes raked over me, speculative and slippery like rotten cooking oil. "What the fuck *are* you?" he mused quietly.

The queen sashayed over to us, still naked. She draped an arm around Gus's neck and pulled him down into a lengthy French kiss that would've scandalized a stripper. When they finally pulled apart, she purred, "My *king*..."

He gave a throaty laugh and growled, "My queen..." before grabbing one of her perky breasts in his large hand and squeezing it gently.

Okay, barf. Their royal foreplay was something I could have lived without seeing.

He caught my eye and gave me a leer that said he delighted in my discomfort, while continuing to roll the queen's dark nipple between his fingers. I glared back at him, refusing to acknowledge his challenge, even when Safeena arched her back and moaned.

"I must go, my love," Gus murmured against her hair. "I need to address our court and inform them of this wonderful development. With me as their king, Fairie's magic is guaranteed to return."

The queen made a sound of protest, and he stopped her words with a searing kiss. "I will return soon. Once the magic is restored, you'll be the first to take my seed and repopulate our realm back to its former glory."

Good lord, what was the fae's obsession with making babies?

"While I'm gone, why don't you prepare this one to join us? I'm already feeling…proliferous." His eyes roamed greedily over my body, and I suppressed a shudder. I wasn't going to give the jerk the satisfaction of a response.

With one last kiss, the queen peeled herself off his chest and sashayed across the room toward the wardrobe.

Gus dropped the adoring lover face he'd been wearing, to reveal an angry glower. I struggled not to back up when he stalked closer. "The last time I saw you, you were lying in a pool of your own innards, *dead*. But since you somehow found a way around that, I need to take a trip to the Fallow Woods to make sure the guardian is just as I left him—with scavengers feasting on his flayed skin until there's nothing left but a pile of bones and one less traitor to follow the dark prince."

I did my best to keep the haughty look on my face; I didn't want him to see my surprise at finding out he didn't know Farranen had been rescued.

"Then, once I've had some fun with my new 'mate,' I'm going to cut you open and see just how that magic of yours works." He laughed at whatever expression he saw on my face. "If you're lucky, I'll wait until the dark prince is here to watch me carve you up."

I clenched my fists and wished I'd had the foresight to stash a weapon in my pocket before I'd been dragged here. What I really wanted was to tell him all the ways Farranen and Lief were going to kick his ass once they found him. But losing the element of surprise wasn't worth the petty satisfaction I'd get from telling him off. So, I bit my lip and tried to look properly cowed, which wasn't very hard, since nobody knew I was here and I doubted anyone would arrive in time to stop him from cutting me up.

With a patronizing chuckle, Gus turned his back on me and sauntered to the dresser, essentially declaring that I was of no importance or threat to him. I couldn't exactly disagree, since I was still magically handcuffed and weaponless.

"The one thing I can't figure out"—he glanced back at me while pulling on a pair of dark gray gloves, which looked bizarre with his lack of a shirt—"is how the contentious dark prince is involved."

The contentious dark prince? Seriously, had he even *met* Lief?

"The guardian's obsession I understand—spending so much time in the Earth realm has obviously spurred his interest in your weaker race—but the dark prince—" His dark eyes narrowed accusingly, like he thought I'd somehow bewitched Lief into being my friend. "It's no matter. His misguided affection will only make him easier to manipulate."

Manipulate Lief? *Ha!* Gus's spectacular misconception was about ten kinds of insane. Apparently, he'd been drinking from the same fountain of crazy as the queen.

I opened my mouth to tell him so, but the words stuck in my throat when the flames in the hearth reflected off the metal object he'd just picked up. *Was that...* No, the fae couldn't handle iron, aside from the enchanted handcuffs and chains that were etched with mysterious fae symbols.

He pulled the top drawer open and tossed in the object in question before I could get a better look. Then, with one last sneer, he pulled off his gloves and tucked them into his back pocket before ambling through the portal, leaving me shaking in the center of the room.

Chapter Twenty

I truly had had no concept of how deep the queen's depravity went until she strove to dress me in something she considered "appropriate for the king's bed."

"That will never fit," I told her with absolute certainty.

She held up another piece of lacey green fabric that I had to assume was a pair of panties. Although, I didn't know how something so small was supposed to cover anyone's backside. I snorted, and she threw them back in the drawer.

"Choose something to wear or be naked; I care not." She waved a hand dismissively before wrapping a silky emerald-green robe around herself. I don't know why she bothered; it was mostly sheer lace and didn't provide any amount of coverage as she took a seat at her dressing table to brush her hair.

"I am wearing something," I protested, while gesturing to my black yoga pants and yellow sweatshirt. After Gus had left, the queen had removed the iron handcuffs with a wave of her hand so I could change. I was starting to think keeping the cuffs on would have been worth it if it meant I could keep my own clothes on.

"You'll get blood on them." She shrugged a delicate shoulder. "Augustus likes to play before we fuck." She met my eyes in the mirror, and I recoiled. The batshit-crazy vibe was still there, more noticeable than when I'd had my first audience with her, but that wasn't what scared me the most. It was the lust that I could see as she watched me. "So do I," she murmured with a smile.

It took me a few seconds to comprehend that she was talking about foreplay that involved bodily harm. With me.

I took an involuntary step back. Maybe I was reading the situation wrong. My brain struggled to recall what Gus had said...*Why don't you prepare this one to join us? I'm already feeling...proliferous.* Well, shit. Why the hell didn't I know what proliferous meant? Stupid fae, always using big words. Damn it, I was a writer and should be better at reading between the lines. Had I seriously thought he was talking about me joining him and the queen for a tea party? Not fucking likely.

I glanced over at the massive bed, and sure enough, I could see blood on the mauve-colored sheets. The crimson spots looked like they had been splattered rather than pooling into one big puddle.

While I'd been silently freaking out, the queen had risen from her stool. She glided across the floor toward me, with anticipation written across her beautiful oval face. The green robe slid from her shoulders, caressing her skin as it slowly fell to the floor at her feet.

"I'd forgotten about you, Theodora Edwards," she murmured. "But now I remember the wild taste of your magic. I've never felt the hum of fae magic in a human shell before. I wonder if it's gotten any sweeter with time?"

Oh, *hell* no! She wasn't getting anywhere near me or my magic. I needed something to distract her. "So, uh—a mating mark, huh? That's new!"

I furiously racked my brain for what Lief had said about the marks. Something about them being rare and only happening when the bond had been consummated with sex.

Thankfully, the queen's eyes lit up with pride, and I knew I'd said the right thing. "It was only a matter of time; the mark is bestowed on the strongest of us."

That didn't sound right; Celesta, the traitorous bitch, had said that Lief had a vision of me dying in Fairie before I could reach the male that would mark me. I'd pretty much dismissed the notion, since my dating life was nonexistent and sex was a necessary prequel to the mark. And I certainly wasn't among the strongest of the fae; I wasn't actually fae at all.

I needed to buy myself some time so I could find a way out of the queen's private torture chamber. As much as I didn't want to, I figured I could go along with her let's-dress-Theo-like-a-slut-and-then-disfigure-her plan until I came up with one of my own. "Actually, it's getting kind of hot in here. Maybe I'll just try some of that lingerie now." And I hadn't forgotten what I'd seen Gus toss in the dresser.

With trembling hands, I opened the drawer and pawed through the pile of naughty scraps of fabric. I wasn't sure if they were the queen's personal intimates, or extras for her consorts; honestly, it was easier not to know. The fabric was silky and cool to the touch, so I noticed immediately when my fingers brushed against something that was hard and heavy. Before I could contemplate the possibility of it being a really uncomfortable sex toy, I pulled the object free, and my mouth fell open.

I needed to change the subject—*fast*. I dropped it back in the drawer with all the pretty unmentionables and smiled brightly. "Can I see your mating mark? I've never seen one up close before."

Predictably, the queen leisurely turned to bare her naked back to me. "Describe it to me, every detail. Tell me of the beauty that my virile mate has branded into my flesh."

I squinted at the shimmery patch of pale skin. "It looks a lot like the way they scramble a person's image on TV to protect his identity for news shows." Yeah, that described it pretty well. It was like looking at a bright light through a kaleidoscope.

She shot me a withering look over her shoulder. "That reference makes no sense. Tell me of the colors and the images that are entwined."

I looked at the spot again, not sure what I was supposed to say. I could make up something that she wanted to hear, but she was a fae and would recognize the lie for what it was. "There's no color, and it just kind of glows...like...glamour?" I snapped my fingers as I realized where I'd seen it before. "It's glamour!"

The queen rounded on me with murder in her eyes. "*Liar!* You seek to taint the bond between my lover and I with your blasphemy!"

I really, *really* needed to learn to keep my stupid mouth shut. Before I could come up with an excuse that wouldn't set off her built-in lie detector, she flew at me. I stumbled back into the dresser, and she wrapped a tiny hand around my throat. My scream was cut off when she squeezed and lifted me into the air.

"You know *nothing!* The mating mark is *sacred* to my people; a mere human could never understand."

I recognized the look in her eye as that of a fanatic. Nothing I said or did was going to change her mind. It didn't matter that the mark was phony. Right then, the only thing that mattered was not dying.

She carried me across the room and threw me on the bed like I weighed no more than a toddler. I sucked in air as fast as I could while scrambling backward across the dried blood splatter. The purple silk flowed and bunched beneath me like I was on a giant slip 'n' slide and I tried not to think about what other bodily fluids I was crawling through.

"My poor mate will be so disappointed when he finds out we started without him." She prowled over to the nightstand and retrieved a large blade that was already stained with someone else's blood.

Please not in the stomach, I thought. I'd already been stabbed in the belly twice, so I knew just how excruciating it would be if she decided to go for my middle.

I'd just about made it to the other side of the bed in case I might stand a chance with the massive wooden bed frame between us. That's when I discovered the body lying on the floor, previously hidden from view on the far side of the bed. I froze. Even in death I'd know that pale blue skin and shocking blue hair. "*Harvey?*" I whispered. There were dozens of slashes across his body, and I could tell by the way his arms were lodged behind his back that his hands were probably tied together. My disgust rose, resentful and sharp, as I took in the careless way he'd been dumped on the floor like a sack of garbage. Like he'd been an expendable toy for the queen and Gus to use and then discard.

She didn't immediately put the knife to use; instead, she knelt at my feet and grabbed my ankle so I couldn't get away. Glancing at the blade lovingly, she smiled and told me, "Don't worry, we'll get to that part soon enough. But first, we're going to play with that stolen magic of yours."

I didn't get a chance to respond, because her magic shot up my leg and wound around my body. I couldn't help but inhale raggedly as it continued to smother me. My own magic retreated, coiling up into the deepest part of me like it was hiding. I couldn't blame it; I wanted to curl up and hide too.

When I'd first met the queen, her magic had been like a warm current flowing through me, ethereal and bright. Now it was a tidal wave, ravaging everything in its path as it sought to root out the magic that had become a part of me.

I screamed, a long desperate sound that made her smile grow wider.

Her magic snaked through me, violating places inside me that I hadn't even known existed, as it continued seeking. It was vile and rotten and couldn't have always been this way. Something so twisted could never have supported and nurtured the beauty of Fairie.

Someone called my name, and I turned my head to where Harvey was kneeling on the bed next to me. "Theo! Use your magic!" His indigo eyes were desperate and behind him Vanessa screamed profanities at the queen. I hoped he hadn't seen the body—*his* body—on the floor.

I didn't want to unleash my magic; I didn't want it

getting anywhere near the queen's contaminated power.

Her beautiful lips twisted into a hideous sneer, and she crawled up my body until she was straddling my thighs.

"She'll kill you, Theo! *Use your magic!*" Harvey sounded frantic, and I looked back at the queen just in time to see her bring the knife down toward my breast. I grabbed her wrist as the knife lowered and sliced a neat path through the fabric of my sweatshirt. The skin above my breast stung, letting me know the blade had drawn blood. The bright burn of pain was quickly drowned out as her magic brushed up against mine.

My magic reacted like a living thing. A pissed-off, snarling, rabid thing that had been violated. Energy exploded down my limbs, tightening my lungs, and I convulsed against the sheets. The queen gripped me between her thighs like a championship bull rider, refusing to be bucked off.

"There it is!" she cackled. I caught the look of ecstasy on her face before her head fell back and she groaned, "*Oh...my...*" Her nipples pebbled beneath my gaze, and my brain recoiled at the thought that she was enjoying this. Her hands were limp at her sides, the knife lost amongst the loose bedding. The feel of her magic shifting against mine was like having a centipede with pedophile tendencies crawl across my skin. I shuddered and squirmed to shove her off. Her hands were small but strong as she caught my wrists and pinned them to the bed above my head.

I struggled and twisted my body, but my useless efforts to dislodge her only ramped up her excitement. I could feel the aroused interest in her magic as it prickled inside my skin. My magic was already fading since I hadn't truly had a chance to replenish it after I'd drained it to rescue Farranen. I had to do something soon or I'd end up like Harvey—a mutilated corpse discarded on the cold floor.

"Use your magic, Theo!" Harvey placed a cold hand on my cheek and gave me a pleading look.

Until then, I'd been trying so hard to keep my thoughts away from how I'd killed the graveel fae by stealing his magic. I didn't want to be a murderer.

But I also didn't want to die.

Something in my face must have alerted Harvey to what I was about to do, because he backed up with a small smile.

I stopped trying to escape the touch of the queen's magic and latched onto it like it was my new best friend. I gave an experimental tug, half expecting her magic to put up some sort of a fight, but it came eagerly, flowing through my body like thick wine. I opened myself to it, beckoning it to fill me. The feeling was heady, and my body became too full, like it was about to burst from the sudden flood of magic. I started to tremble, and then shake.

"Stop…" The queen's voice sounded far away, like she was talking to me from the other end of a tunnel. "Stop it…"

But it was Harvey's voice that finally got through to me. "You're taking too much, Theo! You're going to burn out!"

I stared up at him blearily. Lief had said something about a burnout once before, but I couldn't remember what. Oh, wait—it had been when I'd lost control of my magic and accidentally brought Harvey through the veil. But then I'd had a ghost to pour all of my magic into. What was I supposed to do with it now?

All my worrying was for nothing, because as the queen's magic continued to fill me, my body suddenly reached the point where it couldn't physically hold any more. It exploded out of me like a bomb going off. A wave of light blasted the queen away from me and threw her into the wall beside the bed.

Books flew off the shelves, and all the tiny little bottles of perfectly arranged lotions and powders were swept off the dressing table. The wardrobe, dresser, and high-backed chairs were shoved several feet farther from where I lay on the bed panting.

My entire body was quaking as I slowly sat up and took in the damage I'd caused. It looked like two tornados had gotten into a fight in the large room. The fire in the hearth had gone out. One of the doors on the wardrobe had come open, and several fancy dresses were scattered across the floor.

I'm not sure how long I sat there surveying the destruction in disbelief until the queen groaned and sat up. I was on my feet in a heartbeat, with my eyes frantically darting around the room for a way out. But all I could see was the panel that looked like frosted glass. I wasn't sure if it would work for a human with fae magic, or if it was selective about who it let through. The last thing I wanted was to run through it and find myself in the middle of another realm, or worse, in the middle of a group of fae having an orgy. The mystical doorway could literally lead to *anywhere*.

The queen let out a mirthless laugh as she pushed herself off the floor. Her eyes darkened to a deep plum, and it felt like all the air had been sucked from the room.

"How did you do that?" she demanded. "Pulling magic is forbidden."

I shrugged, since I really had no idea how I'd done it.

"You're going to regret that." She took a faltering step toward me, letting me know that whatever I'd done had weakened her. And she was right about me regretting it—I already regretted every damn minute that I'd been forced into this cursed realm.

The lines of her delicate face had transformed from a playful predator to a fully pissed-off homicidal maniac. When she took another angry step in my direction, I decided to hell with it, the mystery portal was better than hanging around here and waiting for the crazy-pants queen to tear my throat out.

I launched myself the rest of the way across the room, toward the portal. A shocked yelp of surprise escaped me when I bounced off the magical doorway as if I'd hit a solid wall and landed on my backside on the floor.

The queen's laugh reached my ears as I dragged myself to my feet. "Foolish girl. Only the rulers of Fairie can control the portals." It would have been nice if someone had bothered to share that little tidbit of information before I'd nearly broken my nose.

I frantically glanced around the room, but there was only one other door and it led to a lavish bathroom. Damn it, if there was another way out of here, I wasn't seeing it.

My eyes flitted across the mess of spilled clothing and make-up, but there was nothing I could use as a weapon lying among the discarded fabrics and powders. If only I'd thought to replace my hunting knife, or even the little pocketknife that I'd previously taken for granted.

The queen prowled closer, but the luminescent glow that had always radiated from beneath her skin was dimmed. I doubted I'd get a second chance to rip any more of her magic from her, not that I'd ever try that particular trick again. My magic still felt fidgety beneath my skin, churning like it wanted to break free. The bit that I'd used to throw her across the room had taken the edge off, but I was still bloated with it. I was too scared to try throwing her around again. Honestly, I hadn't been the one in control last time—I hadn't used the magic; the magic had used me. I had no reason to think it would be any different a second time.

My hand-to-hand combat skills were just as lacking as my magical abilities, and I'd get my ass handed to me unless I found something to use as a weapon. I doubted the queen kept a loaded shotgun tucked between her mattress and headboard like I did at home—

I sucked in a ragged breath, remembering what I'd seen Gus discard in the dresser drawer. I didn't waste time trying to be stealthy or conceal my intents, I just lunged toward the dresser like a Black Friday shopper who'd finally found the sound system of her dreams.

Behind me, the queen continued to taunt with promises of violence and suffering. I didn't risk a backward glance as I pawed through her panties and assorted intimates. With a triumphant *ha!*, I yanked the cold hard lump of sleek metal out and pointed it at her. She stopped, less than ten feet away and tilted her head to the side curiously.

"Open the portal."

"Why would I do that? I'm just starting to have fun." She smiled.

I hid my cringe. "This is a gun. Let me go, or I'll shoot you with it." I had no idea if it was even loaded, but it had enough iron in it that she couldn't handle it. I'd beat her with the damn thing if I had to.

"No." Her smile grew, morphing into something wicked. Maybe she didn't know what kind of damage a gun could do.

I recognized the challenge for what it was and bared my own teeth.

"If I shoot you, you'll die." Even her immortality wouldn't be able to save her from a shot at close range from such a freakin' huge gun. It was modern, made out of dark-gray metal and almost too big for my hand to hold onto. My gaze went back to where the queen was waiting, and she acknowledged my fierce look with a laugh.

"Augustus has already demonstrated its useful qualities for me."

"But I thought the fae couldn't use iron," I stupidly noted.

"We can't. My lover had a special pair of gloves made so that he might wield it in the human realm in his quest to acquire females for breeding." What the *hell?* Was this the smoking gun from the raid on Marissa's brood?

She slanted her eyes at me in a way that chased some of the insanity from them. "How can you handle the iron with such ease?" Damn, the bitch was observant.

I ignored her question and opened my mouth to tell her that she was an atrocious ruler, that her world was dying because of her selfishness, and that she deserved to be stuck with Gus if she was stupid enough to fall for his pathetic attempts to trick her using glamour, but instead I said, "I get it."

She cocked her head, and I continued, "You want a baby, but you can't have one. I get it." Uncertainty swirled through her eyes, dimming some of the hostility. "I can't get pregnant either." I'm not sure why I said those last few words, but it seemed like the right thing to do. Farranen had already told her about my infertility, so there was no point in trying to hide it.

"My king will sow his seed, and I will be the first to bear the fruits of his labour." The queen ran a hand over her flat belly. "And I will nourish our child with the blood and magic you stole from this realm." Well, she was right about the magic part, since some of the magic buzzing within me had been stolen, but the blood was all mine. If we were going to start keeping score, Fairie should actually owe me some blood for all that I'd spilt at the hands of the fae.

Before I could correct her misconceptions, she launched herself at me, going straight for my throat with her hands. I threw up my arms and squirmed backward until my back hit the wall. All semblance of sanity had disappeared from her face, wiped away by my words. Apparently, reminding her of her infertility had only served to enrage her, rather than endearing her to me. My bad.

I pressed the gun flat against her collarbone, and she made a hissing sound that let me know the sensation of cold iron against her naked skin wasn't pleasant. When she drove her elbow down on my wrist, my scream was lost in the sound of the gun going off.

The deep *boom* echoed off the high ceiling and bounced back to assault my ears a second time. My hand went slack and the gun fell to the floor just as the queen collapsed into my arms. I staggered under her slight weight, and my injured hand screamed in protest when I attempted to push her away.

We both ended up sliding to the floor in a tangle of limbs. I sat there, with the queen unmoving in my lap while I struggled to learn how to breathe again. What the hell had just happened? I blinked, trying to clear my vision, but my eyelashes were stuck together. Using my good hand, I swiped at my face until I could see again. A quick glance confirmed that my sleeve was covered in blood and little bits of bone.

My hands shook. *What the hell had I done?*

I wiggled my way out from under the queen's body and forced myself to check for a pulse. My heart thudded painfully in my chest as I searched for a matching one on her neck and then her wrist, but there was nothing. I pushed some of the blonde and green hair, now a matted crimson, away from her face and let out a whimper when I found the small hole under her chin. And then the even bigger hole on the top of her head. It looked like a cantaloupe that had exploded from the inside, spraying everything with blood and bone and little pieces of brain.

She's dead, I thought. *I shot her, and now she's dead.*

My knees wobbled, and I made myself walk over to the bed and sit on the edge where there was less gore. I bent over and put my head between my knees when I thought I might pass out.

She's dead. I shot her, and now the queen is dead.

I wanted to be relieved. Lief and Farranen were safe. Everybody in Fairie was safe. I should have been relieved.

I wasn't relieved. I was terrified.

Chapter Twenty-One

Gus would be back any minute, and I was still trapped in a room with the queen's dead body and no way out.

Don't panic, Theo.

"Don't panic, Theo." I jumped at the echo of my own thoughts and looked up to meet Harvey's worried gaze. "You've got to get out of here."

I didn't protest when he took my hand and pulled me to my feet. He said something, but I couldn't really hear what it was. His voice was fading into background noise, drowned out by the thoughts in my own head.

I killed her. She's dead, because I killed her. She's—

Something hit me in the face, and I gasped like I'd been holding my breath. Maybe I had been.

"Wake the *fuck* up, Theo!" Vanessa snarled, her face inches from mine.

I blinked, surprised to see that both my ghosts were still here.

"Stop acting like a traumatized little baby and get your ass moving!" she ordered.

I looked around because she was right. I needed to be gone before anyone found me with the body. It wouldn't take a genius to figure out who'd killed the queen. It was like a really poor murder-mystery board game; anyone with eyeballs would know it was

Theodora in the queen's private chambers, with the gun.

I took a step forward and stopped. Where the hell was I supposed to go? The portal was closed, and there weren't even any windows.

Deciding I'd feel better with some form of protection, I tiptoed through the splattered gore that had misted the floor and retrieved the gun. It had avoided most of the blood and brains and was relatively clean. I kept it in my good hand, clinging to the heavy weight of it like a security blanket. I had no idea how to check if there were any more bullets in it, so I kept it pointed at the floor in case I accidentally fired it again.

"Harvey, is there any other way out of here?" I asked in a level voice, even though I felt like I was falling apart inside.

"Not that I know of," he told me apologetically.

Vanessa walked up to the portal and stuck her arm through. When nothing happened, she walked through like she would any other wall. Harvey made a choked sound that he abruptly cut off when she stepped back into the room.

"The hall's empty," she told us and flipped her long hair over her shoulder.

I walked over to the portal and tentatively rapped on it with my knuckles. It sounded hollow, like it was made of glass, but it was definitely solid. "At least you guys have a way out," I told them half-heartedly. I glanced at the gun in my hands and briefly wondered if I could just shoot the damn portal. It was tempting, but there was a pretty good chance the bullet would just ricochet right back at me. I sighed and leaned my forehead on the chunk of glass that was currently blocking my only escape route. "Please, just open," I whispered.

Harvey's startled exclamation made me open my eyes just as the portal dissolved into a swirling eddy. My good hand, the one that was still holding the gun and had been resting on the wall, slid through the liquid silver and disappeared from my view. I tumbled forward with a gasp and landed in the hallway outside.

My ghosts joined me in the hall, and Harvey helped me to my feet.

"This way," Vanessa ordered, with none of her usual impatience. I caught a flash of something sympathetic cross her face before she turned to lead the way.

****

It must have snowed while I was in Fairie. The path was still visible, but there were no fresh prints coming or going from the hawthorn tree.

The sun was slowly sinking across the western horizon, staining the clouds a golden orange through the bare branches of the trees. It looked like I'd only been gone for half a day, but it felt like weeks had passed.

I didn't see Vanessa and Harvey anywhere; they must have gone back to their ghostly realm to recharge. That was fine, since I was still feeling emotionally numb and didn't want to talk to anyone.

Something in the long shadows of the tree moved, and I froze. A familiar whine filled the air, and I let out the breath I'd been holding. Dog shot out of the alcove of roots he'd been curled up in and knocked me over in his excitement to get to me.

I let out a startled "Ow!" and clutched my injured

wrist tighter to my chest.

He forced his big head under my other arm and sniffed at the gore on my sweatshirt. His eyes slanted down when he caught the scent of blood, and he let out a low growl.

"It's okay; it's not my blood," I reassure him. At least, most of it wasn't mine.

His yellow eyes were accusing as he continued to sniff me like I'd bathed in roadkill.

"Can we have this fight at home? I'm freezing." Damn Celesta for rushing me out the door without a coat or mitts.

His expression promised he would hold me to my word, but he backed up and gave me enough room to stand. I made it halfway across the clearing before I realized Dog wasn't with me. I turned back and saw he was pawing at something in the snow where I'd been sitting.

"What did you find?" I asked.

I knelt down and wrapped my hand around the dark gray lump that had captured Dog's attention. I almost dropped it when I realized it was a gun. I quickly patted my back where I'd tucked the gun into the waistband of my pants—yep, it was the gun I'd stolen from Fairie. I must have dropped it when Dog knocked me over.

I debated dropping it back in the snow. I never wanted to see the damn thing again, but with all the foot traffic that had been tromping through my backyard lately, it was sure to be discovered. With a resigned sigh, I kept the gun and trudged toward my cabin.

****

If my feeble old water heater had had lips, I would have kissed them.

I was thankful for every single second of the moderately warm shower that it took to clean the dried blood and brains out of my hair.

Once I was squeaky clean and dressed in something warm, I lit a fire in the hearth and made some supper for Dog. Doing such mundane things felt wrong. I'd just killed someone, and there I was, making sandwiches, when I should have been...I had no idea what was expected of someone who'd just committed such an atrocious crime. Hiding the dead body? Securing an air-tight alibi? Packing a suitcase and boarding a plane to Mexico? I should probably do an internet search.

Nothing in the cabin had been touched since Celesta's visit. The bowl of cake batter was still sitting on the kitchen counter where I'd left it. My bed was still unmade, and the sheets smelled faintly of cinnamon and pine.

Dog nudged my knee with his head; his doggy eyes were sadder than usual.

"I'm okay," I told him.

I wondered how long I had until Gus discovered what I'd done and came for me. Last fall he'd come to my cabin to escort me to Fairie for an audience with the queen, so he knew where to find me. Maybe the PIMPs had some sort of supernatural witness-protection plan I could apply for. I should call Ozzy.

****

I didn't call Ozzy.

The next morning, when it became apparent that all the icepacks and ace bandages in the world weren't going to fix my wrist, I drove myself to the small walk-in clinic in town. After a two hour wait, and some awkward questions about the scars on my arm from Lebolus's attack, an X-ray confirmed that my wrist was broken. The doctor, a nice middle-aged woman, plastered everything from my fingertips to my elbow in a cast and sent me home with a bottle of painkillers. She also slipped me a pamphlet for a hotline that helped victims of domestic abuse. I didn't bother trying to explain to her that most of my abusers weren't even human. She probably would have given me a different pamphlet, one that had the number for a mental illness hotline.

Dog sniffed at my wrist suspiciously, and I patted him on the head to chase away the worried look on his face.

Lunchtime came and went, but I wasn't hungry. I threw some sausages in a pan and cooked them for Dog, and once he was done eating, I crawled into bed.

I took one of the pills from the clinic and fell into a deep, dreamless sleep.

****

The sheets were all wrong.

My sheets were a cozy flannel and smelled like fabric softener. The imposter sheets were soft, maybe cotton or something equally nice, but they felt wrong against my skin. I opened my eyes and my chest filled with a sinking feeling; not only wasn't I in my own bed, I wasn't in my own realm.

I recognized everything from the stone walls and floor, to the tall arched windows. I was in Fairie. The only thing that kept me from panicking was the fact that the room had been constructed from stone too dark to be the queen's castle.

I'd been here once before, when I'd been stabbed

the first time. Farranen and Lief had brought me to the dark prince's castle to be healed by Eddesta, one of the best healers in Fairie. After five days in a magically induced coma, I'd woken in the very same bed.

Shaking off the weird sense of déjà vu, I sat up and looked around. Eddy was nowhere in sight, but I recognized the empty tea cart that was tucked into the corner. The wall of cupboards with glass doors that held medical supplies were just as meticulously organized as I remembered them being. The mountain of bedding that threatened to smother me hadn't changed either. Even the fae asleep in the chair next to my bed was familiar.

With his arms crossed against his chest and relaxed expression, Farranen looked like he was taking a leisurely catnap. The only thing that gave away his defensive wariness was the handle of the dagger in his palm. The blade was tucked between his chest and other arm, so that it was nearly concealed from view.

My heart gave a few painful thumps as I watched his chest slowly rising and falling with each breath he took. He was still alive. I honestly hadn't let myself think too much about the secret mission that Lief had sent him on, knowing that I might never see him again. And I'd been kind of busy dealing with Celesta kidnapping me and dragging me to Fairie.

I gave a slow stretch and was happy to find that my body felt better than I'd expected. I cautiously slid my legs off the bed until my bare toes touched the cold floor. I was contemplating standing, when Farranen opened his eyes.

"Theodora?" He sat up in the chair and uncrossed his ankles to lean forward. His green eyes were alert, and he looked better than the last time I'd seen him, like he'd fully recovered from everything he'd been through.

"Hey," I answered lamely, since I had at least a dozen or so questions but wasn't sure where to begin.

"Are you...well?" he asked tentatively. His hands gripped the arms of his chair like he was scared it would try to run away.

"I feel good," I told him, surprised to find it was true. "Why am I in Fairie?"

"You were unresponsive, so I brought you to the dark prince's castle. Eddesta was unable to wake you." It hit me that the tension in his body was his way of hiding the worry he'd felt at finding me passed out.

"Sorry, I didn't mean to scare you. I took a painkiller, and it must've hit me pretty hard." I looked down at my arm and exclaimed in disbelief, "What happened to my cast?"

"We removed it."

I flexed my hand and made a fist, and when there was no pain, I looked at Farranen in surprise. "Eddy fixed my broken wrist?"

He slowly shook his head and told me, "She tried to, but as soon as she touched you, you hit her with your magic."

"I *hit* Eddy?" I asked in shock. He had to be wrong; I liked Eddy and would never hurt her.

"Unintentionally, yes. You were unconscious and couldn't have known it was her." His eyes were kind, but I still felt his words like a physical blow.

I covered my face with my hands, horrified that I'd hurt the gentle female that looked like a cross between a walrus and a spider monkey. "I'm so sorry! Where is she?" I looked around, needing to apologize. She'd saved my life, and I'd repaid her kindness by letting my magic smack her around. I was a horrible person.

"The dark prince evacuated those who reside in the castle; she left with the rest of his court."

I scrunched my nose in confusion. "Evacuated? Because of me?" How hard had I hit her?

"The entire realm has become unstable, and it appears to be affecting your magic as well."

"Affecting it how?" Dread settled in my belly, as cold and hard as ice.

"Your human body can no longer accommodate the fae magic that continues to live inside you. Bringing you to Fairie has triggered your magic to grow at an accelerated rate." I turned my attention inward and saw my magic had indeed grown. It was tingly and pulsed eagerly, waiting to be set free. "The pressure became too great, and your body was forced to release it. Eddesta is calling them 'magical flares.' You let off several since your arrival, but you should be able to control it now that you're awake."

"Did I hurt anyone else?" I asked in a small voice.

"No." He gave me a small smile that reached his eyes. "The dark prince and I were strong enough to be able to bear the brunt of the flares without any negative consequences."

I wanted to crawl back under the covers and hide for the rest of my life. My stupid messed-up magic wasn't just embarrassing; it was dangerous. Even then I could feel it pressing against the constraints of my human body.

"If it got worse by coming to Fairie, will it get better when I get home?" I asked hopefully.

271

"Theoretically," he hedged, which I took to mean that he had no f-ing clue.

"Well, let's find out then." I stood, belatedly realizing that someone had dressed me in a filmy night shift that seemed pretty darn impractical to be considered Fairie's equivalent of a hospital gown.

Farranen stood as well, towering over me as he swept his gaze across my face. "There was another unexpected change due to Fairie's discord." He held out his hand, and I reached for it, but I gasped when I caught sight of my outstretched arm. The purplish scars that had previously cut across the pale skin were gone. I quickly held out my other arm, and it was just as unblemished as the first.

"What the hell?" I breathed. The skin was satiny smooth beneath my fingertips; even the freckles were gone.

Farranen caught my chin with a gentle finger and tipped my head back. "The vampire bites are gone as well."

"How?" Had Eddy done this? It was unlikely, since I'd walked away with scars the last time she'd healed me.

"The volatile nature of Fairie is affecting everyone differently. I'm unsure why it chose to heal you, but I'm most grateful it did."

I was still on the fence about Fairie's magic making alterations to my body without my consent, but that was something I could contemplate once I was safely back in my own realm.

"Where did you go yesterday?" When he gave me a confused look, I clarified, "The super-secret mission that Lief sent you on?"

His eyebrows rose. "That was five days ago."

My eyebrows climbed my forehead as I mirrored his surprise. *"Five days?"* Holy cow, what kind of painkiller could knock me out for five days?

He nodded. "It took me two days to locate the dark prince—"

"Is he okay?" I asked anxiously.

"He is well. The information he received about Gus was incorrect, and he was led on a merry wild goose chase across the swamp lands."

I smiled at the thought of Lief tromping through a swamp.

"Once I located him and we were able to reunite with his followers—"

"Oh, my God!" I interrupted again. "Celesta is working for the queen! She's the mole!" I can't believe I'd forgotten to tell him something so important.

"Yes, her betrayal has been made known to the dark prince, and she has already been dealt with," he assured me.

I didn't really want to know how it had been dealt with, so I kept my mouth shut and he continued.

"There was an unexpected development that prevented me from completing the dark prince's mission. Augustus of the Light Court has taken the throne."

My magic responded to his dark words, prickling along my body like it was anxious to get out.

"The 'light king,' " I scoffed, trying to hide my guilt with bravado.

"Yes, how did you know?" His face turned shrewd as he looked down at me.

Oh, crap. I shouldn't have known that and

wouldn't have known if I hadn't been an unwilling witness to the mockery he'd made of "mating" the queen. My eyeballs were still burning from the image of Safeena bent over the bed while Gus thrust himself into her like a bull in heat.

"Lucky guess?"

His suspicious frown said he wasn't buying it, so I quickly asked my own question.

"Why would Gus being king stop you from doing whatever secret thing you were supposed to do? And now will you tell me what it was?"

He sighed, and I could see the indecision in his eyes. I waited, knowing he'd either tell me or he wouldn't. Finally, he softly told me, "I was sent to kill the queen."

My mouth fell open. *Holy shit!* "You were going to *assassinate* the *queen?*" I demanded.

"Yes." He was braced for my condemnation, but he couldn't have known the horror on my face wasn't for him at all.

It was because I'd nearly forgotten the horrible thing I'd done in the queen's private chambers. I'd shoved it as far back in my head as I could, stuffing it to the very darkest corner of my brain to be dealt with at a later date, but Farranen's admission brought every gory detail rushing back in vivid detail.

"The act has become irrelevant with the king's manifestation." Frustration rasped in his dismal tone.

The urge to console him was overwhelming, but if I confessed that I'd inadvertently executed his crazy plan, I'd have a mountain of explaining to do.

I had to assume that her body hadn't been found yet, since Farranen didn't know she was already dead.

"So how does Gus fit into all of this?" I asked, trying to look innocent.

"Theoretically, Fairie should get stronger with an added monarch figure to help support the realm," Farranen mused.

"Is that why the magic here has become so unstable? Because there's another king and Fairie's just getting used to him?" Maybe I'd been wrong about the mating mark being a fake.

"Perhaps." He didn't sound totally convinced but didn't seem to have any theories of his own either.

"What if..." I took a deep breath and attempted to sound mildly curious instead of insanely guilty before continuing. "...he's not a king?"

Farranen quirked a brow, and I quickly added, "What if the mating mark...was fake?"

"There was a witness to the consummation," he told me patiently, like he was explaining something simple to a small child.

"Yeah, I'm not saying they didn't 'consummate' the heck out of each other, but what if the mark was forged. Like, they drew the mark on her skin...or glamoured it?" I missed the nonchalant vibe I was trying for by a country mile and ended up sounding cagey instead.

After a moment of consideration, Farranen shook his head. "To maintain such a blatant untruth in front of the entire court would be beyond even the queen's skill."

"What about Gus? Could he pull it off without the queen's knowledge?" I pressed. "He wouldn't have to dupe the entire court if he was able to trick her into thinking it was real."

"It's doubtful…"

His speculative look didn't match his words, and I let the subject drop. He hadn't completely dismissed the idea, so the seed of doubt had been sown.

Chapter Twenty-Two

My guardian glamoured my useless nightgown into pants and a ridiculously soft black sweater, with a matching black cloak that would hopefully help me slip past any of the queen's guards that we might encounter between here and the gate.

He kept hold of my hand once the glamour was in place and led me out into the hall.

"Where are we going?" I asked as we strode past a row of doors that were all shut. The castle was silent and empty of any signs of life.

"The dark prince will want to know you've recovered."

"And then I can go home?" The magic beneath my skin shifted, almost like it was protesting.

"Yes; it will be safer for you in your own realm until the ambiguity here settles," he answered with a small nod, and I gave him a relieved smile in return.

Dog must be going out of his mind with worry; I'm pretty sure he had some form of separation anxiety. Hopefully he'd fed himself while I'd been gone. Five days without food, and he'd be back to the bag of skin and bones he'd been when we'd found each other. And how the heck had I slept for five days? I should call the medical clinic and let them know their onsite pharmacist needed to be fired.

We stopped in front of a section of wall that had no

paintings or artwork. Farranen murmured something I couldn't understand, and the stones of the wall swirled and blurred until a portal formed. He dropped my hand and used his dagger to slice his finger open. Blood welled and slid down into his cupped palm, and he thrust it through the wall.

I'd seen this happen enough times that I didn't even blink when the portal grew to the size of a door. While the portal in the queen's castle had looked to be made of light, this one was made of shadows. They were exact opposites, the differences as stark as the sun haloing a person and a living black hole. Which only served to remind me of the closed portal that had opened for my whispered plea when I'd been trapped in the queen's bedroom. "How does it work?" I asked, gesturing to the wall.

"Only the monarchs of Fairie have the power to create portals. The dark prince has spelled this one to allow me access, just as the one to the queen's private chambers once accepted me." There was remorse there, probably at being labeled a traitor once he'd switched allegiances.

"I'm sorry," I told him, knowing my words were inadequate, but the least I could do was acknowledge the sacrifice he'd made for his realm.

"Worry not; the queen has closed her portal to everyone, not just those suspected of being loyal to the dark prince. She has not emerged from her private room for over a week."

Oh, crap. Crap, crap, crap. Realistically, I knew her disappearance would be noticed, but I'd hoped to be safely out of Fairie by the time people questioned her absence.

Magic slid along my body, prodding without hands as it searched. With a reassuring look, Farranen laced the fingers of his free hand through mine and stepped through the opening.

Lief's room looked like a carbon copy of the queen's private chambers, but the furniture and décor had more of a gothic vibe rather than the queen's spoiled princess look. The bed was in the same place, but Lief's was a simple platform rather than Safeena's intricately carved four-poster. The bedding was black, but crimson sheets peeked out where the bed had been turned down. The wardrobe and dresser were simple and equally dark. A large gray fur rug covered most of the floor, and a fire crackled in the fireplace. Books of every size and age filled the bookcase and covered every horizontal surface. There was even a pile stacked next to the bed.

With the dark stone walls surrounding us, it should have felt like an underground tomb, but I thought it was warm and cozy.

Lief stood in the center of the room with his back to us.

"My lord?" Farranen and I approached Lief, but he didn't move.

"Lief?" I reached out, wondering what the heck he was doing that he hadn't even heard us arrive.

"*Wait—*" Farranen called, just as my fingers touched Lief's arm.

My magic, already antsy to get out, leapt at the contact. It scrambled down my arm and melted into Lief's magic before I even knew it was happening. The room around us disappeared in a blink, and suddenly I was standing in a clearing. It looked to be early spring, all the trees had new little buds and tiny shoots of grass were emerging from the ground. Lief was still standing in front of me, and I gasped and tried to pull away. He turned and caught my hand before I could back up.

"Theo?" His confusion would have been comical if I hadn't been so freaked out by the sight of his eyes. Instead of the clear crystal blue I was used to seeing, the iris was completely black.

"Lief?" I asked in shaky voice. He smiled hesitantly, and some of my fear receded. "What happened?"

"I'm having a vision; you must have accidentally gotten pulled in." His smile thinned, and he tightened his grip on my hand. "Don't let go. I don't know that you'd be able to find your way out without me to guide you."

I nodded; the thought of getting lost here was chilling enough that I took a step closer to Lief until my cloak was brushing his leg.

"What's happening?" I turned to look in the direction he'd been facing, and my breath caught in my chest at the sight of the woman kneeling in the grass.

"Is that…*me?*" I asked breathlessly. The woman's face was obscured by the fall of her hair, but some part of me recognized that it was me.

"Yes." He glanced down at me, and the blackness of his eyes was no longer so disconcerting.

"Now what?" I asked, turning back to the other me. She wore a long white dress with a modest bodice, and the skirt shimmered like it had been encrusted with tiny pieces of diamonds. The back dipped below her shoulder blades, and I could see the top of a pale green tattoo peeking out.

"Now we watch," Lief murmured.

I looked back up and was surprised to see the harsh lines of his face had softened into something that looked like adoration as he watched the other me. Or…maybe it really was adoration? But that didn't sound right. Lief was all talk and no bite; flirting was just a game to him, right? I hated that I was questioning myself and looked back at the other me.

The grass around her body had been slowly growing, and now small flowers bloomed on the carpet of green. Overhead, the trees surrounding the clearing unfurled their tiny buds, and they quickly grew into fat tear-shaped leaves that filled the branches and blocked out the sky. It was like watching a video in time lapse, both lovely and fascinating.

The other Theo looked up, her hazel eyes shining when she found us. I never would have believed that her beautiful smile, so full of secrets and mirth, could have come from my lips. Yet there it was.

The world around us faded, and I clutched Lief's hand tighter. Once everything around us had gone completely black, I realized my eyes were shut and quickly opened them.

We were back in Lief's room, right where we'd started. Lief's eyes had gone back to their normal pale blue. He smirked at my astonished look and then looked around until he found Farranen standing next to the desk with his head bent over a book.

"I assumed you would be nearby since Theo awake."

Farranen looked up at Lief's words, and the worry on his face melted into relief. "You had a vision?"

It wasn't really a question, but the dark prince

nodded anyway.

"I didn't grasp the entirety of the situation until she'd already touched you," Farranen told him, sounding more apologetic toward Lief than I'd ever heard him before.

"It's nothing to worry about; our Theo is none the worse for wear." Lief glanced at me and cocked an eyebrow, as if to confirm his evaluation.

"I'm good. It was just like dream walking," I told him honestly. When he continued to hold my gaze, I suddenly became aware of how tightly I was holding his hand and let go.

"It appears your time in Fairie has done you some good." He traced his eyes lower over the curve of my neck to the perfectly smooth skin where my scars used to be.

I self-consciously held up a hand to block his view. "Yeah, the scars are all gone," I admitted awkwardly.

He shook his head. "Not just the missing scars; your magic shimmers." There was reverence in his voice that I wasn't entirely comfortable hearing. It didn't fit in with his cocky playboy persona, and I was the first to look away.

"What did you see in the vision?" Farranen asked, and I was grateful for the distraction.

"Theo." He smirked benevolently, like he wasn't surprised that I'd been tangled up in one of his visions. "She was in Fairie, kneeling in the glade west of the Light Castle."

"Wait, is that the queen's castle?" I asked. How many freakin' castles were there in Fairie?

"Yes," Farranen supplied.

"Does that make this the Dark Castle?" I asked, a

bit disappointed that the massive structures didn't have cooler names.

"Indeed." The dark prince arched a brow in amusement before returning us to the topic of his vision. "Our dear Theo was marked."

"Marked?" A small kernel of dread bloomed in my gut. Anytime that word got thrown around, nothing good came of it.

"Marked? You're sure?" Farranen demanded, but not nearly as apprehensively as I had.

"It was definitely a mating mark." Lief turned to me before asking, "You saw it in the vision, on your back?"

"The green tattoo?" I'd wondered about that, since I'd never had any desire to have something permanently inked into my skin.

"It was a mating mark. It appeared to be in the shape of a key."

"A key? How could you tell? Only the top was sticking out."

He smirked. "You were wearing a white dress."

"So?" I demanded.

"Fae eyesight is much sharper than that of a human. White fabric does little to conceal what's beneath." His eyebrows rose suggestively, and I tried to remember if I'd ever worn white in front of him. Nothing came to mind, but if it ever did, I'd be sure to smack him.

"So, what does it mean?" I asked, just so he'd wipe the challenging look off his face.

He shrugged. "I don't really know. Most likely, it was just telling me that someday you'll find your true mate among the fae and receive a mark."

I didn't miss the long considering look he exchanged with Farranen but chose to ignore it. I was done talking about mating marks. I needed to get home. If I'd really been gone for almost a week, I wouldn't put it past Dog to find a way into Fairie so he could find me.

As if Lief could read my thoughts, he said, "Before you go, you should see what I found." He crossed to the desk and lifted the book Farranen had been reading. "This is a first-hand account of a changeling who was bitten by a vampire."

My eyebrows shot up, and I joined him at the desk. When I saw the small, neat rows of ink, I groaned in frustration. "I can't read that."

"Of course not; it's fae." Lief laughed. The bastard actually *laughed* at my annoyance.

"Farranen did some glamour thing months ago, and I can still understand you just fine—so why can't I read it?" I demanded rudely.

"Glamour doesn't work that way," Farranen told me gently. Leaning over me, he tilted the book so he could see it better. "The woman named Livitha was kidnapped by someone in the Light Court...Her transition was successful, but she resented being forced to stay here...Then she escaped through the gate. She ran and was able to hide for many years."

Good for her, I thought.

"She was attacked by a vampire and terribly wounded...Knowing she would die without help, she returned to Fairie." Farranen looked over at Lief. "Fae and vampire magic in the same body, just like Theodora."

Lief nodded before my guardian continued reading

from the book.

"None of the healers here could purge the vampire magic from her, and it continued to grow until…" His expression never wavered, but his finger trembled on the page for a heartbeat.

"What?" I asked, dreading whatever answer would make my big strong fae tremble.

"She died," Farranen whispered.

Lief let out a long-suffering sigh and reached over to turn the page. "Keep reading," he drawled.

Farranen focused back on the book. "Then, after two days, she rose to live again."

I gave Lief a look promising payback that would be painful and embarrassing. He just grinned unrepentantly. The big stupid jerk.

"So, the fae magic was what kept Livitha from turning into a vampire after her first death?" I asked.

"Most likely," Farranen mused. "It says she remained a changeling and retained both magics. Her vampire magic should have required blood to sustain it, but she never partook…Instead, she let her fae magic support it."

Huh. It was pretty cool to know I wasn't the only one that accidentally ended up with magic from two different supernatural sources. "Can I talk to her?"

He shook his head. "Livitha died three hundred years ago."

Dang. Still, it was good to know she never fully turned into a vampire or drank blood. Because that was never, *ever* going to happen to me. I hoped.

"The Dark Castle will be the best place to make our stand. You should send word to the evacuees to return now that the danger has passed," Farranen told

Lief, and I looked down at the floor.

Yeah, my magical outbursts had been the danger he was referring to. I should hang a sign around my neck that said WARNING! ROOKIE MAGIC USER! STAY AWAY!

"Did Eddy say why I slept for so long?" I just wasn't buying that one tiny painkiller could knock me on my butt for so long. And my weird hybrid magic being trapped in a human body could explain the magical flares, but not a five-day long siesta.

After exchanging a look with Lief, Farranen answered. "When I found you, your magic was completely depleted. As soon as we crossed through the gate, it started to replenish itself, like you were pulling magic from the very air around you."

My magic hadn't felt empty when I'd gone to bed. After the boost I'd gotten from stealing Safeena's magic, I'd pretty much had a full tank, so what had drained it so fast? I racked my brain, going over what I'd been doing that morning, but all I could recall was the trip to the walk-in clinic, the domestic abuse pamphlet that was still in my coat pocket, and feeding Dog before I fell into bed. I hadn't actually been feeling much of anything. Maybe I'd been in shock? That might explain why my body had shut down.

Farranen and Lief were exchanging looks that ranged from worried to speculative, and my own unease skyrocketed. So far neither of them had questioned my broken wrist, or the painkiller that I'd taken, but it was only a matter of time before they thought to ask. Then I'd have to tap-dance my way around the fact that I'd murdered the queen. I needed to change the subject before that happened, seeing as I was the world's worst liar.

"Did you feed Dog or tell him we were in Fairie?" I asked. At my guardian's contrite look, I sighed. "I need to get home."

Chapter Twenty-Three

Visually, the walk from the Dark Castle to the gate was serene. Verbally, it was like traipsing through a minefield with cement blocks tied to my feet.

The conversation kept turning to things I was desperate to avoid discussing. When Farranen brought up the subject of Gus's rise to the throne, I panicked, thinking he'd figured out what I'd done and was looking for signs of guilt. It took a minute to grasp he was just doing the fae equivalent of gossiping. If I hadn't been so agitated, I would have found it charming.

The only safe subject he brought up was when he told me that the females rescued from the queen's demented breeding program had fully recovered at the PIMP headquarters and had returned home.

When we arrived at the gate, Farranen stopped and reached for my hand. When his fingers brushed against mine, a spark of my magic escaped my grasp and barrelled into him. "Sorry!" I told him with a flinch. My lack of control was mortifying.

His lips curved upward into a smile that said he was more amused than affronted. After a few heartbeats, his face once again grew solemn, and turmoil brightened the green of his eyes. I could stop him right then, before he said whatever was on his mind. But I didn't. I was already running from too many things, so if he was about to confront me with something, I was going to meet it head on.

"What?" I asked softly.

"I wish to revisit the issue of my desire to be 'more than friends,' " he said, equally softly.

"You do?" I asked in surprise. "Want to be more than friends, that is?" In all honesty, I had thought he'd be tired of me and all my baggage. Drama followed me around like a lost puppy dog, and I wouldn't have blamed him for moving on.

"Yes. Theodora, I very much wish to court you," he told me gravely.

"You do?" I really needed to come up with some deeper questions; I sounded like a broken record. "Then why are you acting like we're discussing funeral arrangements for your great-aunt Agnes who just passed away?"

A hint of a smile graced his lips before disappearing. "I am most anxious to hear your answer."

"I…" I paused, knowing something this important required some thought, rather than me just blurting out whatever words popped into my head.

Did I want to risk getting my heart broken all over again? Because that's what I'd be gambling with. I already knew just how painful it was to watch him walk away; I'd done it once before and didn't know how I'd survive if I had to do it again. But for the chance that something good might be waiting to develop between us, it just might be worth it.

Before his disappearance, whatever had been building between us had been like a glowing hot ember; and since his rescue, I couldn't deny that that ember had sparked into a flame. Every minute I spent with him, every shared touch, fed the fire to burn hotter, stealing the oxygen from my lungs. So, yes, for the chance to see how high and bright the flame would grow, it would indeed be worth the risk.

I looked straight into his eyes, letting him see my honesty and all my trepidation about where this might lead. "Yes," I carefully told him, "I would like to see where this goes." I held up a hand when a small smile graced his lips. "But we're going to do the courting thing my way. I don't want to see you walking around without pants on just so you can showcase your male assets in front of me." If pants became optional, it would set a bad precedent for Dog.

"Understood," he told me, with an appropriate amount of seriousness.

While I wasn't real clear on what courting meant to the fae, I was just as unclear on what dating meant for humans. It had been over a decade since I'd dipped my toes in the dating waters, and back then, dating had been lots of movies and fast food, with a few local hockey games thrown in during the winter months. I had no idea what modern-day dating for two people from different realms would look like.

"There's a pretty good chance that I'm going to screw this up," I told him, knowing he deserved a heads-up because I was really good at messing things up.

"Understood," he agreed, without any hesitation.

I briefly debated seeing what else I could get him to agree to, but it was hard to think when he was looking at me with so much hope in his eyes.

My stoic guardian shifted slightly from side to side, the gesture more nervous than anything I'd ever seen from him, even when he'd been facing down Gus with nothing but a hunting knife. "And I would have you know, Theodora, that I am equally likely to 'screw this up.' " He brought my hand to his lips and pressed a chaste kiss to my knuckles. "But given the chance, I will make every endeavour to honor our courtship for as long as you would have me."

"Understood," I told him.

He'd already screwed this up once, but we'd managed to get past it; and I was fairly confident that we could face whatever craziness the future threw at us. When trouble found me, as it so often did, there was nobody else I'd rather face it with.

"Well, okay then…" I smiled, feeling giddy at the prospect of truly getting to know the man in front of me without the threat of death hanging over us. "Let's go home."

****

I'm not going to lie; I was more than a little anxious about the whole courting thing.

The implications of what I'd gotten myself into finally hit me as I dressed in my pjs and brushed my teeth in the bathroom.

After crossing through the gate, we'd made it as far as the backyard before Dog came racing out of the cabin with wary joy in his eyes. When he'd seen I was unharmed, he'd given Farranen a look that conveyed relief and gratitude.

The fridge was nearly empty, so my poor shifter hadn't starved while I'd been away.

Once I was ready for bed—and out of excuses to hide in the bathroom any longer—I crept into the bedroom. Farranen was already tucked under the blankets, looking for all the world like he'd always belonged there. His smile was hesitant as he lifted the covers for me to crawl in next to him.

I was worried that it would be awkward, that we'd have different sets of expectations regarding the sleeping arrangements, but he let out a small hum of contentment when I snuggled up next to him proving my fears had been unnecessary.

His lips brushed my forehead in a subdued motion, and I tilted my face up in invitation. I felt, rather than saw his brief smile, before he swooped in and claimed the kiss I'd been offering. Delight shot through me as his tongue slowly slid against mine, like we had all the time in the world to explore each other.

And while it would take time before I'd be ready to share every part of me with him, I was more than happy to share this part. My hands were just beginning to explore the roadmap of scars on his chest when the bed suddenly jolted. Two hundred and twenty pounds of shaggy black wolf settled across the foot of the bed.

Dog glanced between the two of us and gave us a wolfish grin.

I debated whether he'd find us if we decided to sleep at Farranen's cabin.

I grinned back at my unrepentant shifter. Or maybe I'd start making salad for breakfast.

A word about the author...

Born and raised on the beautiful Canadian prairies, Everlyn prefers to spend her time outdoors with her family kayaking, skating, fishing, and hunting.

She loves reading and writing about vampires, witches, fae, and zombies that get to find their own version of happily ever after.

www.ingramcontent.com/pod-product-compliance
Lightning Source LLC
Chambersburg PA
CBHW051143030726
47504CB00004B/1008